Violet
The God Of War

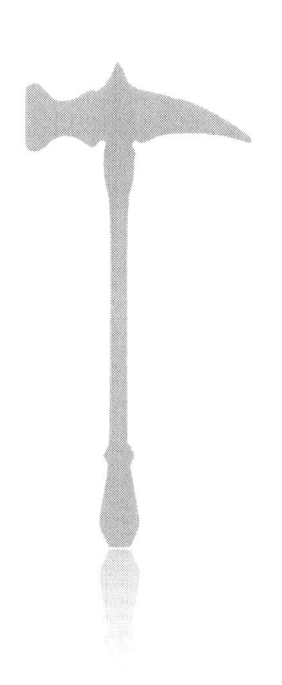

DOUGLAS SHORE
Copyright © 2021 Douglas Shore

All rights reserved.

Copyright © 2021 Douglas Shore.

All rights reserved. No part of this publication may be reproduced, distributed, or transmitted in any form or by any means, including photocopying, recording, or other electronic or mechanical methods, without the prior written permission of the publisher, except in the case of brief quotations embodied in critical reviews and specific other noncommercial uses permitted by copyright law.

This book is sold subject to the condition that it shall not, by way of trade or otherwise, be lent, resold, hired out or otherwise circulated without the publisher's prior written consent in any form of binding or cover other than that in which it is published and without a similar condition including this condition being imposed on the subsequent purchaser.

ISBN: 979-8-7852-7274-3. (Paperback)

Any references to historical events, real people, or places are used fictitiously. Names, characters, and places are products of the author's imagination.

Cover image by Artist Rebeca Covers.

Printed by KPD, Part of Amazon

First printing edition 2021.

To Kayleigh, from whom Violet was born.
To Mum, for my love of books.
To Dad, for all your support.

CONTENTS

	Acknowledgments	i
1	The Incident in Manhattan	Pg 1
2	The White Steps of Washington	Pg 23
3	London's Calling	Pg 39
4	The Eyes Have It	Pg 54
5	The Past, Present & Future	Pg 70
6	Deadlines	Pg 87
7	The Party In Paris	Pg 100
8	The Jilted Decision	Pg 118
9	Complete Chaos	Pg 134
10	Trouble in Tokyo	Pg 150
11	The Council of Petaria	Pg 167
12	The Traitor Lives	Pg 181
13	The God Of War	Pg 196
14	The Lunar Assault	Pg 209
15	Return to Eco	Pg 226
16	The Three Rings of Nova	Pg 239
17	The Nexus	Pg 252
18	Travel Through Time and Space	Pg 267

19	The A.I Army	Pg 285
20	War Has Begun!	Pg 299
21	Into The Caves	Pg 314
22	The God slayer	Pg 327
23	Flee!	Pg 341
24	The Wrath Of God's	Pg 358

ACKNOWLEDGMENTS

I want to start my thanks to my advanced reader (and fellow writer), Nik; I would never have written this book had I not been inspired by you and your journey.

Thank you to Carol (or, as I know her, Mum) for your proofreading. Capitalisations are not my strong suit.

Thank you to Rebeca for the fantastic cover design. I cannot imagine this book any other way.

And most importantly, thank you to Kayleigh for pushing me, even when I couldn't face another day of writing.

— CHAPTER ONE —

THE INCIDENT IN MANHATTAN

As the summer rain fell hard upon the steel containers, the Delta team prepared their zip wires for the ground descent. The clock just struck midnight, and the streets were barren, eerily so for this usual bustling metropolis.

Now was the time to attack, under cover of darkness in the dead of night, their aim to be unheard and unseen as they stalked their prey. The U.N-Eighteen Yellowhammer glided through the air, gradually slowing to a stop.

There it remained, silently hovering just above the Manhattan dockyards. It was close enough to the ground for them to zip wire down in seconds, yet far enough up to stop any intruders that may have been lurking in the shadows from climbing aboard.

The Delta team would soon be leaving the safety of their jet, staring down death; an uneasy tension gripped them to their chairs. The sirens rang. The cargo bay door began to lower as the pistons hissed into motion. A bright red light flashed in the night sky as the door completed its opening sequence flooding the cabin with a sudden rush of crisp fresh air.

Scrambling at the jump-off point, poised and ready for action, aligned in their standard combat formation, the team awaited further instructions. A familiar voice from the comm-link rang through.

'Delta team! On my mark, you may begin your descent.'

The voice was soft and calm yet strong and commanding; this was the unmistakable voice of Major Violet Villin.

Quickening her pace, she began to reel off several codes, each relating to a specific member of the Delta team.

The cadets plunged from the Yellowhammer with each finished code, the zip wires slowing them down as they landed swiftly upon the ground.

The cargo doors began to retract, dampening the warning sirens emitting from the jet; the red flashing light gradually faded from view, leaving nothing in sight except for the faintest outline of the Yellowhammer.

'Activate the cloaking field,' Violet ordered, maintaining her calm composure.

As the command came through the comm-link, the outline of the Yellowhammer faded from view, blending into the pitch-black of the midnight sky until all that remained were the ghostly moonlit clouds drifting through the air.

'Delta team! You may begin your search.'
Not wasting another second, they began moving swiftly, splintering around the cargo containers, snake winding as they went to avoid any potential threats. They kept their weapons close as they hunted through the storage bay, leaving no corner unturned.

'The signal is coming from the northern quadrant sector thirty-two, cargo bay four.' Violet remained calm and in control as she relayed intel via the comm-link.

The Delta team re-routed to the coordinates as instructed, the heavy rain falling around them suddenly stopped. Their footsteps, no longer masked by the rain, crunched on the ground as they walked. The element of surprise was fading fast.

'Major! We have located the cargo unit, switching to visual now.'

'Roger, that Commander, visual is online; you may proceed with caution.'

The Delta team now stood head-on facing the front doors of the shipping container, the air stiflingly still, darkness shrouded the container as they inched ever closer towards the doors.

'Major, I'm detecting volatile levels of energy. It's coming from the container! I request to call off the assault.'

'Negative, Commander! Proceed as planned.' Violet ordered.

The Commander waved his hand above his wrist, materialising a small holographic screen. The screen receded only to be replaced with a long chrome bar as he selected the required item.

Gripping the pole firmly in his hand, he pressed his thumb upon the centre of the black screen. Instantaneously, the end of the bar began to spark with flashes of blinding green light.

'Clear the area, remain in your formation and be ready.' the Commander shouted as he thrust the pole into the doors of the cargo unit piercing the steel shell.

The door bent on contact, expelling an ear-piercing shriek as sparks of jade green swarf littered the floor.

Despite this horrendous noise, the Commander continued to carve a hole in the door forming a human-sized entrance.

Suddenly, a stream of burning black light emitted through the gaps he had traced, radiating pure heat, melting the doors before their eyes, and turning the solid steel into a thick bubbling soup.

The Commander jumped back, shielding his face from the insurmountable heat; with a flick of his wrist, the chrome bar dematerialised from his hand, replacing it with his U.N.N standard-issue automatic rifle.

'Target located! Major, are we clear for use of force?'

'Affirmative Commander! Bring it down.'

Violet stood atop her central command post; she could see and hear everything from deep within her London base. She was dressed in her military-grade all-black catsuit. Her hands were firmly clasped to her hips. She flashed a crooked smile as she paced back and forth; her intense violet eyes seemed to glow as she glared at each ten-foot screen that walled the oval room.

Behind the command post were rows of desks, each occupied by one of the seven black-ops members, quietly monitoring the situation as the events unfolded.

Violet would be sat down, enjoying a lemon and ginger tea whilst pre-emptively congratulating herself on another well-done assignment if it were any other mission. However, this was no ordinary mission, and Violet couldn't afford another mistake.

'Major! We're receiving some feedback on the line.' Caspian said.

Violet turned her head, breaking her view from the screens to look at Caspian in the eyes. A relatively tall and slender man, his chalk-white hair held rigidly in place, reflected his posture as he sat firmly upright in his chair. He was dressed in his standard military intelligence uniform, consisting of Royal blue trousers, a t-shirt and an army jacket. Each piece was embedded with the silver symbol of a sword piercing a book. His ghostly pale skin contrasted his deep hazel eyes that were now fixed on Violet as he awaited her response.

'Clarify the visual!' Violet snapped, turning her back on him as she returned to the mission at hand.

Each of the ten-foot screens that illuminated the room once crystal clear now began to flicker; the white static clouded the display, distorting the images rendering them useless.

'Trying as best I can, Major, but the screens are unresponsive.' He said, frantically tapping the glass pane on his desk. 'Switching to drone now.'

With a swipe of his arm, the screens switched from a static-filled haze to immaculately clear as the drones jettisoned from the Yellowhammer.

Violet watched on intently as they rapidly approached their target.

'How close can we get?' Violet asked, keeping her eyes fixed to the screen,

'I'm not sure. The energy from the target is interfering with the electronics!' Caspian replied, moving his hands over the glass pane in rapid-fire.
Just as the drones approached their target, a surge of dark energy expelled from the container, knocking back the Delta team and frying the drones out of the sky.

'Damm it!' Violet said, slamming her fist onto her desk shattering the glass top, 'Commander, can you hear me? I repeat! Commander, can you hear me! We have lost visuals.'

'Major, the comm-link is down. We have lost contact.' Caspian said, his screen flashing red and white as it reeled a list of damages the Delta team had sustained.

Violet continued to stare at the blank screen, willing for it to reconnect, wishing for the comm-link to kick back in,

'Major, we're picking up a visual from the Yellowhammer, bringing it up on-screen now.'

A blurry image slowly came into focus on the screen closest to Violet.

'Amplify the sound!'

'Sound amplified.' Caspian responded.

The noise of rapid-fire gunshots filled the comm-link, shortly followed by the harrowing screams and manic shouting of the Delta team; Violet knew the mission was in jeopardy.

'Fall back! Abort the mission! Commander, do you hear me? Get your men out of there.' She shouted into the comm-link until all audio fell eerily silent.

'Major.' Aster said, daring his luck to interrupt; he pointed his finger towards the vitals indicator.

Violet tore away from her screen in disbelief to face Aster. Standing at six and a half feet tall, Aster was well-toned and much older than his boyish good looks would lead you to believe. Dressed similarly to Caspian but in all black, each piece of his uniform embedded with a gold sword piercing a decayed skull. His jet black and rather fashionable hair grazed his eyebrows, framing his pale azure blue eyes that were now transfixed on the vitals indicator.

One by one, the green man-shaped icons on the screen turned red, the ear-piercing alarm of the vitals meter rang through the room as it dropped into a droning flatline.

'Zoom in and clarify visual.' Violet commanded, her face tense and unyielding as she swung back to face the screen.

The pixelated display gradually smoothed over until the view of the container and the ground surrounding it became clear, revealing the bodies of the Delta team lying cold and motionless, scattered across the floor. Violet paused, dropping her head for a brief second whilst contemplating her next move.

'Zoom in on that gap in the crate. Whatever this thing is, it's in there.'

Lifting her head, she leant in towards the screen, squinting her eyes as the camera focused on the gap.

The screen began to flicker as the images turned static, the white snow clouding her view. Then, suddenly, it was clear that a young girl's appearance flashed before her eyes, wearing a tattered grey dress that rustled in the breeze. Her face was shrouded in a faint black mist, preventing any type of identification, except for a few tendrils of white-blond hair that whipped in the wind.

Violet watched on, edging closer to the screen, her eyes transfixed on the girl as she burnt the image in her mind. Then, moments before her nose touched the monitor, amber sparks shot from the wall of screens, the harsh sound of firecrackers came as it plunged the room into darkness.

'Major! We've lost visual, the comms are down, and all vitals are red. It's over!' Aster said, pushing his desk to the side.

Violet slammed her fists into her desk again, causing the solid steel frame to bend out of shape; clasping it with both hands, she flipped the desk across the room, letting out a scream of pain, unlike anything her comrades had ever heard.

'This is not how it ends,' Violet said, regaining her composure, turning from her command post to look around the now darkened room. Her eyes caught sight of the Nexus portal in the distance; cracking a wicked smile from the corner of her mouth, she stepped away from her post.

'Major! The Nexus is untested. We still don't know the full ramifications...' Caspian trailed off as Violet lept from the post. Now, running at full speed past him, followed by Aster and the rest of the Black-ops team.

'Gentleman! Line up! If all goes as planned, we should be there in a blink of an eye.' Violet said, grinning as she faced the Nexus control panel.

The Black-ops team stood anxiously on the transport platform waiting for the Nexus to kick in, Violet pushed the activation button, but nothing happened.

'Caspian!' her shout echoed across the darkened room towards his solitary figure watching on in disbelief.

'*Mon Dieu.*' He mumbled, now jogging towards the Nexus.

'Begin the transport sequence!' she commanded, impatiently tapping her foot against the steel grates of the raised platform.

'Transport Sequence in three, two, one. See you on the other side, Major,' Caspian said as he inputted the code into the control pad.

The oval framed machine started up with a clang as the lights dotted around the portal began to flicker like fireflies in the fog. The frame started to rotate slowly but gathered speed at a tremendous rate.

Then, a sudden flash emitted from the centre of the empty frame, shots of deep purple thunderbolts fired across the room, striking at the steel grates and network of pipes and wires surrounding the machine.

A thick purple haze began to form from the centre of the oval. With each passing revolution, the mist grew thicker and heavier, creating a wall of fog that started to swell, enveloping the occupants of the platform. Then, with a sudden flash of blinding light, the black-ops team were gone, leaving the

Nexus portal empty, except for a single wisp of smoke that faded into nothing.

'Major! Verify location.' Caspian said over the comm-link as he turned on the spot, now running back to the central command post.

'Manhattan dockyards, sector thirty.' she replied, holding back her excitement.

Caspian let out a sigh of relief as he collapsed onto the chair.

'Switching to visual.' he said, flicking his wrist to activate his holo-screen.

'Visual active. Get me a read on that energy spike.' Violet replied, clipping her H.U.D eyepiece to her left ear.

'The strength is weak but still active; re-routing coordinates to H.U.D.'

'Roger that.' Violet said as she turned her head to the rest of her team, 'Shoot to kill, we take this thing down today.'

Violet, followed by her team, ran towards sector thirty-two; a thick haze of black smoke drifted towards them, forming a wall of ominous dark energy.

'Switch to air filters.' Aster said as they passed through the wall of fog.

'Caspian! I need an update on the energy readings.' Violet said, now approaching the shipping container.

'It's all around you. I can't pin it down.'
Just as the words left Caspian's mouth, the image of the young girl came into full view, her porcelain face splashed across the screen.

'One hostile, dead ahead!' Caspian blurted out as he fell from his chair. The image of the girl began to crackle and blur as his holo screen began to buffer.

'Bring her down!' Violet shouted, flicking her wrists to activate her Nano bands. Within seconds, two guns began to piece together bit by bit until they formed into her trusty M-eights.

The black-ops team aimed, each armed with their weapon of choice and began firing at their target; the girl slid back into the smoke, disappearing from view.

The black mist began to retract, leaving a girl shaped void. Then, she released a barrage of black lightning bolts upon her assailants. Each one landed precisely onto their targets, shattering their weapons and forcing them back in different directions, preventing a coordinated assault.

Violet, predicting this type of attack, jumped out of the way. She spun into a backflip, landing perfectly just out of reach of the wayward bolts. Then, raising her arms, she locked onto her target, pressing firmly and confidently on the triggers; she began her barrage against the unknown hostile.

With each round fired, the bullets appeared to connect with the target. Violet was no lousy shot, yet the girl continued to stand still, unphased by Violet's barrage.

'Caspian! I need intel; why is she not taking any damage?' she asked over the comm-link, keeping up her relentless attack.

'She appears to be bulletproof,' Caspian replied, transcribing the data from her H.U.D.

'Find me a weak spot.' Violet said as she stepped forward, slowly approaching her enemy.

Keeping her eyes fixed on the young girl, the H.U.D switched from its usual green crosshair to a startling red, darting around the target, desperately searching for any weaknesses it could exploit.

'I'm not getting a response; there doesn't appear to be any,' Caspian said, continuing his analysis. 'Everything has a weakness!' Violet replied, honing her eyes to her target, 'I'm switching to explosive rounds.'

Flicking her wrists simultaneously, both M-eights began to flash with strips of green light as the new bullets loaded into the clips, flowing in a steady stream straight from her Nano-bands.

There was only a brief second from her break in fire before she started to shoot again. The new bullets, now exploding a vivid neon green upon impact.

Violet continued her attack until both clips ran empty.

'How about now?' Violet said shortly.

'I'm not getting any readings, Major!' Caspian replied, his words shrouded in a thin veil of self-doubt.

Plumes of bright green smoke had formed around the girl, a by-product of the explosive rounds. Violet stood motionless, her hawk-like eyes glued to where her target once stood. Readying herself for round two, she loaded her weapons with a new bullet. Her M-eights lit up with strips of flashing blue lights as the clips filled in a single swift motion.

As the neon clouds cleared, the girl in grey remained, standing completely still. Her pale skin, still immaculate, despite the scathing attack from Violet.

The girl flashed her pitch-black eyes towards Violet, lifting her arm into the air; a sleeve of dark energy began to form from her shoulder to her wrist. Then, with a single swipe of her arm, she sent a stream of black thunderbolts right at Violet.

'Major!' Caspian blurted out,

'I see it.' she said, lunging out of the way of the bolt, landing hard upon the ground with a mighty thud. She turned her head in time to watch as the bolt struck the container behind her, slicing it cleanly in half.

Violet jumped from the floor to her feet. Then, raising her weapons, she began returning fire.

A sea of electric blue bullets shot through the air connecting with their target, bursting into purple flames on impact. Then, they released their micropower as the ultraviolet lights began to freeze the dust mid-air forming solid violet crystals, cementing the girl on the spot.

'It's not working, Major! fall back.' Caspian said as he watched the girl make the slightest movement, shattering the crystals with little force.

Violet, ignoring the comm-link as she continued to fire at the girl who had now started to walk towards her. The girl's slow and timid footsteps grew large and bold as she broke out into a run. No matter how many bullets Violet launched, the girl refused to slow down.

In a last-ditch attempt to neutralise her target, Violet flicked her wrists, the M-eights in her hands de-materialized, reforming to the S.I.N.N full assault mode rifle. Violet flicked a loose tendril of her purple hair from her face, hitting the safety and assuming her assault stance. Her lips curled into a toothy grin as she firmly pressed down on the trigger.

A bombardment of bullets showered her mark, each one turning to dust upon contact of the girl, who was gathering immense speed as she headed in Violet's direction.

Realising that the S.I.N.N had no effect, she lowered her weapon. Thinking fast to devise a solution.

'Caspian! I need a readout on any form of energy that may be surrounding her.'

'I'm trying, but—'

Just as Caspian began to speak, the girl leapt from the ground into the air. Then, raising her arms above her head, she locked her sight onto Violet.

Violet jumped back in time, avoiding the girl's fists as she slammed them into the ground cratering the concrete upon impact. Then, spinning on her heel into a back kick, Violet landed a strike squarely to the girl's chest. Stunned for a brief moment, but then, regaining her composure, the girl began to glow, emitting the faintest shade of purple light.

'The energy spike has returned.' Caspian said.

'So, that's how she kills!' Violet replied, watching on, fascinated by the display before her eyes.

Standing in the middle of the cargo bay, the purple glow surrounding the girl in grey began to fade. The dark energy amassed in the dockyards began retracting inwards towards her, the mist gradually absorbing into her body as the air around the docks cleared.

The girl was no longer visible, her body shrouded by a thick layer of dark pulsating energy.

Black lightning bolts fired down onto the land around her, encasing her in a cage of deadly thunder.

'Major, the comm-link is starting to fault, Ca.. … h… .m.'

'Caspian! She's going to redirect that energy at me.' Violet said, unsure if her message got through.

'..to. .f …e.' Capsian replied as the comm-link faded to a low hiss.

Violet scanned the dockyards for the best place to take shelter. Finally, her eyes rested at the edge of the pier. Glancing down to the water below, she knew what she had to do. Running as fast as she could towards the edge of the dock, a bolt of black thunder broke through the clouds above, whipping at her feet as she ran.

A wisp of dark energy shot from the girl in grey, lashing at Violet's face, slicing her cheek in a clean line, a steady stream of crimson blood began to flow from her wound.

Violet, not daring to look back, pushed herself faster than she ever had, all her focus on reaching the edge of the dock. An earth-shattering noise sounded from the girl's direction. She had begun to form the dark energy into a single ball, suspended in mid-air.

She leant forward, moulding the black sphere into her liking, then, with a quick tap of her finger, she sent it flying through the air towards her target.

The energy ball moved quickly, burning the ground as it passed, making its way to Violet, gathering extreme amounts of speed with each passing second.

Violet leapt into the air, nose-diving into the sea, the dark energy just scraping at her back, melting the catsuit and searing her skin like fresh meat on the grill.

The sound of explosions filled the air as it struck the main dock's loading arm, engulfing the neighbouring sector in a sea of pure black flames, liquifying anything it came into contact with.

'Major, do you copy?' Caspian shouted frantically over the comm-link.

The link was silent. Caspian held on, waiting with bated breath.

Then, finally, the comm-link hissed, the sound of a broken voice came through; it was faint, but it was all Caspian needed to know Violet was ok.

'I ..py ..u. C....an .. y.u ..ad .e.'

'Major?' Caspian said as he tweaked the frequency of the comm-link.

'Yes, I re.d y.u.'

'The comm-link is damaged, and the visual is offline. Are you ok?'

'Y.s!'

The final word was spoken as the comm-link disconnected.

Caspian breathed a heavy sigh of relief as he sank into the Major's chair, holding his head in his hands.

Pulling herself up onto the dockyards from the water below, Violet collapsed on the ground, her energy all but spent.

Lifting her arm and pushing through the pain, she pressed the EMT radar attached to her Nano-bands, alerting the cleanup and medical crew to mobilise on her location.

Violet pulled herself up, steadying her legs until she was eventually vertical. As she witnessed the damage and utter catastrophe the attack had left behind, she noticed the target was gone.

All that was left were the bullets wedged into the steel containers, and the lifeless bodies of the Delta team scattered about the ground.

Violet searched in what remained of the dock for the rest of her black-ops team, finding them unconscious around the yards many meters away from where they were first attacked.

'Major!' a voice came from across the platform.

'Aster!' Violet said as she craned her neck to view him.

'Glad to see you're ok, boss,' Aster said with a grin across his dirt-covered face, 'I know you like to win, but this takes things to a whole new level.' He said, scratching his head as he looked around in disbelief.

'It got away, Aster! Delta team is dead.' Violet said her words sliced at him like a gust of ice-wind on a cold winter's morning.

The smile from Aster's face fell as he slumped to the floor
'We failed?'

'Again!' Violet replied as though to finish Aster's sentence.

'Major! We just got word from Washington; the General wants an update on the situation.' Caspian said as the comm-link re-activated.

Violet sighed heavily, tilting her head back; she fell silent as Caspian's words ran through her head. Then she shot a glance in Aster's direction.

'Let me guess! Contemplating our next steps? The big master plan of yours!' Violet jeered.

'No!' Aster replied sharply, 'Just realising our failure.' he said, shuffling his feet on the ground.

The summer rain began to clear faster than what felt natural. The sound of U.N.N jets filled the night sky as the clean-up and investigation crew began to arrive. High-powered spotlights illuminated the ground around the dockyards, displaying the tragic battle's remnants.

The clean-up crew were quick to action, setting their sights on the total devastation of the surrounding lands and the recovery of the bodies of the Delta team, taking pictures of the destruction and loading the dead onto slabs of floating steel.

Violet walked towards the Yellowhammer as it landed gracefully in front of her.

'Report back to base. I will liaise with the General; we debrief at seven hundred hours.' She said, boldly stepping onto the transport platform.

With her words still ringing in Aster's ears, he watched on as the doors sealed shut, the jet began to hover, rising vertically into the sky high above the city of Manhattan. Then in the blink of an eye, it was gone.

— CHAPTER TWO —

THE WHITE STEPS OF WASHINGTON

The Yellowhammer pulled into the docking station behind the White House; Violet looked out from the window of her passenger seat, witnessing the wonder of the city of Washington in all its sparkly splendour. The lights from the megacity below glimmered in the dark as private, and public transports flew high in the night sky, carrying all manner of dignitaries, politicians and other respective people of significant power.

'Washington!' Violet said to herself, crumpling her face in distaste.

'Landing sequence complete, Major.'

'Thank you, Captain, have a good night,' she replied, standing from her seat.

Approaching the transport door, Violet inhaled deeply, first cracking her neck then her knuckles as she readied herself for her second battle of the night.

The door hissed, swinging open to reveal a tall, broad and very stern-looking man dressed in full military regalia. His eyes shone a deep chocolate brown as he flashed a smile of his luminous white teeth, each one framed perfectly by the heavily curated handlebar moustache he took pride in displaying.

He patiently waited for Violet to exit the jet, wearing his all green military uniform displaying five silver stars.

'General!' Violet said, standing to attention, saluting the man in front of her.

'Major!' he replied, in his thick Texan twang.

Stepping off the Yellowhammer, she walked boldly towards the General, her eyes fixed upon the path ahead, not daring to look up, expecting a dressing-down if she were even to catch his eyes.

'Well! You've seen better days, V. I'll give you that.' He said, removing his hat and placing it under his arm as he rocked back and forth on his heels.

Violet remained silent, holding her rigid posture, too afraid to relax under the potential outburst that could be coming at any moment.

'Shall we?' he said with a heavy sigh, gesturing his arm towards the ivory white steps of the White House.

Violet led the way as the General followed; she had been to the White House more times than she cared to remember or at the very least care to admit.

With every passing step, she could recall each visit, the many wins she had claimed in the name of the U.N.N, each medal gloriously pinned to her jacket of honour. But this time, it was different; each step fell heavy as she climbed the white steps of Washington, each growing heavier than the last until, finally, she reached the top.

'Present identification!' A soft female-like voice came from the imposing steel clad door that both Violet and the General were standing in front of.

Lowering his face towards the red glowing orb centred in the door, a red laser scanned the General's eyes.

'Identification verified. Welcome, General Hill.' With that, the door slid swiftly to the side, granting them access.

The door opened to a grand hallway lined with plush red carpets. Solid gold sconces emitted a warm homely glow, the pure white walls embellished with lavish oil paintings seemed to stretch on for countless miles, each one of a past General, all of whom had served under the U.N.N.

'Have I ever told you the story of General Lee and his brilliant strategic last stand against Russia?' the General boomed as they wandered down the lush, if not tacky, hallway.

'I believe you have, sir,' Violet said in confusion, 'A few times if I'm not mistaken.'

'Yes, yes, it's one of my personal favourites; even with all that firepower and the mediocre technology of the twenty-third century, he was able to achieve victory over those Russian bastards! Still, he had to sacrifice his own life for the fate of the world. Now that! That's a leader! Don't you agree?' he said, reaching for the handle of his office door.

'One must give their all in the line of duty, for mankind and country.' Violet said, reeling off a sentence drilled into her from the younger days she spent as a cadet.

'Agreed!' he replied, entering the office, 'Close the door behind you.' He grunted as Violet passed the threshold.

'Please! Take a seat.' He gestured towards the tan and steel studded armchair situated in front of his dark solid oak desk.

Violet sat as General Hill fussed with an E-file he had retrieved from the bookshelves across the other side of the room. Then, sitting in quiet, she gazed around the large square room, making a mental note of the emerald green walls, the plush red carpet, the dozens of trophies and medals that lined the bookshelf, along with his most prized possession. The personal letter from the President, taking pride of place at the centre of the cabinet, right next to where the General currently stood.

Clearing his throat, General Hill turned to face Violet, 'Yes. So here we are, would you be so kind as to read aloud the first line of this page for me?'

Handing over the E.file, he sat behind his desk, waiting for Violet's response.

'Four nine nine five U.N.N, Case operative Major Villin, designate black-ops - Operation mosquito, E.DOC; four nine nine six U.N.N.'

'Thank you.' he said, taking back the E-file.

Violet sunk in her seat as the General pressed a button on his desk, the blinds turned from fabric to steel, the door bolted with a sudden clunk. The solid oak desk lowered into the floor, replaced with a holographic display unit showing past and present information, videos and still images relating to operation-mosquito

'Let's take a trip, shall we?' then, with a slight gesture of his hand, causing the screens to double in size, he said, 'Do you remember the first day I assigned you to this mission?'

'Affirmative, General.' Violet replied.

'Cut the crap V! I ain't got the time!' the General hissed as he spoke.

Violet rolled her eyes, standing from her seat to meet General Hill's stern glare.

'Yes! I do. I also remember the words you said to me! I believe it went along the lines of, "A year at best, I reckon, don't worry, y'all got this in the bag!" Tell me does that sound familiar?' Violet mocked, her face turning red as she clenched her fists.

'Enough!' he spat, tensing his shoulders as he puffed his chest, 'We can take shots at each other till we're both red in the face, but I'm sure you would agree, that will get us nowhere!'

Violet sighed, cracking her neck to relieve the pressure; she tilted her head back, choosing to focus on the small black smudge that marred the perfectly white ceiling.

'It was never my intention for this to go on any longer than a year—'

'And yet! Here we are five years later, the case still active, innocent people still dyin', and you and your pathetic band of useless followers still completely clueless!' the General snapped, cutting Violet off mid-sentence.

Sitting still, frozen to the spot with anger, Violet could feel the rage building up inside, fighting back the desire to shout; she swallowed her pride, keeping herself quiet.

'I need somethin' V. Anythin that tells me you're close to finishin' this.' he said, breathing a heavy sigh, taking a moment to calm himself.

'Listen V, the President—'

'Don't you talk to me about the President; I'm fully aware of her expectations!' Violet hissed, tilting her head towards General Hill, her icy stare bearing down on the shocked General.

'I get it; I put you forward for this; I wouldn't have done it if I didn't think you could do it.' He said, realising his misspoken words.

Violet crossed her arms, leaving the comfort of the chair; she began pacing around the office. An uneasy quiet fell over the room as Violet ruffled her hair, scratching her head.

'Fine!... Tonight was the first night I've come anywhere close to that thing; from my evaluation, it's not human.' Violet said, pressing on a still image of the girl enlarging it to an almost blurry scale.

'So we're dealing with some kind of alien?'

'Potentially yes, I now have insight into how she kills, and during our little altercation, I have managed to get a physical sample of the dark energy she produces.' she said, pointing to the scar on her cheek.

'She?' the General repeated in surprise.

'We've been tracking the energy via satellite data, but now we have a physical sample we can run it through B.I.O.N.A; this will allow us to track the energy movement before it spikes.' Violet continued, ignoring General Hill's interruption.

'I see! So you're goin' to be there before it kills again?'

'That's the plan.' She said, daring a brief smile.

'I gotta say; I expected more from you, V.' Violet uncrossed her arms, placing them on her hips, listening intently as the General continued to talk.

'Tell me, how do you intend on catching it once it does reappear?'

'With force!' Violet sharply replied.

'That didn't work out too well last time, now did it.' He scoffed.

'We have more intel on the effects of weapons against the subject; it would appear there is some sort of field of energy protecting her. Some invisible force deflected the bullets; even when I could get a hit, they just disintegrated. I've never seen anything like it.' She sighed, swiping at the holo-display to reveal a motion image of her attacks.

'MAGNA force technology?' Hill said, investigating the image in minute detail, 'How is this possible? We've tried MAGNA tech before but could never control the cylindrical effect, not to mention all the crushed bones from the rogue warping field.'

Violet paused, staring at the holo-display.

'Curious.' Violet mumbled to herself.

'What?' General Hill asked, breaking his gaze from the screen.

'Nothing!' she said, snapping out of her trance, 'I will ensure a full report is completed, filed and on your desk first thing tomorrow morning.'

'You mean today! I will also need a copy of your action plan and timeline of completion.' He said, updating the E-file, sliding it back onto the shelf in the corner of the room.

'Violet! If you fail to bring this thing under control, you and you alone will face the consequences. I don't want to be calling in the full strength of the Nova guard just to eliminate one hostile. Am I making myself clear?'

'Perfectly!' Violet replied.

Nodding her head, she began to excuse herself from the General's office. Then a soft but firm knocking came from the other side of the office door.

'Yes!' General Hill shouted as he pressed a button, reverting the room back to normal.

The door of the General's office swung open to reveal a tall slim blond-haired woman, her hair only just grazing her shoulders in a chic, sleek bob. She wore a black and white pinstripe dress cut just above her knees. Her black and red platform heels clicked on the floor as she strode elegantly and confidently into the room. The woman's ocean blue eyes caught Violet standing across the room from behind her stylish all-glass frames.

'Violet? I'm sorry, Major Villin, I didn't expect to find you here so late.' The woman said in a fluster.

'Ms Myers, How may I help?' General Hill asked, sinking back into his chair behind the imposing desk.

'Right! General, I have the results from the first trial phase of the E.X.O suits and the statistics on the proto-gen BIO-weapon.'

'Thank you, Ms Myers, please accept my apologies for the late request, urgent matters, I'm sure you understand.' He said, in the softest gentlemanly tone that he could muster, flashing her a wink as she handed him the E-file.

'Right, good thing I was already in the office, well! If that's all, I'll be on my way, General! Major!' she said before turning on her heels to leave the room.

'Oh!, Ms Myers before you leave, would you be so kind as to update me on the Nexus project?' he asked, flashing a sinister smile towards Violet.

'Certainly, General! The initial testing of large non-biological transportation is going well with generally positive results. There have been some phasing issues, but it's relatively minor.' She said, turning to face the General.

'And what of human transportation? How's that goin?' he asked, his crooked smile still glaring directly at Violet.

'Human trials have yet to begin, sir; we are still many months, potentially years from that phase.'

'Ahh, I see, well then, perhaps you should schedule a meeting with Major Villin; after all, her use of the Nexus is showing auspicious results.' General Hill said, returning to his work.

Myers shot a glance towards Violet, her eyes pinning her to the spot.

'Thank you, General. I will make sure to set one up A.S.A.P.' She said through gritted teeth, swiftly stepping out of the office.

'General,' Violet said, saluting as she left the room, closing the door behind her.

Violet walked into the corridor hastily trailing behind the flustered woman.

'Are you kidding me?' she snapped, spinning on the spot to face Violet.

'Look, Serena! We had no other choice; what else was I supposed to do?' Violet said, startled by Serena's sudden outburst.

'I don't care, V, what were you thinking!' she said, her anger growing by the second, 'And the worst part of all of this is I have to hear it from him.' She said, thrusting her finger in the direction of the General's office.

'Look, if you're worried about your precious little project then—'

'How dare you!' Serena snapped, cutting Violet off before she could finish her sentence. 'So that's how little you think of me! You truly believe that I care more for a bunch of nuts and bolts than you.' Serena clenched her fists, turning away from Violet, fearing she couldn't control her anger any longer.

'Do you even know how dangerous it is?' Serena said, her voice quivering in frustration.

'It was the only way; we needed to be there before the signal went; the Nexus provides instant transport. So what was I to do? Fly there? We didn't have the time.' Violet replied, trying her best to bring calm to the situation.

'I can't keep doing this V, Every time I hear another story about how brave you were, another day where you fly off to save the world whilst I sit on the sidelines, waiting for that inevitable call telling me you're gone! I just can't do this anymore!' Serena said, her eyes welling with tears.

'Serena, please—' Violet begged, extending her hand towards Serena.

'No!' She replied, slapping Violet's hand away. 'We can talk about this later; right now, I'm busy!'

she said as she stormed away from Violet, leaving her standing in the White House halls alone.

As Violet walked towards the exit; her day going from bad to worse, the sound of her name echoed in the distance; turning her head to face the direction of the voice, she squinted her eyes, trying to make out the shape of the person approaching from the bottom of the White House steps.

'Major.' The sound became more apparent the closer the person got.

'Aster?' Violet said as he came into clear view. 'What are you doing here? My instructions were clear!' she said in a mixture of frustration and confusion.

'They were Major. But, when I got back to base, I was instructed to meet with the intelligence team to relay the information we gathered on the current mission.' Aster said, his face now back to its pristine, dirt-free self.

'Intelligence?' Violet asked, still confused, 'That's not your area. Where is Caspian?'

'Back at the base, Major. I'm here in his place.' He said, raising a single eyebrow.

'Who called you in?' she said briskly, her eyes pinning Aster on the spot.

'We received a memo from Deputy Director Wren asking us to submit our data files on the current operation. I just dropped them off at the east wing now. Is there a problem, Major?'

'No! I guess not.' Violet's mind began to wander as she turned to look back at the empty hallway of the White House, her thoughts still lingering on the row she had just had with Serena.

'Major?' Aster said, awaiting her order,

'Right, the debrief.' Violet said, shaking herself out of her trance.

'Are you sure you're ok, Major?'

'No. Yes. It's just… Washington!' she said, shrugging her shoulders, trying to wake herself up.

'Should I call for the Yellowhammer?'

'No! We can take the O.D.T.S.'

'Why? The Yellowhammer is much quicker,' Aster said, his brow furrowed in confusion.

Violet made her way across the promenade, walking briskly towards the entrance point of the O.D.T.S located under the landing zone of the White House docking station. Approaching the entrance point, she pressed a button on the side panel. The dark-tinted glass doors swung open almost instantly, revealing two white chairs in the middle of an all-black cabin.

'Get in, Aster!' Violet said, rolling her eyes as he jogged behind her.

Upon entering the cabin, a single-camera lens dropped from the ceiling producing a red laser that scanned the room.

'Scan complete. Welcome Major Villin, Commander Voss, please confirm your desired location.'

A holographic keyboard appeared at waist height in front of Violet.

'Destination confirmed...estimated travel time to London is... Seven minutes.'

'Seven minutes! There must be traffic,' Aster grunted.

Violet sighed as she and Aster took their seats; once the final belt buckled, the doors to the carriage snapped shut. The oval room illuminated a soft shade of seafoam blue, the engine began to power up, a low hum filled the cabin, and with that, they shot into motion, descending deeper underground.

'So, how did the meeting go?'

'Now's not the time Aster, perhaps you should practice your peace and quiet!'

'Well, I figured whilst we have a spare seven minutes.'

'Fine! If you insist,' she said, closing her eyes, relaxing into the seat. 'Not good.' She finished abruptly, bringing the conversation to a stop.

As they sat in uncomfortable silence, the low and strangely comforting hum of the carriage filled the air. Violet breathed another heavy sigh as she continued to replay the Manhattan attack over and over again in her mind.

'One minute to the final destination.'

'Finally!' Aster rejoiced, slapping both his thighs as he unclipped the safety belt.

Violet opened her eyes, focusing on the doors to the carriage as it slowly came to a stop.

'You have reached your final destination! Central travel hub, London, level ten. The local time is six AM. Please ensure you collect all your belongings and take care when exiting the carriage. Thank you for travelling the Omni-directional travel system. Have a great day!'

The doors to the cabin swung open, flooding the room with the burning heat of the summer sun.

Violet and Aster walked out, feeling the warm morning air on their skin.

'Another beautiful day in London!' Aster said, throwing a wide toothy smile in Violet's direction.

— CHAPTER THREE —

LONDON'S CALLING

As Aster and Violet walked along the cobblestone streets of London, the sounds of the hustle and bustle one had come to expect of the fiftieth century London filled their ears.

The surface pods swept past in their early morning rush, whilst passers-by on the street, adorned in the most fashionable clothes, waved and spoke amongst themselves, blissfully going about their daily business. The early morning birds chirped their blissful song as the scent of oak and maple spun in the clean, fresh air.

'I see the new trees are growing well,' Aster said as they walked along the pavement.

'Yes.' Violet mumbled, taking no notice of Aster as she walked towards the platform lift.

Situated on the side street of London's central travel hub, the glass elevator stood hundreds of meters tall with no end in sight. Every mile or so had a platform suspended in the air, floating ominously in the London skyline. Violet pressed the button calling for the sky elevator. The glass doors opened smoothly with a satisfying swish, revealing a gold and silver walled cabin large enough for four people to fit inside. Located in the centre of the cabin were four white leather chairs bolted to the floor by a thick chrome pipe.

'Platform selection!' The voice came from the speakers of the cabin.

Violet selected from the fixed number pad on the chair arm.

'Platform forty-two selected!'

The glass doors came to a swift close, then the carriage shot through the tube, climbing faster with each passing level. Relaxing into the chairs, Violet and Aster began taking in the spectacular views of the many platforms of London.

'You know! It would be easier if we just took a sky-ship.' Aster said, turning to look at Violet.

'I know.' She sighed, cracking her neck, her mood steadily shifting at the sight of her hometown.

'Sooo, why the long trip?'

'It gives me time to think! And besides, the commute is pleasant, is it not?' Violet mocked, a slight grin cracked from the side of her mouth.

The cabin slowed to a complete stop at platform forty-two. The glass doors slid open, locking to the platform.

Aster and Violet left the cabin, continuing their walk past the many old-fashioned shops and market stall carts littered with people setting up for the day ahead.

There they passed the high rise buildings of the financial district until they reached an imposing red-bricked building that stood alone at the edge of the platform.

'I've never seen inside your place before.' Aster said as he tried to comprehend Violet living like a normal person.

'Who said you were invited?' she sneered.

'What are we even doing here?'

'I require a change of clothes,' She said, pointing at her back towards her melted catsuit, 'Wait here, I'll be right back.'

Aster strolled over to the park facing the building, sitting on an old wooden bench; he watched on as the ducks swam and quacked peacefully in the pond.

Approaching the doors to her building, Violet paused; an uneasy presence crept into her mind, turning on the spot; she could feel the eyes of someone watching her. With a flick of her wrist, she materialised a small orange marble branded with the character Ψ throwing it into the air; the marble froze in the sky. Then, levitating just above her head, it began to pulsate, emitting an orange wave of energy for every second it stayed air-born.

A holo-pad materialised on Violet's arm, displaying her exact location. A series of low pitch beeps began to emit from the pad as it revealed the radial image of the grounds around her.

'Aster, confirm your current location.'

Aster turned from the pond to see Violet poised and ready for battle in the middle of the entrance path to her building.

'OVER HERE MAJOR, WHAT'S UP!' he shouted, waving his arm in the air, a confused look etched across his face.

'Never mind,' she said, deactivating the marble catching it as it dropped from the air, 'It's been a long day.' Violet said to herself, drawing a deep breath.

The entrance doors to the red-bricked building creaked as they opened; Violet spun round to see a gaggle of people leaving, talking and laughing rather loudly as they passed. Violet continued to walk towards the complex doors, unable to shrug off the uneasy feeling of being watched.

'Lifeform scan commencing, please present identification!'

Violet flicked her wrist, a holographic I.D. projected from her arm, raising it towards the camera lens; a green light scanned the 3D image.

'Welcome, Violet Villin!' The speaker said as the doors slid open to reveal a perfectly square room.

The warm glow of golden lights pathed the floor as the red brick walls stood boldly encasing the circular-shaped polished copper reception desk in the centre of the room.

As she passed the desk, making her way to the closest glass elevator, located in the middle of the wall, she flicked her wrist, calling for a cabin to land. The copper door lift opened to reveal a solid oak room adorned with black and white pictures of London, all lit up with a single soft glowing light that flickered as through to emulate a real candle.

'Good morning Ms Villin! Please select your destination.' The sound of a softly spoken British gentleman emitted from the speakers above as she entered the required location.

'Floor three two four, section A.' Violet said into the intercom.

The lift began to rise, leaving the ground with a slight clunk; moving slowly at first, it started gaining speed the further up the building it went; as the lift reached floor ten, its rate of acceleration increased.

The cabin, now moving so fast it was but a blur to anyone viewing it with the naked eye.

As she reached floor three two four, the cabin slowed to a complete stop, then jolting back, it darted horizontally past each letter of the alphabet, finally arriving at section A.

'You have arrived at your destination, have a pleasant day!' The British man said as the doors from the elevator opened straight into Violet's apartment.

Walking through the hallway of her two-story duplex, the sights and sounds of home overcame her senses. The scent of orange blossom filled her nose as she moved from the hallway to the living room. Her eyes landed on the pictures of her and Serena on vacation, the image of her graduation from L.N.U. She cracked a faint smile as she stopped at her and the Black-ops team on their most recent celebratory night out.

She breathed a deep breath, shedding the weight of the past twenty-four hours. However, as quickly as the moment passed, an uneasy tension now filled the air. She sensed the watchful eyes of an invisible person again. Attaching her H.U.D, Violet scanned the room for any visible signs of life.

'Read complete, detecting zero visible life levels!' The HUD said via the comm-link.

'Scan for non-visible!' Violet said, darting her eyes from side to side.

'Read complete, detecting zero non-visible lifeforms!'

Violet readied herself for a potential attack, flicking her wrists, activating her M-eights. She knew she was not alone. As she crept through the ground floor, her footsteps creaked along the floorboards, making her way from the living room to the kitchen; the hot morning sun beamed through the many windows warming the room, illuminating every nook and cranny.

Violet cleared the ground floor making her way to the central stairwell. Keeping her steps slow, she silently climbed the concrete slabs arriving at the second floor's landing, walking along her bedroom corridor, keeping her guns pointing dead ahead, ready to fire on any assailant in her way.

Finally, reaching her bedroom, the H.U.D continued to show no signs of life, human, or otherwise! Reaching out, placing her hand on the handle of the bedroom door, slowly and firmly twisted it until it made a click. Pausing for a brief second, she could sense something or someone in her room. As she pressed her ear to the door, the room was deathly silent, but this was of little comfort.

Violet stepped back, calming herself; she closed her eyes, gathering her thoughts she ran through her plan of attack. The door was now unlatched, ready for her to strike, with a single kick to the centre, it flung open.

Violet, pressing her advantage, switched the H.U.D to combat mode, the green crosshairs changed to red, now, with the room in full view, before Violet, stood a man almost seven-foot-tall. His hair was as white as snow; his eyes glimmered like starlight in the night's sky; he wore a robe that grazed the floor, its colours ever-changing.

Violet, without second-guessing, opened fire on the man; a stream of glowing blue bullets shot from her M-eights, each one connecting with their target. The man fell back, his body pinned to the floor as the shots froze his limbs on impact. Continuing her barrage, she moved closer to her target, her fingers rasping on each trigger. Then with a flick of her wrists, her weapons began to glow green, firing a single shot at the intruder; the vivid green bullet sped towards him, landing a perfect hit. The shell burst into a cloud of acid green flames engulfing her target, sending him across the room.

Violet ceased her fire, waiting for the smoke to clear. She held her aim, slowly approaching her mark, guns firmly in hand, her eyes squarely fixed upon the intruder now lying motionless on the floor.

'Identify yourself!' she commanded, a slight quiver in her voice.

He remained still. Violet gritted her teeth as she slowly crept forward, readying herself for another attack; she knew the fight was not over yet.

'I said identify yourself!' She repeated, bending down to tap him with her gun.

Suddenly the intruder spun into the air; rising rapidly, he snatched the guns from Violet's hands whilst landing a kick to her chest. His strength was unlike any modded human that Violet had fought before, flying across the room, her body connected with the wall just outside the bedroom. Slumping to the floor, she raised her head, staring down her enemy; with a flick of her wrist, the M-eights dematerialised from the assailant's hand, instantly reforming back into hers. Each gun clicked as they glowed their familiar blue colour; Violet smirked as she opened fire again.

'Enough!' the man said, swiping his arm in Violet's direction.

The weapons stopped firing. Violet struggled to move; willing her limbs to stand, she felt an invisible force bear down upon her. Unable to move a single limb, she strained with each forced breath as she refused to let up.

'Much better.' The man said, slowly lowering back to the ground.

'Who are you?' Violet strained, pushing her words through gritted teeth.

'A friend.' The man said, chuckling to himself as he brushed off his robe, smoothing his hair back to the side.

'What?' Violet gasped, struggling to breathe in her frozen state.

'Fine!' the man said, flapping his arms in defeat. 'I can forgive the amateur dramatics, but you have to promise me, if I release you, you'll put a stop to this whole shoot first, ask questions later attitude!' he said, sauntering over to Violet.

'Agreed.' She strained, feeling the blood rushing to her ears muffling the man's soft voice.

'Very well then!' the man said, snapping his fingers; the tremendous boom echoed across the room.

Violet felt the pressure release as she sprawled across the floor, swallowing air by the droves as the sound of tinkling bullets lightly dropped to the ground around her.

'Now! I think introductions are in order, my name is Aeon, and whom may you be?' the man winked, laughing hysterically as he finished his question.

'Why are you here?' Violet said, her words still through gritted teeth.

'I was just passing by. Thought I'd stop by and say hi!' he said melodiously,

'What do you want?' Violet said, her face glowing red in anger, forcing herself to not lunge into another attack.

'Nothing from you, Violet! But you will be thankful for this,' his tone shifted from light-hearted to serious as he threw a small golf ball size crystal towards Violet, 'It may just come in handy in the future.'

'What is it?' she asked, catching the ball and turning it in her hand, watching the light bounce around the room from its smooth surface.

'A gift.' he said in the sternest of ways.

'What?' Violet said, looking up at Aeon.

'You will understand when the time comes, and when it ends!' a broad smile spread across Aeon's face, laughing as he turned on the spot, disappearing as though he had just walked behind an invisible curtain.

The room went from dishevelled, the bed still smoking from the explosive round back to normal in an instant.

Violet pulled herself up from the ground, gingerly walking into the bedroom, still on edge waiting for another surprise attack. She looked around the room, her hands still firmly gripped, onto the crystal, nothing, not a sound, she realised she was now alone.

'Major, what's taking so long?' the voice of Aster took Violet by surprise.

'Yes, Aster, I will be there momentarily!' she said, snapping back to reality, her thoughts, returning to the mission at hand.

Grabbing a bag of clothes next to her bed, Violet stuffed the mysterious crystal ball safely into the side pocket, hastily rushing out of the apartment.

Arriving at the courtyard, she found Aster lying on the grass next to the pond of her apartment complex.

'Aster! on your feet, let's go.' Violet hissed as she marched towards the O.D.T.S.

Aster stood straight up, looking Violet up and down, witnessing a somewhat dishevelled Violet stomping off ahead.

'What happened to you?' he blurted out, instantly regretting it.

'Nothing, let's go! The debrief cannot wait any longer, now call the Yellowhammer and let's head to base.' She said, her words in a fluster.

Flicking his wrist, Aster activated a homing beacon. Moments later, the Black-ops jet appeared hovering overhead.

'See! much faster!' Aster said, smiling at Violet. But, unfortunately, the smile was not returned.

'Get on the ship Aster.' Violet said, her eyes burning into him with her icy cold stare.

'Welcome aboard. We will have you back at base in no time!'

'Thank you, Captain.' Violet said, taking her seat in the cockpit.

The Yellowhammer doors slammed shut as it rose vertically from the ground; as the engines kicked in, it spun in the air towards the coordinates of the Black-ops base. With a final blast, the engines emitted a jolt of yellow thunder, pushing them at high speed towards their destination.

As they whipped through the sky, Violet stared out the window, taking little interest in the passing ships. Instead, deep in thought, she pondered the same questions that plagued her mind. Such as, Who was the man in her apartment?, Who is the girl in grey? How was she going to solve this case? The Captain, interrupting her thoughts, announced they had begun the landing sequence. Violet shook herself back to reality; gathering herself together, she stood from the cockpit, making her way towards the doors.

The Black-ops base was known for being the most secure place in all of Uropa. However, its location was top secret, known only to those working within the division. Situated on the lowest platform of London, the base was accessible only to those carrying Black-ops credentials. It was so secret that there was no access lift or landing platform.

Instead, it used cloaking field technology to hide in the open with only a single entrance point for authorised carriers. Those who managed to access the lowest floor could see only a single door, framed in black steel and nothing more.

A holo-post illuminated the door requesting verification. As Violet walked towards the entrance, the sound of thunderous waves from the waters below filled her ears. The sun grew gloriously hot as it raged down upon the steel floor; the scent of hot metal filled the air as they prepared their credentials.

'Present identification!' a mechanised voice said.

Violet leaned forward, allowing the newly formed lens to focus on her eye; with a single click, the doors opened.

'Welcome, Major Villin.' The mechanised voice rang through the speakers as Violet and Aster walked into the scanner located on the other side of the door.

The base was vast and dark, dimly lit with single white lights and no signposts. Walking down a series of crowded corridors littered with soldiers, technicians, medicare providers, and numerous other workers, the sound of innate chatter filled the air as their boots clunked upon the steel floor.

They made their way to the access lift for the central command post deep within the base.

Arriving at the doors, they walked into a perfectly oval room, filled floor to roof with computer screens; the bright white light of the displays illuminated the room.

Aster followed behind Violet, trailing off to his station, standing along with the rest of the assembled Black-ops team.

Violet continued to walk down the centre of the room, passing each steel desk. Then, making her way to the central command post that stood atop of the rows of work stations, her steps rattled as she walked with purpose over the steel grates, the noise filling the deathly silent room. The eyes of the Black-ops team fixed upon the command post as Violet made her way up the steps. Turning on the spot as she reached the top to face the group. Her violet hair glistened as it swung, her hands now firmly placed on her hips. She flashed her luminous violet eyes towards the Black-ops specialists; sharpening her gaze, she took a deep breath.

'Gentleman!' her voice boomed around the room,

'Major!' they replied, standing to attention, saluting in unison.

'Let us begin!'.

— CHAPTER FOUR —

THE EYES HAVE IT

Violet scoured the room. The Black-ops team took to their seats as they began their long-awaited de-brief.

'The General is requiring immediate action; we must provide him with a swift resolution on this case; I expect you have all had enough time to prepare your individual action plans.'

All eyes focused on Violet as she sat, crossing her legs, ready for their statements.

'Caspian! Intelligence update!' she said, facing him directly.

'Major! We have re-formatted the satellite as per the incident in Manhattan; it will now include the molecular structure of the energy she emits when active; after my video call with Ms Myers, I can now inform you all that the B.I.O.N.A is fully operational. We have run the residual energy sample collected from the crime scene through B.I.O.N.A; I'm expecting the results very soon.'

'So, we are ready for the next attack?' Violet replied, her stern voice echoing around the room.

'Yes, however! We won't know if the re-calibration of the satellite will work until a physical detection has been made. By that point, we could be too late.'

'Any suggestions on how to fix this?' Violet asked, scanning the rest of the room.

'We could trace the energy that remains in the bodies of the Delta team. If it caused death, then the sample must be stronger than the one collected from the ground. If we feed that through B.I.O.N.A, we could locate the target before she strikes again.'

'Good work Caspian! feedback to me immediately once complete, this could be vital to our success.' Violet said, flashing him a brief smile.

Caspian set about working on the task at hand as Violet turned her chair to the next specialist.

'Leo!' she said, casting her gaze upon the broad blue-eyed man, who sat just behind Aster. He wore a similar uniform to the others. However, his was a distinct shade of blood-red, with each piece adorned with a golden gun and brass sword as a mark of the weapons guild; his golden blond hair lay messy as he grinned his cheeky smile.

'Any information as to why our weapons were so ineffective?' she inquired.

'I have run diagnostics, replicating the fire sequence from your M-eights, aligning them to the exact biometric composition of the target. There are no signs that show the prevention pierce. In short, it shouldn't have stopped the bullets from hitting.'

'So why did it?'

'I have no answer, Major.' Leo said, his head dropping to the floor.

'Not good enough Leo!, You have had ample time in which to get me the information. I expect answers; failure to provide them will result in your removal from my team. Am I making myself clear!' like a parent scolding a child, Violet scowled at Leo from atop her command post.

'Very clear, Major,' He replied, now scrambling to develop a solution, 'I will work on the ammunition and weapons specification to improve performance. I am confident there is some hidden data on MAGNA tec somewhere in the archives.'

'Fine!' Violet said sharply, slowly turning to her next operative.

'Zyair.' She said, looking behind Leo towards the dark-haired man. He wore a light grey military-style doctor uniform branded with a platinum caduceus. His deep brown eyes gleamed in the dark as he held the Major's gaze.

'Your extensive knowledge on explosives and BIO human engineering could aid Leo in actually providing some form of usable intelligence,' She said, raising a solitary eyebrow. 'Can I trust you both to come up with a solution?'

'Yes, Major.' Zyair replied.

'Takeshi, I will need you to develop the tactical response plan for our next encounter, use the information provided by Caspian, remember no mistakes this time!'

Takeshi stood from his chair, saluting the Major, as he did, his immaculate green uniform, bearing the tactical division logo of a silver map with an arrow underneath, glistened in the dark. His short jet black hair lay smooth atop his head as he removed his hat in respect of the Major.

'Yes, Major.'

'Jax!' she said, focusing on the man in a tan uniform bearing the insignia of a silver fighter jet.

'What developments can we expect from our current transportation. I'm sure you can agree it was highly ineffective!' her devilish glare was now pinning him to the spot.

'I have run diagnostics on the effects of the registered energy against our technology; it appears to have some form of ionic effect. Anything emitting an electrical pulse is neutralised during the burst. There are multiple options we can take. The most effective would be to look into the integration of nanotech among the already commissioned carriers!' he replied. His bronze eyes focused straight ahead as he avoided her enveloping stare.

'Good work Jax, I look forward to reading the results.'

Violet craned her neck to view the final man, who sat quietly working on the desk furthest from hers.

'Oren, your update, if you please.'

Oren stood to address Violet. He wore a similar uniform to the others. His was all-white, bearing the black emblem of a planet encircled by a ship. His vivid green eyes glowed as he spoke; his soft voice was smooth to the ear as he relayed his analysis.

'I have analysed the attack patterns, energy formations, muscular composition and fabric density of the target in question. A scan from the archives has shown that this person is not from Nova. From what I have deduced, it is some form of subhuman entity.'

'So it's not from earth?' Violet asked, her eyes widening,

'Definitely not, it may have human form, but everything else is extraterrestrial.'

'Continue the research; if we can link its origin, we may have a better chance of taking it down!' Violet said as she stood from her chair.

'Yes, Major.'

'Gentleman, you have your assignments, now, get to work!' Violet said as she made her way down the platform.

'What assignment do you need from me, Major?' Aster asked from across the room.

'Come with me,' She said, striding past his desk. 'You know more than you are letting on Aster! I'm going to need that information.' Violet narrowed her eyes as Aster walked towards her, her stare burning through him like a hot knife to the chest.

The room fell silent as each person worked on their plans, the soft thump of fingers on glass echoed across the room.

Zyair stood in a sudden outburst 'Major! I have made a discovery.' His shocked voice cut through the stillness of the room.

Violet turned from Aster, looking Zyair dead in the eyes,

'Go on!' she said, making her way towards his desk,

'I have been analysing the body's of the Delta team to see if there were any specific kill marks—'

'To the point, Zyair!' Violet said, rapidly tapping her foot on the steel grates.

'There is a specific kill mark we found on each victim; it's small but present on each person, a darkmark of sorts.'

Zyair moved his hand over his wrist, activating his nano-chip. A holo-screen materialised, with a flick of his finger, the image appeared on the screens surrounding the room.

'It's a symbol.' Aster said, leaning closer to the screen as he inspected the mark.

'Omega,' Violet said, her voice breaking the tension, 'Where is this mark located?'

'The eyes Major, both of them on each body.' Zyair replied,

Aster sat down on his chair, staring intently at the screen, not breaking any attention from the marks in the victims' eyes, until he noticed something quite peculiar. The walls began to melt. Then, the room slowly dimmed until everything faded, and Aster blacked out.

*

Opening his eyes, he found himself surrounded by lush green fields; the crisp air filled his lungs as he breathed in deeply, a familiar scent drifted through the air as the heat from the orange sun beamed down from the sky.

'Eco.' Aster said to himself, his eyes welling with tears.

Aster could barely believe it, pinching himself to make sure he wasn't dreaming; no matter how hard he squeezed, he didn't wake up.

'This must be real!' Aster said as he began to explore the all too familiar surroundings of his now distant homeland.

He walked among the green fields, the sound of fresh grass crunched under his feet as the ground yielded to his presence. He would stop to admire the colour of the delicate flowers scattered across the land. He would look up to take in the vast azure sky and listen to birds' songs as they played their melodic tunes. Aster had all but forgotten what it was like to be on Eco and just how much he missed it, it had only been five years, a mere blink of the eye for an Econian, but on earth, it felt like a lifetime.

As he made his way through the field, the ground below began to smoke; the acrid fumes filled his lungs as the sky started to turn a vivid shade of blood red. He choked as he dropped to his knees. His heart began to beat fast as the memories of Eco's final days came flooding back.

'This is not the Eco I know!' he sputtered, his eyes growing wide as he witnessed the horror breaking out before him. The sound of women and children screaming filled the air, their cries for help overwhelming his senses. Aster shook his head, begging to wake from his nightmare, the village ahead now engulfed in a sea of black flames.

The ground beneath him began to crack as flames shot forth from the field. Then a ball of dark energy suddenly formed at his feet. It was too late to escape.

The explosion sent Aster into the air, the force pushing him hundreds of miles further past the fields towards the lands of his home town, landing on the ground with a hard thud.

The blood now rushing to his head, Aster stood as the painful memories came flooding back. He was back in the Eco he knew, the Eco ravaged by war. An overwhelming sense of dread filled Aster's body as he took off running in the direction of the grand citadel, a glorious castle amid the rubble of destroyed houses.

As he ran past many men fighting in the streets, a mix of both Econians and alien creatures battling to the death, he remembered the dismembered and bloodied now littered around the grounds. Then throughout the death and destruction, Aster heard a voice call his name,

'General Voss, the city is overrun; we cannot hold them any longer. We must fall back to Rittia.'

'No!' Aster shouted, unable to stop his actions, 'Hold the citadel, we've lost too much to flee now.' He said, unable to stop the words as they left his mouth.

'General, the western border is taken, we have pushed them towards the east, but we cannot hold the line. She is here; the Executioner has entered the —' The comm-link fell silent. The voice of the unknown person rang out as the sound of explosions could be heard in the far off distance.

'General! your orders!' said one soldier,

'General! We await your commands!' said another.

Aster looked on in horror as his entire battalion began to fall. One by one, they were slain as droves of aliens flooded the city.

The world began to darken, the peoples' faces became unrecognisable, the words they spoke stopped making sense. Aster could feel himself blacking out.

The world came back into focus; finding himself bound in chains, he struggled to move. The world was blurry. He could barely make out the events now unfolding before him.

'For your horrific crimes of high treason, I sentence you all to death!' the voice boomed from a man unrecognisable to Aster.

His vision returned, but only for a brief moment, just long enough for him to see a figure of a young woman, clad in grey armour, appear from a cloud of black fog; her long blond hair flowed freely in the breeze.

'You!' Aster shouted, unable to contain himself.

The girl ignored Aster as she slowly stepped forward, making her way towards the blurry man whose voice continued to boom across the city.

The Alien army surrounded the young girl, their weapons aimed directly at her, ready to take her down upon their Commanders orders.

'Send that bitch back to hell.' The man's voice boomed as the ground quivered in fear.

The woman clicked her fingers, a rush of dark energy gathered towards her, wrapping around her body until all that remained was a mass of black smoke.

The sound of a click came from the centre of the dark mass; then, she unleashed the energy from around herself, firing it upon the surrounding army, killing all who stood in her way. The dead bodies flew past Aster, the face of a slain soldier flashed before his eyes.

'Omega.' He said in shock, 'That symbol, the marking, the woman, this has happened before!' So he said to himself as the winds picked up, engulfing him in a tornado of black fog.

'ASTER!' Violet slapped her hands together in front of his face, jolting him back into the room.

'I don't expect to call you five times before you answer. What are you daydreaming about anyway?' Violet asked, clearly annoyed by his ignorance.

'The past.' He said, his eyes still semi-glazed from his vision.

Violet furrowed her brow staring at Aster.

'Do you care to share with the group?' she said impatiently.

Aster looked around the room to see fourteen sets of eyes all firmly placed on him. It was rare to see anyone fail to answer Violet on her first call; this naturally caught the team's full attention.

'The mark in eyes. I've seen it before, back on Eco, during the rebellion.' Aster croaked, shaking his head.

Violet paced the room, processing the information she had just received.

'Aster, I need you to tell me what happened on Eco?' Violet said, her voice shaking with anticipation.

Aster explained to Violet the events that just unfolded, how he found himself back on Eco, how he fought as a General in the rebellion and how a woman in grey showed up slaughtering an entire army.

'It's not enough. How did the war start? Who were you fighting?'

'I...I don't remember; there are gaps in my memory; I can't explain it. It's like the longer I'm away from Eco, the more it fades.' Aster said, his head in his hands.

Violet pressed her fingers to her temples and began to rotate them; she knew there had to be more to this than what Aster had told them.

'Thank you, Aster,' Violet said, turning to Zyair, 'Is there a way to extract the mark from the victims' eyes?'

'There has been a trial on the excavation of the cornea. However, as soon as one of the lenses was pierced, the mark faded. We have yet to continue any further tests.' Zyair swiped up on the nano pad bringing the video of the surgery on screen.

'Malignant energy,' Violet said as he watched the video playing on repeat, 'Aster, you said that the energy she emitted killed everyone around her?'

'Correct.'

'Zyair, I need you to scan the bodies with B.IO.N.A, if this truly is a form of energy B.I.O.N.A will generate a chemical structure, knowing that we should be able to find a way to siphon it from the body's before it evaporates.'

'Yes, Major, I will head to the testing lab now.'

Violet paused, her thoughts rushing a mile a minute.

'Aster, I need you to visit Serena Myers, see if there is anything in her lab that can help bring back your memories.'

'Yes, Major, right away.' Aster said, slowly standing trying to find his footing,

'Leo, I need you to pull the data from the tracker satellite and run a virtual reenactment of last night.'

'I can, but the data won't match the lab sample sequence; it only tracks the dispensed energy, it could skew the results.' Leo words slicked with sarcasm.

'That's why you also pull the thermal data from our Nano cam's and the vitals report, cross-reference the three to get a near-perfect result! Do you have any other stupid questions?' she said, her words hitting Leo like a punch to the gut.

'No Major.' Leo sulked.

'Takeshi, I need the reports of all infantry victims over the last five years and coroner reports on causes of death specifically.'

'Yes, Major.' He replied, standing from his chair in respect,

'Jax!, walk with me; there is something I need from you.'

'Yes, Major.' he said, rushing to catch up with Violet and her usual fast-paced walk.

Violet made it to the exit of the command room before Jax caught up. Then walking in complete silence, they passed the threshold of the doorway of the central command room.

'Jackson, what progress have you made on the Nexus portal?'

'The trial phase of BIO matter has been successful nine out of ten times. Progress on return phasing has been an issue, but I'm confident I can work out the kinks by the end of the year.' He replied.

'What information has been given to Serena?' Violet asked as she leaned in closer to him,

'Just the non-Bio matter transportation results, all BIO data has been kept under Black-ops control.'

'Good, continue your development, remember Jax, this stays between you and me,' She said, her steel gaze pinning him to the spot, 'Oh, and I need one more thing from you. Can you analyse this for me?' she said as she produced the crystal ball from the side pocket of the bag.

'It's a glass ball.' He said in confusion.

'It's crystal, from what I can see. It was given to me by an acquaintance; it may be of some use in the future!' she said, ending the conversation.

Jackson left the corridor heading back to his workstation, leaving Violet alone in the dark hallway.

'Leaving for the day, I see?'

'Yes, it's been a long day!' Violet said, turning to face the person speaking, 'Serena!' Violet said, shoving the bag in her direction.

'Thanks.' She said, slightly startled by Violet's reaction.

'Look, about before; you must understand Violet, usage of the Nexus during this critical point could mess everything up. So until I know it's safe, I can't run the risk of you using it.' Serena said, her words rushing from her mouth.

'I know, listen, you don't need to worry about me, have I not made it this far, and look at me, perfectly fine.' Violet said, her face turning soft, her eyes shining like amethyst gems in the night sky as she smiled at Serena, grabbing her hand to reassure her.

'Yes, by sheer dumb luck!' she said, holding back her laugh, 'But let's get one thing straight, you wouldn't have got this far if it weren't for me!' she finished her smile beaming back as she broke out giggling,

Violet embraced Serena as they stood in the corridor,

'I will see you later.' Violet said, kissing Serena on the forehead, letting her go as she turned to leave the base.

— CHAPTER FIVE —

THE PAST, PRESENT & FUTURE

The sun was setting on another busy day in London. The birds rushed back into their nests, the streets slowly emptied as the stalls and shops closed for the day, and Violet finally arrived back at her apartment complex.

As she strolled towards the steel doors, the soft golden lights embedded in the ground illuminated the path she walked, guiding her back to the comfort of her home.

The carriage from the lobby pulled into the docking station of section A, the memories of her encounter with Aeon suddenly came flooding back.

Preparing for the worst, she attached her H.U.D, rapidly tracing the apartment for any potential intruders.

'Scanning complete, zero detection for active life forms!'

Violet narrowed her eyes, her trust in the H.U.D waning since her last surprise encounter. The doors to the cabin swung open, revealing the dark corridor. Passing the threshold of the doorway, Violet flicked her wrist, enabling her nano pad. With a few taps, the warm glow of soft lights illuminated the pitch-black room. Closing the door behind her, she did so slower than she ever had before. Creeping around her apartment, ensuring her footsteps didn't make a sound, she moved from room to room, making her way into the kitchen, meticulously checking in each cupboard for signs of any intruders.

'All clear.' She whispered to herself with the slightest sigh of relief.

Slowly moving towards the stairwell, creeping up the concrete steps, she swiftly entered the hallway.

With a flick of her wrist, she enabled a single M-eight; the familiar rush of blue lights illuminated the hall. Pointing the weapon directly in front of her, she prepared herself for the third battle of the day.

'Is anyone there!' she said, her stern voice masking her fear.

Listening intently, she awaited a response.

'Hello.' She tried again, gripping her weapon firmly, her knuckles turning a ghostly shade of white.

No sound came from the room, the H.U.D was clear, there was only one thing left to do. Violet gripped the door handle, slowly she pushed down till the door unlatched, with a swift kick to the door it swung open.

'Nothing.' Violet said to herself as she lowered her weapon, sinking to the floor in relief.

Sitting in bed readying herself for a well deserved night's sleep, she realised it had been two whole days since her last full night's rest; her eyes grew heavy, her head throbbing in pain. Finally, she lay down and closed her eyes; she fell asleep as soon as her head hit the pillow.

Violet woke to find herself in the middle of a grassy plain; the wind whipped through her hair as it flowed freely in the breeze. The light from the orange sun reflected in her eyes as they shone brightly in the daylight. The crisp fresh air filled her lungs as she breathed a gasp of wonder.

'Where am I?' she said out loud, looking around for any recognisable signs.

As she took a step forward, her feet crunching in the rustling grass, the soft ground yielding beneath her, she felt as though it must have been some sort of heaven. The sweet sound of birds chirping filled her ears as she came about a stream of crystal clear water rushing down from the field's above.

Violet squared her eyes, looking off into the distance, just barely making out the figure of a man.

'Tall, dark hair, is that... Aster.' Violet mumbled to herself in disbelief.

The figure came slowly into view, his jet black hair dishevelled, his dark eyes bloodied, his body beaten and bruised.

'Aster!' she shouted, breaking out into a run trying to catch up to him, her heart beating fast, her breath falling short, her head filled with so many questions, where were they? What happened to him?

'Who did this to you? Aster, talk to me!' she shouted, grabbing him by his arm, holding him up in his broken state.

Aster stumbled, choking up fresh blood as he desperately tried to respond. Suddenly, the sound of a high pitched whistle rang through the air. Violet looked up, facing the direction of the whistle. The ear curtailing sound grew in pitch until it wailed like a banshee at sea. Turning to face Aster, she grabbed him by the shoulders,

'Aster, come on, we have to get moving!' her voice shook in fear.

The wail reached ear-splitting levels; as the sound grew ever closer, Violet looked into the sky. It was too late.

'NO!' she screamed, her face splattered with crimson blood.

Aster stumbled forward, his head flung back, his terrified eyes growing wider by the second as he stuttered to speak. A magnificent golden spear protruded from his chest, its engraved, ornate design slowly filled with Aster's blood. Violet took a step back in horror, watching as Aster fell to his knees, gasping frantically for air.

The high pitch whistle she had once heard now began again, faintly at first far off in the distance. Then, gradually, it developed into the familiar screech that chilled her to the bone. Before she had the chance to move, a second golden spear shot from the sky, striking Aster in the back of the head. The malefic weapon pierced through his skull; the sheer force of this holy spear was so strong it pushed him into the ground pinning him in place.

Aster lay motionless, the grass around him now dyed a vivid shade of red as the blood pooled around his body, the sound of his gasps for air had stopped, Violet knew he was dead.

Flicking her wrists, She activated her nano bands.

'What.' She said in shock as the bands remained still.

Violet flicked her wrist again; the bands failed to respond.

'Come on.' She said, her eyes filled with tears, her hands shaking with fear.

Her breath turned erratic, and her eyes stung from the tears. She turned from Aster, running away as fast as she could. The tears froze to her skin as they ran down her face until suddenly she felt the most unbearable heat. Flames shot forth from the ground.

The fires of hell burned at her feet, the smell of black smoke filled the air choking her as she ran, the sky turned black. The soft sounds of chirping birds began to warp into violent screams that grew louder and louder, flooding her ears, disorientating her, until she could run no longer. Finally, Violet dropped to the ground, her head in her hands. The screams tormented her as she cried out in pain.

Suddenly, there was complete silence; as though someone switched off the sound, the fire disappeared back beneath the ground, and all that existed became consumed in total darkness.

Violet opened her eyes; the outline of a man came from the distance; his presence alone produced an overwhelming amount of pressure. There he stood, clad in pure gold armour adorned with many rubies, shimmering by their divine light. He carried a golden hammer, the handle as long as he was tall, the hammerhead studded with purest of white diamonds, his eyes glowed a burning red like two fireballs in the lightless void, they burned into her as he made his approach, his voice boomed, shaking her to the core.

'Die now.' Came the voice as he clasped both hands to his weapon of war, swinging it behind to gather force, then thrusting it forward at breakneck speed.

Violet watched on, frozen in fear. She closed her eyes, waiting for the hammer to hit until the blunt force of the object stuck her in the chest. At first, there was a crack, then a scream. Violet fell back, hitting the ground hard, her body paralysed as she let out a cry of pain.

'Humans, you're all so…fragile.' The man said as he grinned his toothy white smile.

He raised the hammer high above his head, then forced it down towards her with as much strength as he could muster. Closing her eyes, she let out a scream louder than she had ever screamed before.

The hammer struck her again in the chest; the wind knocked from her lungs, the sheer force pushing her head up from the ground, her eyes forced open.

*

There she lay motionless in her bed; a cold sweat had seeped its way into her clothes. Her eyes fixed to the ceiling of her bedroom as she dug her nails into the mattress. She knew it had been a dream, but it all felt so real. She began frantically checking herself for marks and bruises, pulling off the damp covers, but there were none. Finally, she reached over for her nano bands on the bedside table, knocking them to the floor in her half-asleep haste.

'Damn it.' She grumbled as she crawled out of bed, her head still fuzzy from the lifelike dream.

Lying on the floor, she reached under the bed for the bands, feeling around using her hand for sight. Moving her arm around, she brushed over a smooth yet hard surface. It felt spherical and cool to the touch. Grasping it in her hand, she pulled it out from under the bed.

'What?' she said in confusion.

It was the crystal, the same one she gave to Jax; only now it began to glow a soft amber as she held it in the palm of her hand. Bringing it closer to her face, it began to emit tiny wisps of golden smoke; it remained cool to the touch as the light increased in intensity, growing brighter and brighter as the golden smoke enveloped the room.

Violet could barely see her hand in front of her face. Finally, the fog began to compress into a human shape, taking the form of a man. Violet, sure she was not dreaming as she stepped towards the man-shaped cloud. Its golden glowing state changed, taking the shape of a familiar face.

'Aster?' Violet said out loud as she continued to stare at the man before her.

The light from the crystal faded, the figure now dissipating, until the sphere was left clear, and the Aster imitation had vanished entirely.

Violet sat on the bed as she realigned her thoughts; She knew only that the root of this case now revolved around Aster, but why?.

As she arrived at the Black-ops base, Violet thrust open the doors to the central command room, storming past the desks. She failed to acknowledge her team, who were now scrambling to stand by their stations.

'Aster, with me!' she boomed as she stormed off towards the exit at the back of the command post.

Violet opened the door to her private office. A small room with a glass desk and two chrome chairs positioned at either end of the desk. On the wall were two pictures, one of her mothers and a single image of a maple tree in a green field. 'Close the door!' She said as Aster gingerly passed the threshold.

'Yes, Major.'

'Take a seat,' She said, gesturing towards the empty chair, 'Now we're in a more private place, tell me, Aster, just what exactly are you hiding?' she said, leaning forward from her chair, her eyes connecting with Asters.

'What do you mean, Major? There is nothing to hide!' he replied, breaking his gaze away from hers.

Breathing a sigh of frustration, Violet stood from her chair. As she walked around the desk towards Aster, she held her penetrating stare.

'Listen!' she said, perching herself on the corner of the desk, 'For the past five years, we have worked together, and until very recently, I have had no problems. But now, Aster, many leads in our unsolvable puzzle keep leading back to you. I need answers, and you know more than you are letting on! So if you don't mind. Your story, please from the start.'

Sitting back in his chair, Aster could feel his heart beating rapidly through his chest.

'Fine!' he said, putting his head in his hands. Then, taking a deep breath, he cleared his throat before beginning to speak.

'I can't remember fully, but it starts with the war on Eco.' He said, standing from his chair.

'Your homeworld?' she interjected.

'Yes—'

'So what happened then? You said there was a revolution?'

'This is going to take forever if you keep interrupting!'

'Then get to the point!'

'I know, better I show you.' Aster said, clapping his hands together.

'What?' Violet said, taking a step back.

'Just let me do it. It's been a while, though. I, think if I just—' Aster said as he extended his arm towards Violet, placing his hand on her cheek.

'Get off!' she said, slapping his hand away.

'Look, this will go a lot faster if you just let me do this!'

'Fine!' Violet said, crossing her arms as Aster placed his hand on her cheek.

The walls began to twist and melt as the room started to spin. Violet closed her eyes to stop feeling dizzy.

'It worked.' Aster said in shock.

Violet opened her eyes to the soft azure blue sky. The sound of people going about their daily business filled her ears as she slowly took in the new world.

'Welcome to the Golden Citadel.' Aster said, extending his arm for Violet to grab hold of.

'How did we get here!' Violet said, slapping Asters hand out the way as she stumbled up the golden steps.

'It's a gift. Well, sort of, all Econians have it. How can I explain it? You see, the mind can play tricks on us, or at least how we remember something. So we developed a technique that allowed us to see into a person's mind; we can replay events with no lies, no exaggerations, as long as we were there, it's in the head. Cool, right?' he said, flashing a wink at Violet.

'Sure, so why here? What's so special about this place?' Violet said, looking around the castle grounds.

'This is where it all started; this place will give you the answers you're looking for.'

As Aster placed his hand on a sensor, the gates to the castle began to move, the golden bars lifted from the ground to reveal a stone path surrounded by many ornate and stylish homes.

As they continued to walk in silence through the golden city, Violet gawked in amazement at the sights around her, its golden walls ascending to the sky, the silver-clad homes glistening in the sunlight, the vivid green grass surrounding the walkway.

'Amazing, What happened to it all?' Violet asked, knowing of Eco's eventual demise.

'That's why we're here, come on, you will see soon enough.' Aster said, ushering Violet into the main castle of the grand citadel, then up the winding staircase making their way towards the quarters of the supreme ruler.

'In there!' Aster said, pointing towards the imposing doors.

'In there what?' Violet said in confusion.

'The answers to which you seek.' He said as he turned to walk away,

'Hey, where are you going? Aster!' she shouted, 'Fine.' She said, turning back to face the door.

Placing her hand on the door handle, she took a deep breath and pushed the door open. The golden light from the orange sun filled the room, illuminating the grand tapestries that covered the walls. The jade floor glistened as she walked upon its smooth polished surface.

Violet could hear the voice of a man from across the room. As she moved to inspect, the grand doors slammed, locking her in the round room, the earth-shattering sound reverberating across the rounded walls. Violet spun on the spot in fear the sudden noise may attract unwanted attention. But, instead, footsteps came from one of the corridors leading to her location; she turned back just in time to see the shadow of a man leaving through one of the many bronze doors.

Violet took off running, aiming to intercept the man and question him. But, as she passed the doorway, she realised she had just stepped into the chambers of a King.

The solid gold room, lit up by the golden glow of floating lights, housed the finest jewellery she had ever seen, diamond-encrusted crowns, a solid gold sceptre encrusted in many gems along with other kingly possessions.

'There you are.' The voice of a man came from behind Violet,

As she turned to explain, she found herself frozen to the spot.

Standing before her was the tallest man she had ever seen. He loomed over her at eight-foot-tall. His dark skin radiated pure energy. His hair was as white as winter first snow; his eyes were blood-red like two fireballs in the void. She had seen his face before. Yet, there he stood, staring down at the man facing the opposite direction, just past Violet.

Shifting her eyes, she focused on the man who stood facing away from her. His gold-lined cape hung on his broad shoulders; there, he stayed motionless and proud. The golden crown upon his grey hair glistened in the warm light as his shadow danced along the wall in the golden room.

'I knew it wouldn't be long till he sent his henchman to kill me. After all, that is why you are here, is it not?' the king said, turning slowly on the spot.

The red-eyed giant laughed; his booming voice shook the castle walls as he crossed his arms, taking a step closer to the king.

'I'm glad to see your memory is intact, Xelios! Tell me, my friend, when did you get so old!' he mocked, laughing as he spoke.

'When did the lord above all send a minion to do his dirty work? Tell me, Bellium, do you still believe you hold the title God of War? Better he send the Executioner; after all, she has seen more battle than you.' The King sneered, flashing a wicked smile.

'Listen to me, pathetic, old man. I am not here to trade insults with a being of no worth to my presence,' He said, his words dripping with disdain, 'You have debts to pay, old man.' He said, winking at the King,

'A debt is only as good as the payment received; he failed to deliver what he promised. Therefore, I have no debts for a cowardly fool!' Xelios spat, his hand grasping at the hilt of his diamond sword.

'So proud is the great King of Eco, you truly think yourself a God amongst men,' Bellium said in a hushed tone, 'I'm going to enjoy painting these halls with your blood!'

'You seem to be under the grand impression that I would offer up my life so freely?' Xelios said, unsheathing his sword.

'You fool.' Bellium bellowed, his laugh sending shockwaves across the castle.

The walls cracked as the roof began to cave, the ground shook, Violet gripped onto the wall as rubble started to fall about her.

'What do you think you would do, kill me! A mere mortal, kill a God! Your delusions will truly be the making of your own death.' Bellium snarled, producing his golden hammer from behind his back.

Violet sank into the shadows; she was sure she was invisible but did not want to take the risk.

'Guards!' Xelios shouted.

As the doors to the King's chamber burst open, a sea of soldiers dressed in a brocade of gold and red armour flooded the room; aiming their golden guns at the red-eyed giant, without hesitation, they opened fire.

'Bring him down!' Xelios bellowed, fleeing from the room.

'Fool's!' Bellium shouted, swinging his hammer directly at the soldiers, killing them all in one single stroke.

'Xelios, you pathetic mortal!' he said, outstretching his arm.

He began to grow in size, almost doubling his height. He opened his hand wide, reaching directly towards the king as he ran down the hall. Violet felt a sudden burst of pressure fill the room, the weight of a thousand tonnes began to bear down on her, she dropped to the floor unable to stand, looking out she witnessed Xelios also lying on the floor, his screams of pain filling the room.

'Xelios, you simple, old, man, die now and consider your debt paid.' Bellium said, clenching his hand into a fist.

The pressure was too much; the building began to break down as the gold walls shattered into a thousand pieces.

The floor started to break away as rubble turned to dust before it hit the ground. Violet's vision turned red as blood began to pour from her eyes.

Letting out a scream, she could feel her bones break as the pressure built to an unbearable level. Finally, the pressure dropped, the world around her turned black, and she faded out of consciousness.

— CHAPTER SIX —

DEADLINES

Violet opened her eyes to a blinding light that shone directly above her. Then, as her vision began to clear, she could make out the shape of two spotlights dangling down near her face.

'Where am I?' she groaned, moving her head from side to side.

As she looked around the room, blurry images came into view. Violet squinted as her vision came back into focus, first she rested her sight on the table next to her, then the person working in the distance. Finally, the sound of slow, intermittent beeps rang in the still room as Violet focused on the vitals indicator next to the bed.

'Am I in the hospital?' she said aloud, hoping to catch the person's attention, quietly working away at the other end of the room.

'Your awake, I see.'

'Aster?' Violet said as she turned her head towards the direction of the voice.

'Yea, it's me, glad to see you're ok,' he said with a bright beaming smile, 'We had to rush you in after you collapsed!'

'What happened?' she asked as she struggled to sit upright.

'It's my fault. I thought it would work. Looks like humans are more fragile than they appear.' He said, cracking a weak smile.

'Evidently so. Aster, what happened?' Violet asked, massaging her temples, trying to relive her headache.

'You collapsed?' Aster replied in confusion.

'No! On Eco, what happened after the King's death? And, for that matter, how does this relate to the here and now?' she asked, her questions blurting out in rapid succession.

Aster paused, looking Violet directly in the eyes, 'Fine, are you sure you're ready for all this?'

'Yes!' she said, turning to dangle her feet off the bed,

'The once-great ruler of Eco. The divine lord Xelios ruled as the fifth supreme leader. Whilst his intentions were to rule a fair and prosperous civilisation, that sentiment doesn't always translate to the purest of actions. Wishing for eternal life, he summoned the Gods of old, entering into a pact, for all that he could pledge would be made as payment for immortality!'

'But he never received it.'

'No, he deceived the Gods, taking them for fools. Many gifts were granted to Xelios. But in his greed, he refused to give them all he had pledged, the God of War was sent to kill him and take back what was rightfully theirs.'

'Bellium!'

'Yes, the King's pride got the best of him. His actions caused the war, resulting in the destruction of the world!'

'But where does the girl in grey come into this?'

'I'm getting there; give me a chance!' Aster snapped. Collecting his thoughts, he proceeded, 'During the final days of the war, we were pushed back into the golden citadel. The last of our men were either captured or already dead. Bellium dispersed what was left of his army around Eco, leaving a small squadron at the citadel. The battle was over once the Executioner took the main gates. As we were sent for execution, she appeared, the girl in grey, destroying all that remained of his army.'

Violet stood from the bed, regaining the strength in her legs, 'So you took that moment to escape?' Violet asked as she stretched.

'Yes, she killed the exact same way as she did in Manhattan, but it was different back then. Stronger, more malicious. I still don't know why she was there or why she did what she did, but they fear her!' Aster finished with a heavy sigh.

'God's, army's, cruel and greedy Kings!' Violet said, a million questions filling her head.

'There is a lot about this universe that you know very little about, Violet.'

'Clearly!' she said, lost for words, 'So how does one go about taking down a God.' Her eyes widened with every word.

Just as the words left her mouth, there was a loud rasp at the door, which was followed by the sound of clunky footsteps filling the room.

'Ah, Good to see you up and about Major, quite the incident if I do say so myself.'

'General.' Violet said, swiftly turning to salute.

'The Doctor called me in, but I can see now that the call was unnecessary!' he said with a sly grin across his face.

'Completely, Sir, My apologies for interrupting your hectic schedule.'

'What happened, V?'

'It was just an experiment gone wrong.' She replied shortly, brushing off the General's question.

'And has this "experiment" led you to any answers on this case?' he asked, looking Violet up and down as he stroked his prized moustache.

'Not yet. However, updates are at noon; we will have more answers then.'

'I hope so, V. Remember, we cannot afford any more mistakes.'

The General turned on his heel and left the room. Striding down the corridor, he made his way towards the exit lift.

'Oh and Violet,' He said from the end of the corridor, 'I expect a full resolution of this case within the next twenty-four hours; you have been warned.' his smirk still tattooed across his face as he entered the lift.

Violet sighed; running her hands through her hair, failure was not an option. She flicked her wrist to enable the nano band, switching it to speaker mode.

'All black-ops specialists to the central command post ASAP!' She ordered, flicking the nano band to close.

'Let's get to it.' Aster said, jumping to his feet.

'Not you, you must continue your work with Serena, there is more to this than you've let on, and if you think we're going to replay your little mind trick, you can think again.' Violet said, swiftly leaving the room.

Entering the central command room, Violet could make out only one figure, sitting alone and backlit by the wall to wall screens,

'Caspian?' she said, as she approached the lone worker,

'Major!' he replied, his tired voice echoing across the room.

'So it is you, glad to see one of us is hard at work.' She said, flashing him a rare smile.

'Thank you, Major.' He said, returning her smile,

As soon as the brief exchange began, it was over. Violet returned to her command post, crossing her arms and facing the doorway, tapping her left index finger on her right forearm as she impatiently waited for the rest of her team to assemble.

'Sorry I'm late, Major, the traffic in the hallways is getting ridiculous, also; why is the General here?' Leo asked as he bounded into the room in his usual unpoised manner.

'Never mind that,' Violet said, her sharp tone returning, 'Take your seat!' Violet moved her arm, extending her finger to point at Leos chair.

'Yes, Mam.' Leo said, shuffling to his seat, like a naughty schoolboy corrected by his teacher.

'Caspian, dial out to the others; we are wasting valuable time.' She ordered, stretching her neck, shaking off the last of Aster's trance.

'No need, Major.' Jax said, running into the room, shortly followed by Oren, Takeshi and Zyair.

'Good, now that we are all present—'

'Hold on, where's Aster?' Leo said, craning his neck to scope the room,

'IF! You'll let me finish,' Violet said, her patience running dry, 'Aster will not be joining us; he is on a vital assignment, Leo! you will be taking second for the interim period.'

'Sweet.' Leo said, only to cower in his chair from the death stare now emitting from Violet's piercing eyes.

'Gentleman, your updates if you please! We have twenty-four hours as per the General's most recent orders.' Violet scanned the room, waiting for the first person to speak up.

'I have checked all archived information on subhuman entities; there is no match from the database. However, we have successfully traced back the B.I.O.N.A data to that of planet A.C54100, located in the Andromeda galaxy. There could be a potential link.' Oren said as he flashed images from his research across the screens of the Black-ops command room.

'Great, I will need more information about that planet, any biological information, to the potential for human life. Also, see if anything in the data archive matches the Omega mark we found in the victims' eyes. There may be some hidden history behind it.' Violet said, clearing the screen with a swipe of her finger. 'Who's next!' she said, patrolling the room with her unyielding eyes.

'Major, I have formulated a tactical operation sequence. I believe this would be optimal for our subsequent encounter with the unknown entity.'

'Where did we get the data from?' Violet asked

'From the recordings in Manhattan, we have analysed her moves and attack sequence, considered her body composition and use of the "dark energy", as we have come to call it. As a result, we should see a vast improvement in our success rate.'

'How can you be so sure it will work?' Violet asked as she honed in on Takeshi, pinning him to the spot.

'We have formulated a plan based on the critical factors as listed before. My simulations have achieved a ninety-nine per cent perfect plan.'

'Hold on! She barely moved last time, and now you got this foolproof plan!' Leo mocked, spinning in his chair.

'I have run the current data through the diagnostic amplifier; it has managed to sequence the event into a statistical data sheet, from that we—'

'Ok, ok, I get it, no need to go on!' Leo impatiently interjected.

'Will it work, Takeshi?' Violet asked, ignoring Leo's outburst.

'As with any intel on an unknown hostile, we have no definitive proof. However, with this plan, we are in a better position for victory,' Takeshi said, his eyes securely fixed on Violet. 'Gentleman, your nanochips have been updated with the plan already, Major we have sent this to your Nano-bands.'

'Thank you, Tak,' Violet said, her tone softening, 'Well then! A plan is all well and good, but if we can't hit this thing, it's DOA, which brings me to you, Leo.'

'Right!' He said as he jumped from his seat, sauntering towards the centre of the room. Violet rolled her eyes, regretting ever giving him the title of second in command.

'Gents, Lady. I have done some tinkering and deduced that our weapons are perfectly capable of destroying anything in our way—'

'Enough of the bravado, can we hit this thing or not!' Violet said impatiently.

'In short Major…No,' Leo said, now witnessing the look of anger flowing from Violet's eyes, he began to regret his own words, 'However, there have been some interesting developments that I would like to share with you all—'

'GET ON WITH IT!' Violet shouted from the command post.

'Yes, Major, we have successfully extracted the energy stored in the victim's eyes, a closer inspection has revealed it to be some form of antimatter!'

'Does it match with any of our current records on anti-matter?' Violet asked, her tone shifting from anger to intrigue.

'No, we have managed to sequence the data by cross-referencing with the data maps in B.I.O.N.A. It's completely unique!'

Hearing these words, Violet began to think, her eyes so focused on Leo it appeared she was looking directly through him.

'Major?' Leo said, trying to regain her attention.

'Carry on.' She said, continuing with her deep thought.

'Right, well, during the sequencing, we were able to mimic the molecular structure. We have omitted the replication effect to control it, but we have now successfully implanted the energy into your brand new, state of the art, MAGNA rounds.' Leo said with a wink pulling off a white cloth covering the ammunition arranged neatly on his desk.

'Spoken like a true salesman.' Caspian said, shaking his head as he stood to inspect the new weapons.

'How do we know it will work?' Takeshi said, grabbing the bullets from the table.

'Ahhh, well, we won't, until it, you know, all goes down,' Leo said shiftily, 'I have updated your inventory already; this is just a sample. Oh, Major, the update will be on the Nano bands momentarily.' He said as he sat back down.

'Thank you, Leo.' Violet said, blinking heavily, trying to shake off her thoughts.

'Zyair, do you have anything to add?'

'No, ma'am.' Zyair replied as he remained sitting quietly behind his desk.

'Very well, Jax, you're up!'

'I have run diagnostics of our current equipment, the dark energy does, in fact, produce an ionic effect, to counteract this, I have switched out the main electrical pulsar that emits from the nano-core of the Yellowhammer, I have also replicated this with our comm-links and recording equipment.'

'So, no more interference?'

'To a fashion, yes, keeping with this theme, I have added the next-gen BIO marbles to your inventory; they work without an electrical pulse.'

'So her "forcefield" will have no effect?'

'Hopefully, Major, but the only way to find out is on the battlefield.'

'Perfect, Caspian, if you please.' She said, taking a seat at her desk, atop the command post.

'Thank you, Major; we are currently tracking the energy across the globe. It has had modular appearances but nothing near close to the spike levels in Manhattan.'

'So what are we looking at now?' Violet said as the screens around the room lit up with a picture of earth shrouded in black clouds with reels of data running across the display, far too quickly for anyone actually to read.

'This is the current energy field across Nova; as you can see, there are no trends and no spikes.'

'But that's not what we're looking for,' Violet said in confusion, 'We were meant to be tracking the energy before it gathered. Remember a pre-emptive strike.'

'Yes, but there is no data to suggest any form of gathering; it's ever-present in the atmosphere, this energy is vast Major, on a global scale we won't know where it is until it's there.'

'Then what is that?' Violet said as she pointed towards the Uropa region.

'It's just the clouds, Major!' Leo said from across the room, still swinging on his chair.

'No, it's not, it's an onset Columbus formation, and that's not a cloud; that's the dark energy!' Caspian said, standing from his chair.

The dark clouds on the screen slowly began to form across Uropa, amassing over the island of Paris. As it gathered in speed, the numbers on the screen started to flash in red as the warning signs lit up into action.

Violet looked at the screen, her heart pounding in anticipation. As she looked around the room at her Elite soldiers, she broke out into an infectious smile.

'Gentleman, suit up, Paris it is.' She said, signalling the Yellowhammer.

— CHAPTER SEVEN —

THE PARTY IN PARIS

'ETA in thirty seconds, Major.' The Captain said from the cockpit of the Yellowhammer.
'Do we have clearance?' Violet asked from the main passenger hold.

'Affirmative! beginning landing sequence now.'

The Yellowhammer lowered to the ground of the Camp De Mars park. The doors hissed as the pistons activated, swinging open the door allowing the Black-ops team to dismount in single file. The sun shone brightly in the afternoon sky as the dark clouds began to gather above them.

'Caspian, I need you to keep an eye on that energy formation; as soon as it begins to spike, you let me know.'

'Yes, Major, it's beginning to tornado above the Eiffel Tower. However, energy levels remain low.'

'Perfect! We might just get there before she does! Gentlemen, stick to the plan at hand. We bring her back, dead or alive.'

'Major!, it's gaining momentum.' Caspian said, pointing towards the dark energy now encircling the tower.

The sky turned grey as black thunderbolts raged through the clouds, the faintest drops of rain began to fall. It was Manhattan all over again.

'Move! Now! To the peak.' Violet said, flicking her wrist, activating her nano-bands to produce her M-Eight's.

Violet and her team made haste towards the tower, running as fast as possible to intercept the energy before it spiked. As they entered the tower's reception, an all-glass room crowded with hundreds of people, Violet knew now was not the time for pleasantries. Flicking her wrist, she activated her nano speaker.

'U.N.N MILITARY, I NEED YOU ALL TO EVACUATE NOW!' Violet shouted as they stormed inside the tower reception. Then, smashing the fire alarm, she made her way towards the hyper lifts.

'Zyair! Get everyone out, head towards the evacuation point!' She shouted over the deafening sounds of people rushing in a panic to exit the building.

'Yes, Major.' He said, flicking his wrist, activating his nano-chip.

A holographic image appeared just above his wrist. With a swipe of his finger, all the screens in the building displayed a flashing warning sign announcing the evacuation sequence.

The hyper lift doors opened, people ran from the cabin screaming and shouting, rushing to escape the tower. Each person was shocked by the sight of the five men and one woman standing in full body armour brandishing military assault weapons on the ground floor.

'Please exit quickly and safely. We need you to assemble further back....!' Violet heard the voice of Zyair outside as he worked to wrangle together the crowd of frightened people.

Entering the cabin, Violet equipped her H.U.D, activating the crosshair to begin its scan.

'Caspian, how long till we get a spike?' Violet asked as the doors slid shut, the ten-man lift blasting off from the ground, rapidly making its way up to the tower's peak.

'I'm unsure, Major, it's in slow development, but that could change.' He replied, continuously monitoring the energy levels on his holo screen.

The cabin pinged as it reached the peak of the Eiffel tower. The doors opened with a soft hiss, revealing a ballroom void of its people, the tables littered with birthday decorations, the floor now a sea of string and bits of confetti, with abandoned plates and glasses from where the guests had been celebrating.

'Looks like the party's over, hey Major.' Leo jested as they slowly walked into the room.

'Quiet.' She said as her H.U.D scanned the empty room, 'Now is not the time. Remain vigilant. Caspian! Anything?' she asked, anxiously awaiting his reply.

'No, Major, The spike is returning to normal levels.' He huffed, deactivating his nano-chip.

'Damn it.' Violet said, lowering her weapons. 'Well, this was a—!

At that moment, the tip of the tower cracked, the steel frame began to bend out of shape as a fully formed tornado struck the floor directly in front of the Black-ops team.

'GET DOWN!' Violet shouted.

Lunging backwards, avoiding the airborne table now encircling the room.

The tornado gathered momentum, the decorations once lining the room ripped from the walls. The presents once scattered on the top table were sucked into the air. Wayward thunderbolts struck the room, smashing tables and chairs, obliterating anything in sight.

Violet gripped onto the nearest steel beam clasping on for dear life; she knew what was to come next.

Focusing the H.U.D directly onto the tornado, the crosshair switched from green to red.

'IT'S HER!' Violet shouted, hoping her voice would catch the ears of her team.

The wind stopped, trailing back up to the skies above, the thunder receded, leaving behind nothing but destruction and a short petite blond girl hovering in the air, dressed in all grey, her hood covering her face.

'Bring her down.' Violet said, activating the new MAGNA rounds.

Aiming at the girl in grey, her weapons of choice now glowing red, she opened fire upon the target. The bullets flew towards the girl, bending around her body, hitting the steel beams behind her. Seeing this, Leo ran towards her, flicking his wrist to produce a dura-steel blade, slashing the blade in bold swipes, each one narrowly missing her as she ducked and weaved from the sword edge. She moved swiftly, faster than Leo's eyes could see. Then, grabbing the blade shattering it in her hand, she proceeded to sweep her arm back, a sleeve of dark energy emitted from her shoulder to her wrist.

'Crap!' Leo said, realising his grave mistake as she gripped him by the neck, cutting off his air supply.

'Leo!' Violet shouted as the girl prepared to swipe at his neck,

Violet produced a small black marble from her nano-band. Eyeing up her target, she threw it directly at the girl in grey. As it sailed through the air, the girl noticed the incoming pellet.

Throwing Leo aside, she moved to intercept the pellet, but it was too late; the marble struck her hand, forming a jelly-like seal that started to grow. It encased her arm whilst slowly creeping around her body. As she tried to break free, spinning violently in the air, she produced a trail of malefic energy.

Gathering it in her free hand, she launched the dark mist upon the ground. Four dark figures emerged from the now dissipated fog; slowly, they began to walk towards the Black-ops team.

'What on earth are they?' Leo croaked as he picked himself up off the floor.

'It's called reinforcements!' Caspian said, producing his A.R.T U.N.N rifle.

'Aim for the shadow men, leave the girl to me!' Violet said, jumping out of the way of an oncoming black thunderbolt.

Now virtually covered in the jelly substance, the girl began emitting thick black energy that slowly formed into a sphere, then the jell hardened, creating a glass orb, pitch-black in colour.

'Major, we have a situation over here!' Leo shouted from across the room.

Violet spun around to see Leo firing at his target, the bullets passing directly through the shadowy figures.

'Switch to UV Freeze rounds!' Violet shouted, returning her attention to the black sphere.

With a Flick of his wrist, Leo switched from the MAGNA rounds to UV, aiming at his target; he opened fire upon the shadow man. Then, landing a hit directly onto the chest of the shadow man, they began to freeze in patches bullet by bullet.

'It's working!' he shouted, getting the attention of his comrades.

The jell-sphere began to crack. A sudden and explosive bolt of black lightning fell from the sky, hitting the floating sphere, smashing it into a thousand pieces. The sheer force caused a radial blast around the room, throwing the Black-ops team towards the heavily damaged walls.

Violet jumped up from the floor spinning the holo-screen above her wrist. The jell-glass dust began to re-form back into the black marble, shooting back to her hand at breakneck speed. As she dissolved the ball back into her nano-band, she scanned the room, checking on her team.

'Assessing raw data, analysis recovery time… three minutes.' The mechanised voice sounded in her comm-link.

'Hold them back. I'm out till the data is compiled.' Violet shouted as her black-ops team rose to their feet, producing their weapons and firing the UV rounds again upon the shadow men.

'Aim for the feet.' Violet commanded, desperately buying time for the analysis to complete.

They did as instructed, firing towards the ground, freezing their enemy on the spot.

'Major, the energy levels are spiking.' Caspian said, his holo-screen now flashing red.

Violet looked up to see the girl mid-air, absorbing the black energy just as she did that night in Manhattan.

'Take cover; this is how she kills.' She said as her H.U.D began to flash red, displaying its emergency protocol.

The shadow men broke free from their bonds, fading into thin wisps of smoke. Then, shooting past the Black-ops team through the wreckage of the top floor, they began their descent towards the civilians on the ground.

'Major, I have multiple hostiles heading down from the tower.' Zyair said through the comm-link.

'Reinforcements are on route!' she said, gesturing to the Black-ops team to immediately evacuate the tower.

'Activate your extension ZIP's.' Leo said as he gripped the exposed steel beam.

A small mechanised pole shot out from his nano-chip. Gripping it with one hand, he arched his arm back, and with all the power he could muster, threw the pole directly towards the ground below. The bar exploded with a bang as two metallic ropes protruded from each end, one firing into the ground. The second hurled back to Leo, who had to duck, missing the rope as it snagged itself onto the steel pike.

'Gentlemen with me.' Leo said, zipping down the wire directly to the civilians below, shortly followed by the rest of the Black-ops team.

Violet ducked for cover behind the main support beam preparing for the imminent attack. Looking at her wrist, she checked the time left till the analysis was complete.

'Come on! one minute left.' Violet said to herself, bracing for impact.

Stretching out her arms, the girl formed the dark energy into a flat, geometric disk of swirling red energy that loomed ominously in the air. As she pulled her arm back, she focused her stare on the main support beam. Finally, thrusting her arm forward, she stuck the disk, causing a blast of radial energy to disperse, coating the Parisian skyline turning it to a harrowing shade of blood red.

It shattered the glass and shook the buildings as it passed. The shadow men hit the ground, followed by Leo and the Black-ops team, crash landing as the sky lit up a vivid shade of blood-red.

'Freeze!' Zyair said, raising his gun towards the shadow men that were now approaching fast.

Opening fire, using the MAGNA rounds, he realised fast how little damage they did. Panicked, he switched to explosive rounds, firing directly upon his targets.

A thick grey cloud of smoke formed around the field, hiding everyone and everything from view. The shadow men swept past Zyair undetected. Then, producing black blades, they began to cut down the civilians standing defenceless in the field. Zyair turned upon hearing the screams from the crowd behind him, witnessing the bodies of the dead falling to the ground as the shadows swept silently across the park.

'ZYAIR, GET OUT OF THERE!' Leo yelled, running full force towards him.

Opening fire, he released a barrage of freeze bullets onto the shadow men trying to slow them down.

'On my six, stop them now!' Leo shouted, his anger taking control, as he witnessed each of the hundreds of people falling to the ground, the red mist of blood spraying in the air.

The Black-ops team rallied to Leo's side, readying themselves to open fire, only to realise no civilians were left to defend. The shadow men were gone, evaporating back into the sky.

'We need to get back up the tower.' Takashi said, turning to view the red energy radiating from the tip of the dishevelled tower.

'Major, do you copy.' Caspian spoke into the comm-link.

As they stood waiting for a response, suddenly, the red energy stopped, receding in a swift and seamless motion. The comm-link remained silent for what felt like a lifetime, then the sound of gunfire began to ring through.

'Sounds alive to me.' Leo said as he took off, running towards the tower.

'Do not enter the tower, I repeat, DO NOT ENTER THE TOWER!' Violet's voice came clear as day as Leo froze on the spot.

'Major, do you require backup?' Caspian said in disbelief, turning to face the rest of the team.

'Negative, remain grounded.' She said as the comm-link shut off in an abrupt break.

The analysis was complete. Violet was back in the game, encircling her target whilst relentlessly firing the MAGNA bullets, hoping one would eventually strike her down.

The girl in grey watched as Violet fired. She flashed a small smile towards her, this sudden break in character caused Violet to stop firing. Hardly believing her eyes, the usually lifeless, emotionless girl just flashed a smile at her. She thought to herself, what could this mean, slowly stepping towards her target; Violet tried her luck.

'Who are you?' she asked, not knowing what to expect.

She continued to smile at Violet, her grimace in plain sight.

'Answer me!' Violet shouted in an explosive outburst.

As the words left her mouth, the girl's smile shifted from grim to sinister. She stretched her arm back into the air behind her, then launched it forwards with a tremendous thrust.

A black bolt of lightning shot forward, striking Violet directly onto her chest, slamming her back against the pillar at the edge of the tower. Violet stumbled, pulling herself up from the floor, then by surprise she felt a hand grab her by the neck, the girl had disappeared from the centre of the room, reappearing directly in front of her, the flash movement was far too quick for the human eye to detect.

Violet struggled to breathe as her feet lifted from the floor, the girl's grip tightening as her arm pulled her up into the sky.

'Pathetic.' she said in a soft and quiet voice.

Violet felt a chill to her bones as she heard the words ring in her ears. Then, still holding Violet by the neck, she threw her with a tremendous amount of force, straight from the edge of the tower.

Falling fast, unable to slow her descent, Violet flicked her wrist, spinning the nano-band, trying to locate something, anything to break her fall. Leo witnessing this from the ground, activated his hyper mod, jumping into the air far higher than the ordinary man, grabbing Violet as she fell.

Next, Zyair produced a green marble from his nano-chip; as he threw it directly at Leo, it burst into a cloud of foamy green padding, encapsulating the two as they hit the ground.

'Major, are you ok?' Zyair asked, running towards Violet as she lay on the ground next to Leo.

'I'm fine!' Violet grunted, steadying herself as she slowly stood.

'I'm fine too!' Leo said, reaching his arm out for anyone to help him up.

Violet looked past her surrounding Black-ops team, looking over to the dead who lay in the field.

Growing increasingly desperate to finish the mission before any more casualties, she flicked her wrist, activating her nano-band.

Just as she turned back to her team, the relentless girl appeared in front of them, her sinister smile still plastered across her face.

'Replication of data analysis complete.' Violet's nano-band announced.

'We have the formula. Hold her back. I need some time to finish this.' Violet said, enlarging the holo-screen, trying to sequence the code.

The girl, suspended in mid-air, slammed her hand into the ground producing the shadow men once more. Then, swooping forward, they lunged towards the Black-ops team.

Tackling them as best they could, each ops member was pulled away from Violet, unable to protect her whilst she worked. The girl in grey honed in on Violet, striking at her with bolts of black thunder. Violet flung herself back, dodging the bolts as they hit the ground around her. Returning fire, using her MAGNA bullets, the rounds continued to miss their target as they flew in all directions away from the girl.

Violet flicked her wrist, de-activating her M-eights, replacing them with a shockwave grenade; pulling the pin, she threw the grenade at the target lunging back to avoid the explosion.

The grenade drew in the air, pulling the girl towards the small green object on the floor. Finally, it clicked, exploding into an electric blue soundwave sending the girl many miles back towards the tower, slamming against the steel beams.

Silently, she slid to the floor. Her smile faded from view as she pushed off from the ground, rising high into the air. The red mist began to descend as it gathered around the girl. Violet turned to warn her comrades that an attack was imminent, only to see the shadow men disappear, leaving the battlefield empty. Her black-ops team stood alone, confused about what had just happened.

'Take cover; she's preparing for a second attack!' Violet said, running towards her team.

Just as Violet reached them, she produced three blue marbles from her nano-band. Throwing each one upon the ground, they burst into a sea of light blue jelly, encapsulating each person in a cocoon of toughened jell-glass.

The girl's red energy began to turn black as she condensed it down to a single floating dot. Then with a single tap of her finger, it expelled its dark energy in a sphere, stretching on for miles, gathering in speed as it went, eviscerating the Eiffel Tower, and destroying what remained of the city of Paris, killing all that remained of its occupants.

As the jell-glass began to melt, Violet stood looking around to see the mass destruction the girl had caused. What was once the proud city of Paris was now a sea of black flames, fumes plumed into the sky muddying the air, the mix of toxic smoke and the scent of freshly melted steel loomed within her nose.

Before Violet could take in the true extent of the destruction, the girl in grey appeared directly in front of Violet. With a swing of her arm, she expelled her dark energy, striking at the members of the Black-ops team. Each person was forced back in multiple directions, disabling them in the process.

Gripping Violet by the neck, she formed a black blade from her arm, then, in a seamless motion, sliced Violet down from her grip.

Violet fell to the floor, unable to move her arms or feel her legs, her body broken and bleeding as the burn from the cut ran deep. Violet opened her eyes, looking at herself on the floor. A cut from her face stretched down to her legs. Bleeding heavy, she lay motionless on the ground, the pain becoming too unbearable to suffer.

'Activate E-tec band!' she screamed.

Her nano-band spun into action, a long thin strip of a neon green material shot from it latching itself to the cut. Violet let out a scream of agony as the band applied instant pressure, sealing the wound.

Violet rolled back, mustering all that remained of her strength; she jumped up, then, spinning on the spot, kicked the girl back. In her final act of defence, she produced a small violet marble, throwing it at her enemy. The flash from the marble illuminated the land stunning the girl in grey just long enough for Violet to escape.

Violet ran as fast as she could, fearing death if she were to falter. A high-pitched whistle came in the distance; its earth piercing screech felled Violet's ears.

Violet lept from the ground, spinning in the air; She reached out to intercept the spear the girl had formed before it could do any harm. It was too close!

Violet put her hand towards her face shielding her eyes as the spear pierced her hand, protruding out towards her face. The spear was thrown with such force that it dragged her down to the ground, pinning her to the freshly scorched floor. Violet let out a blood curtailing scream as smoke emitted from the spear. She looked over to her hand, the smell of burning flesh filling her nose as the spear melted her skin. Unable to move, her veins began to turn black as the energy leached into her wound.

The girl strolled towards Violet, her stern face returning to a menacing smile. Violet looked up into the girl's soulless black eyes, watching her as she raised her arms, forming another black spear.

Finally, the girl tilted her head towards Violet, her face warped from its menacing grin to a sad frown.

'I'm going to miss you, pathetic girl.' She said as she thrust the spear down towards Violet's head.

— CHAPTER EIGHT —

THE JILTED DECISION

The sound of steel-capped boots clanged in the bunker as General Hill stomped into the war room.

'Update on the situation!' The General said, taking his seat next to the President.

'We are still sketchy on the details. However, at thirteen hundred hours, the Eiffel Tower and a thirty-mile radius of Paris has just been destroyed. We have traced this back to an unknown energy source detected at the epicentre of the explosion. It replicates the same one from Manhattan just a few days ago.'

'What scale of casualty are we looking at here?' The President said, sitting forward in her chair.

'About twenty million, the full scale is yet to be determined, Ma'am.' the agent replied.

'So you're telling me Paris just exploded out of nowhere?'

'Intelligence suggests the last team in that area was the Black-ops division.' The agent replied as he silently tapped on his hollo-board.

'Your black-ops division!' The President said, glaring at General Hill.

'Has an evac been called?' Hill asked. A hint of concern washed over his voice as he ignored the President's intrusive stare.

'No sir, the lines are dead. We've been unsuccessful in locating any member of the team.'

Just as the agent finished his sentence, a green dot began to flash on the screen travelling fast towards the now destroyed Paris.

'Incoming UFO, identify yourself.' The agent said into the comm-link.

'U.N.N - PO 1334, Aster Voss,' He replied, racing forward in the M.K.One speedster, 'On route to blast location.'

'Abort the mission Commander Voss, that is an order!' Hill boomed.

'No can do, General, I have a team to save!'

'If there's even a team left to save Aster, this mission is too dangerous, you—' He started to say until the line cut dead.

'General, I think it's high time we sent in the weapon.'

'But, Madam President, if Violet is alive, we would be signing her death note.' General Hill replied in shock.

'In life, much like war, one must be ready to make many sacrifices, you, General! Understand that, more than any man in this room,' She said brazenly, 'I am not prepared to allow whatever has caused this to continue. Initiate sequence zero.'

'But Madam—'

'My orders are clear. There is no one there worth living anymore.' She said as she briskly left the room.

The General flicked his wrist, activating his holo-pad, a blank screen appeared shimmering in the darkened room. As he placed his hand on the holo-screen, the room illuminated into a sea of red flashing lights; warning sirens alerted from the ceiling as red and yellow signs splashed across the wall of screens.

'Launch sequence active, select coordinates.'

The General entered in the coordinates of the now desolate land where the proud Eiffel Tower once occupied.

'God damn it, V.' He said, sinking into his chair.

*

Aster clicked the auto-pilot on the M.K.One. As he readied himself for battle, the screen on the speeder began to flash, alerting him to the missile launch from Washington.

'No! No! no!' he said, grabbing the speed booster, pulling it back. The speeder engaged its hyper thrust, pinning him to the chair. 'Holy shit, that's fast!' he said as the speeder approached the destruction zone.

Aster spotted Violet in the distance, her body pinned to the floor as the girl in grey stood above her twirling her black spear in the air. Aster struck the disengage button jettisoning him from the cabin many miles into the air.

The M.K.One rushed towards the girl; just as she thrust the spear towards Violet's head, the speeder struck the girl in grey, now dragging her and her weapon of malice many miles off into the distance.

'Major!' Aster shouted as he disconnected his safety belt, jumping free from the chair that remained floating in the air.

Landing upon the ground, he ran towards Violet as fast as he could, suddenly the air filled with an ear-splitting whistle. Aster jumped out of the way just in time as the black spear struck the ground next to him.

'Guys, I need you to secure Violet.' he said, continuously dodging the spear as it relentlessly pursued him.

'Yes, Commander, we are on route.' Caspian replied, pulling himself up from the ground, slowly making his way across the battlefield.

After much dodging of the swift and nimble spear, the girl in grey appeared before Aster. Striking at her with his fist, he released a barrage of punches and kicks, all landing perfectly onto his target. Unphased by Aster's attack, the girl sent a single black bolt from her hand, smiting him in the chest. Aster fell hard upon the scorched ground, jolting in pain as the black bolt paralysed his body.

'Major, we're here.' Caspian said, grabbing the spear that pinned her to the floor.

Letting out an almighty scream, he fell to the floor; the dark energy burnt his hands, the smell of scorched flesh filling the rotten air; as the burns travelled up his arms.

'Don't touch the spear.' Zyair said as the rest of the team assembled around Violet and Caspian.

'So your plan is what, leave it in?' Leo jeered, reaching for the fell weapon.

'No!' Zyair shouted, slapping Leo's hands away, 'Let me do it!'

Zyair flicked his wrist, two nano gloves formed over his hands, firmly clasping at the spear; he pulled it, releasing it from the ground, freeing Violet from her bond.

Just as he threw the spear, it evaporated into a thin black mist, catching the wind it blew back towards Zyair, invading his nostrils. Collapsing to the ground, he let out a half-choked scream, gasping for air; the world around him turned dark as he drifted from consciousness.

*

Aster gritted his teeth, the black thunder still jolting through his body, pushing through the immense pain; he slowly found his footing, pulling himself up from the ground. The girl in grey waved her hands, moving the spear through the air, focusing on Aster; she motioned her hand, striking at her weakened target.

Unable to fight back, Aster flicked his wrist, activating his nano-chip, producing a green marble, then throwing it in the air; it burst into a cloud of lime green dust, rapidly it turned to foam encasing the spear in the air as it slowly drifted to the floor. But he was not done yet; pressing the call button on his holo-screen, he sent the M.K.One towards her. Activating the assault mode, it unleashed the full power of its Meta-rail wing-mounted guns upon her.

The bullets showered down, passing past the girl hitting the ground behind her. Then, throwing her newly formed spear, she pierced the speeder's engine, causing another explosion, knocking her out of the sky.

The rubble from the blast fell to the ground, knocking Aster back to the floor, trapping him beneath. As he lay under the smouldering remains of the decimated speeder, he let out a small laugh, mustering all that remained of his strength; he pulled himself free. Now looking up into the smoke-filled sky, he began to lose conscience.

'Fine, if that's the way you want to play it!' he said out loud, closing his eyes, lying motionless upon the ground.

The girl appeared above him, her fresh face glaring down at the lifeless Econian, forming a black spear; she thrust her arm into the air and then shot the spear down towards Aster with tremendous force.

The spear chimed as it struck a solid object, the sound of steel on steel screeched in the still air, the girl's face changed from vacant to angst, her eyes widened at the sight below.

There stood Aster; his eyes changed from their azure blue to a deep soulless black. His hands were the shade of steel blue, his face twisted to a maniacal grin as he grasped at a black blade of his creation, smouldering in the same dark energy of her spear. Drawing the spear back, the girl clicked her finger, duplicating the spear as many times as she could, the sky now filled with spinning weapons of destruction.

Aster, not wasting another second, jumped from the ground, slashing his blade through the girl, slicing her in two. Then, turning mid-air to witness his victory, the girl remained airborne, her body intact and her spears turned in unison to face him. Asters face dropped. He was sure his attack had worked; spinning the blade in his hand, he threw it directly towards her.

The slender steel whistled in the wind as it shot faster than light towards the girl in grey.

The blade flew through her like a bullet through the clouds. She smiled at Aster as she slowly faded from view.

Aster landed upon the ground, confused by the events that had just unfolded.

'Thirty seconds to impact.'

Aster remembered the missile launch ordered by the President; thinking fast, he produced a single yellow marble.

'Come on!' he said, clasping the marble firmly in his hand.

As the missile sped towards him, Aster breathed a deep breath readying himself. Then, crushing the marble in his hand, he swung his arm in an upwards motion.

The yellow dust shot from his hand in a cloud-like formation just as the missile flew above his head. It hardened instantly, freezing the rocket on the spot. A thick amber-like structure encapsulated the rocket, abruptly stopping in the air.

'Holy crap, it worked.' He said to himself, remembering to breathe.

'Violet!' he said in a moment of clarity.

Aster ran towards the bodies of his comrades, his eyes regaining their familiar colour, the steel blue of his skin slowly faded away.

He slowed to a stop, leaning over Violet to check if she was still alive.

'I'm picking up a faint pulse.' Aster said, scanning her body with his nanochip.

Pressing the call button on his nano-pad, the sound of jets slowly filled the air as the cleanup crew began to arrive on the scene.

*

Violet opened her eyes. The lights above blinded her as she winced in pain. The room was plain, its steel walls bare and lifeless, the sound of a hydraulic pump thumped in the distance. Trying to sit up, she realised she was unable to move, her legs like dead weights, her arms failed to respond as she willed them to move, her head fixed in the one position facing up to the ceiling.

'I am nothing short of impressed!' the sound of a woman's voice filled her ears. She recognised the voice instantly.

'What?' Violet choked as she tried to speak.

'I wouldn't try to speak if I were you V. You may do more damage.' The woman, her soft tone, fluttered into Violet's ears.

'The things you do for this world, and for what? No recognition, no fame, no thanks! Sad, isn't it.' The woman said as she slowly appeared in Violet's line of sight.

'Alexi—'

'Shhhh V, save your strength!' the woman said, pressing her finger to Violet's lips. Her plump, ruby red lips pursed as she removed her finger, pressing it against her own.

'It is nothing short of amazing, the lengths you go just to piss me off.' She said as she flicked her long tumbling auburn hair to the side. Her piercing emerald eyes bore down on Violet as her sultry voice filled the room.

'I have to admit V, I didn't see all that happening, and that, as you very well know, is quite unusual for me!' she said with a flippant laugh.

'Do you remember V, that day when I told you your future, I do! Would you care for me to re-tell the story?' She stared into Violet's eyes, her face stern and terrifying as a wicked smile crept across her face.

'Ohh, look at me, runs a whole world but forgets the smallest things.' She giggled, 'Blink once for yes and two for no.' She said as she leaned in closer to

Violet's face. The tip of her nose just grazing Violet's cheek.

Violet, unable to move, blinked twice.

'Two ones, no need to repeat yourself V, Yes it is.' She said, clasping her hand around Violet's neck; her red nails dug into Violet's skin as she slowly tightened her grip.

'In the future, a pretty purple-haired girl tried to save the world. Sound familiar?' she said, grasping tighter with each word.

'She flew through space, off on another valiant mission, her brothers in arms surrounding her, protecting her, giving their lives for her!' she continued her grip unyielding.

'Then the silly girl crash-landed on a new planet, with her guns in hand and battalion by her side, she attacked the Gods, bringing nothing but death and ruin!'

Violet began to panic as she struggled to breathe; her eyes began to bulge as she gasped for air.

'The Gods feared this Violet warrior. And so, to teach her a lesson, they took back their favourite creation, humans. One by one, man, woman; child by innocent child, the Gods enacted their revenge, slaying all who took a breath until finally, just the warrior remained!'

Violet could feel herself blacking out, unable to scream, unable to move. She could only see the red-haired woman lying on top of her as she slowly ran out of air.

'In the end, V, they all die. I will not allow my planet, my people, my life, to become pledges of sacrifice for you and your lofty ideals of world domination.'

The woman's soft face turned hard as she clasped her second hand over Violet's mouth and nose.

'Heed my warning V. If you live, we all die.'

As the words left her mouth, the door to the isolated room swung open. Aster jumped from the doorway to the hospital bed. Turning his arm towards the woman, he landed a direct hit knocking her back off Violet. Then, flicking his wrist, he equipped his U.N.N assault rifle, aiming at the woman.

'Madam President.' Aster said as she pulled herself up from the floor.

'Aster Voss! I knew you were stupid, but I didn't realise just how stupid you truly were.' She said, clicking her fingers. The sound of multiple guns loading came from the hallway behind Aster.

'Enough of this!' the General said as he stormed into the room, pushing past the President's secret service.

'Stand down, Aster.' He said, forcing the gun towards the ground.

'General, I would suggest—'

'Enough of your suggestions Madam President,' He said, his face turning a flush shade of red, 'Clear this room immediately.' He boomed, his voice ricocheting around the room.

Aster stormed from the room, dematerialising his gun.

'Madam President, you're not exempt from my rule. Have we not just entered a state of war.'

'I needn't explain to you my actions Hill, nor do you have the privilege of questioning me,' She spat, each word full of venom, 'I expect an immediate resignation for your insubordination. Am I making myself clear?'

'Crystal,' General Hill said as he took to guard Violet's bed. 'Oh and one more thing, Madam President, do not re-enter this room!' he said, flashing her his sternest stare.

'You have no piece to play in this game Hill. Mark my words, she lives, we die!' the President said, brushing off her coat as she stormed from the room.

Gliding down the hallway, she reached the end of the corridor.

'Madam Prez, I didn't recognise you without my Major's neck under your hands!' Aster said, turning the corner to reveal himself.

'Listen, alien, I have bigger things to tend to, stand down, and it spares your life!'

Aster, enraged by the words from the President, clapped his hands together; pulling them slowly apart, he produced a black blade.

'I hadn't realised it before, in all the speeches, the television shows, the swarms of crowding fans, hanging on every word!' Aster said, inching closer and closer.

His eyes turned black; the room began to feel small, as though the walls were caving in. Then, finally, the President stepped back, her eyes wide with shock.

'Then it hit me; you've done all this before, lived this life on repeat. Tell me, Alexis! How long have you been hiding your true self?' Aster finished his sentence, swinging his sword arm back.

The black blade shot flames from its sharp steel edge, the dark energy emitting a tremendous heat.

'Reveal yourself, witch.'

With a sweep of his blade, Aster fell forward as a shower of bullets struck him from behind.

'Let me make this clear to you, Aster! You have no idea who you are messing with.' The President said, her wicked smile turning into a menacing grin, her eyes narrowing upon Aster as he fell to the floor.

The blade disappeared in a cloud of black smoke as pools of red blood flooded the hall.

Aster craned his neck, scoping the hall for his assailant.

'So, you think all these men are enough?' he said, slowly rolling onto his front.

'Pathetic.' Alexis said as she stormed down the hallway towards her armed guards.

Aster jumped from the ground, lunging towards the President, his black blade re-materialising in his hand. Suddenly a shock of blue light struck him in the chest, sending him back towards the door of Violet's room.

'Finish him off.' Alexis said as she ran towards the safety of her guards.

Aster paused, now focusing on the swarms of men running down the corridor towards him; he let out a small smile. Then, lunging from the door at a rapid speed, he swiped his blade in a single wave, cutting down the President's guard that stood in his way. Then, with a flick of his wrist, he produced a single gun. Pressing firmly on the trigger, he shot down the President's entourage.

Now slowly making his way forward, his black blade smouldering with a coat of black flames, he swiped the sword up, sending a stream of fire towards Alexis, knocking her from her feet as she ran to escape.

Aster arrived at the President's feet, rolling her over. Alexis returned his stare, her grimace bold as she cackled lying on the floor.

'Let me tell you your future, General Voss. As the last storm of Nova begins, the world will cry in pain; no man nor woman shall fate you their life. Time will standstill. He will collect her. You will pay the price; the creator will claim his possessions for once and for all!' as the last words left her mouth, the room turned cold, the lights began to flicker as a howl of wind invaded the hall.

'Let me tell you your future, Alexis, or should I say Vata, you don't have one!'

Swinging the blade into the air, Aster looked down at his enemy, his black eyes full of malice, then in a swift motion forced the sword down towards her head.

— CHAPTER NINE —

COMPLETE CHAOS

Caspian looked up from his desk deep within the Black-ops base, surrounded by the warming wall of screens. He sighed. The images of their fight in Paris played out around him as he continued to gather intelligence in the hopes to relay it back to Violet.

'Yo Caspian, any news on Major?'

Caspian spun in his chair to face the man now entering the dimly lit room.

'Leo, yes, we have news. She is awake. The General confirmed back about an hour ago.'

'How're the hands?' Leo said, holding back a faint laugh.

'Yea, doing fine, thanks for asking.' He replied, looking down at his nano-encased hands.

'So is it just you? Where's everyone else?' Leo's voice boomed through the base.

'Do you mind? Some of us are trying to sleep.'

'Sorry Tak, Oren, I didn't see you there,' Leo said, blushing in embarrassment, 'You could have told me the base was now a campsite.' Leo said, punching Caspian on the arm.

Caspian shook his head, turning back to his private holo-screen, trying to focus on the task at hand.

'So, what's the plan?' Leo asked, looming over Caspian's shoulder,

'You're second, you tell me!'

'Yea, second in the battlefield, this intelligence stuff is all you.' Leo said, grasping at Caspian's shoulders.

'Get off!' he said, shrugging his shoulders as he stood from his chair.

As he walked towards the central command post, muttering under his breath, the plan began to unfold within his mind.

'Ok, Leo, I need you to do me a favour.'

'Sure thing.'

'I need you to collect the extraction samples we collected from Zyair.'

'No probs. Before I do, he's not dead, right?' Leo asked as a rare look of concern washed across his face.

'He is fine Leo, after removing the old lungs, we replaced them with nano-tech ones. He started breathing again by himself almost instantly. But those extraction samples could show me how the dark energy affects the body and how best to combat it.'

'Awesome! I'll head down there now.' Leo said, exiting the room.

The room fell silent again as Caspian walked back towards his desk.

'What do you need from us?' Jax asked, sitting up from his makeshift bed.

'Nothing, just continue as you are. There's not much we can do now anyway.'

As the conversation finished, the room erupted into an ear-piercing alarm. Red flashing lights began to pulse, illuminating the darkroom. The screens wiped as they displayed a flashing red warning sign.

'Red alert - commence evacuation sequence one.'

The sound from the alarms continued to ring as Caspian typed furiously on his holo-board.

'I.D. Two zero, zero seven. Command unit black operations, senior Caspian Snow, replay pre-evac footage!'

Images of the lower level testing facility filled the screens surrounding the bunker. The sound of screams filled the comm-link as Caspian recoiled in horror. The images flickered, slowly filling with a haze of black mist. Then the sights of men and women fighting against an unknown assailant came into focus as a solitary shadow man relentlessly struck each person down.

'All black-ops specialists to the testing bay now.' Caspian said into the comm-link.

Just as he and his comrades made it to the bunker doors, the lights in the room began to flash green, the alarm growing louder with the sudden colour change.

'Green alert - full sequence lockdown will begin in sixty seconds.'

'Move now.' Caspian shouted as the Black-ops team made their way into the corridor of the base.

As he pressed the call lift button, the doors swung open to an empty five-person cabin.

'State your level.'

'Lower level two-fifty.' Caspian said as the doors closed sharply, the cabin now plunging towards the ground at breakneck speed.

The doors snapped open. The testing bay was dark. A trickle of black mist swayed in the air as the emergency lights continued to flash green.

'Activate air filters.' Caspian said, taking the lead.

The Black-ops team made their way around the testing bay laboratory, trying to keep silent not to disturb what was hiding in the dark.

'Craaapp!' Leo hit the wall with a thud, sliding down to the ground. The Black-ops team rallied to his side.

'What are you doing here alone!' Caspian said, dragging him up from the ground.

'I was collecting samples for you! Then whatever the hell that thing is, happened!' He replied, pointing at the shadow man standing across the room.

Caspian shot a UV round towards the dark energy, but it was useless. The bullet flew straight through, bursting on the wall behind it.

'It's not the same, Casp. I already tried.'

'Get out now to the upper floors!' Caspian shouted, retracting his gun.

Running from the room, they jumped into the lift cabin, the doors sealing shut firmly behind them.

'Medical bay now.' Leo said in a panic.

The lift arrived at the medical bay. Bursting into the room, there they were greeted by Zyair standing in his full combat gear.

'Green alarm and you all run here, feels promising.' Zyair said, flicking his wrist, activating his standard-issue assault rifle.

'The black energy is on the loose.' Caspian panted.

'How?'

'Not sure, I haven't had the chance to run any diagno—'

'Now's not the time, boys!' Leo said, opening fire onto the shadow man who had just materialised in the room.

Using the MAGNA rounds, Leo sent a barrage of bullets through the air, each one passing through the shadow man as he confidently walked towards the team.

Takeshi, seizing the moment, produced a black marble from his nano-chip.

'Cover your eyes!' he shouted, throwing the marble directly at the shadowy figure. A sharp blinding light emitted from the marble as it landed on the floor, inches from its target.

Then a cyclone of air began to whirl as it ensnared the dark energy, sucking it into the small black sphere.

'Small but useful. Remind me to thank Ms Myers; her gadgets are truly revolutionary.' Takeshi said, picking the marble up off the floor.

The sound of nails on glass filled the room as the black marble began to crack, the foul whistle growing louder with each second.

'Get down.' Takeshi said, throwing the marble across the room.

The marble exploded with the force of a newly formed tornado, throwing the Black-ops team around the room, disposing of them one by one until the dark energy took form, once again free to do as it wished.

*

'Warning, amber alert, base zero, zero two is now compromised. Total shutdown in sixty seconds.'

The lights around the weapons bay began to flash amber as the warning sounded throughout the intercom.

'Make sure the blast doors remain sealed. Shut down all transport links from the lower levels. Isolate all evac points from level three-hundred to this floor. Commander, now is the time to activate the E.X.O's.'

Serena had managed to lock down the entirety of floor one. A level dedicated to weapons development and strategic defence. It was also the room she spent most of her day in, doing what she did best, creating technology unrivalled by any other. Securing herself and the Omega team inside the room, they prepared for whatever danger may present itself.

'We have confirmation on location - Med bay, lower level one five five.' Serena said, applying the finishing touches to the B.I.O weapon she held in her hands.

'Ms Myers—'

'Serena, Commander, if we're gonna die, we might as well go out on a first-name basis.' She said, flashing him a smile.

'Right, Serena, we have confirmed it is from the dark energy retrieved from the lungs of Zyair Nkosi.'

'I'm familiar with Zyair and his procedure. But this was not merely enough. Mass cannot multiply out of thin air!'

'It's a guess, but we think the energy gathered from the Delta team may also have contributed.'

'Fine! What are we working with in terms of casualties?'

'Currently, six, no other signs of life have been found.'

'And the other levels?'

'Evacuated, just us and the Black-ops combatants!'

Serena picked up a small silver bangle from the counter. Placing it over her wrist, it began to emit a soft blue light that pulsed every few seconds. Then a tiny holographic ball flew across the room, centring itself directly in the middle of the floor.

As it expanded into a large sphere, images displaying each base floor flashed across the screen, revealing empty room after empty room.

'There med-bay, zoom in, keep all cameras locked on that thing.'

'Yes, Serena, but what are you going to do if that thing gets up here?'

'When Commander! Not if! There is a contingency plan in place. Follow my lead.'

'Understood, and it's Cody.' he smiled, producing his E.X.O inbuilt rifle.

Serena rifled through her desk, grabbing a small block of unknown material. It glowed with the faintest of red lights. It appeared to be moving and bending with a mind of its own.

'Serena, you may want to take a look at this!' Cody shouted from across the room. His eyes fixed on the holo screen.

Serena turned her head, witnessing the events now unfolding in the rest of the base.

The shadow man slowly moved towards the medbay door passing through it with ease. As it entered the corridor, it stood still, focusing on the central lift.

'It's on the move.' Serena said, gripping onto the red box with as much force as she could muster.

Sparks of red lights shot from the box as it slowly began to melt through her fingers.

'Not to ask too many questions, but what is that thing?'

'Anti-matter, or at least a synthesised version. Stable enough to stop it from destroying everything it touches. My trump card, if you will.' She said with a wink.

The red energy formed into a shape mimicking the shadow man, who was now flowing through the next level in search of any lifeforms to kill.

'Go now, stop it from getting any further!' Serena said, staring into the red abyss as it made its way towards the blast door.

'Impressive, to say the least, but how do we know it will work?' Cody asked, watching as the red man phased through the door.

'We don't.' Serena said, loading the B.I.O weapon aiming it at the door in preparation for an oncoming attack.

'Keep your eyes on that screen, Cody. We must be ready.'

'Serena!' Commander Cody said in shock, enlarging the screen displaying lower level five.

The shadow man gripped hold of the red replica, slowly filling it with its dark energy until all that remained of Serena's anti-matter weapon was a wisp of red light that slowly faded into the deep depths of the underground base.

'Biomass replication. So it feeds off other energy, fascinating.' Serena said, narrowing her eyes towards the screen.

'It's here!' Cody shouted, aiming at the door.

The black energy flowed to floor one. The dark mist passed through the doors reforming into a single shadow man.

'Light it up!' the Omega Commander said as a blaze of gunfire filled the room, the bullets moving through the mist swiftly. They proceeded to bounce off the heavy steel doors chiming across the room. Witnessing the failed gunfire, Serena took a single shot from her B.I.O weapon, a bolt of vivid green energy shot across the room, striking the shadowy figure in the chest. Slowly the green energy began to overtake the black as it swirled around the shadow man, freezing him to the spot.

'Direct hit, we'll make a soldier out of you yet!' The Commander laughed.

'It's far from over.' Serena replied, reloading the weapon, her eyes fixed upon the shadow man.

The now green man jolted as he walked, falling to the floor he burst on impact. The green mist evaporated into the air as the energy dissipated.

'Nice work Serena.' The Commander said, breathing a sigh of relief.

Serena watched on as a faint wisp of black smoke began to linger in the air. It slowly fell to the floor, followed by other wisps, each thicker than the last.

'It's reforming.' She said in a low, calm tone.

Rushing towards her desk, she grabbed a solid silver ball. Not wasting another second, she threw the ball on the ground towards the gathering mist.

'Shield your eyes!' she shouted; her nano band spun into action, forming a black shield in front of her.

The ball opened at the centre, emitting a thin blue light that shot up at the ceiling. As it grew in size, the blue light became more potent until the room filled with a light brighter than the sun.

Suddenly the light dropped to the floor, producing a radial effect, the seismic energy released covering the whole room.

'Take cover.' Cody shouted, throwing himself on the floor as the energy vaporised anything in its way.

All that could be heard was the sound of steel on steel as the light screeched its way around the room, destroying everything in its path. Then, finally, the silver sphere stopped, the light dispersed, and the room was left empty. Serena deactivated her shield.

Holding the B.I.O weapon close, she scanned the room.

'Commander Cody, respond.'

'Don't worry; we're all here.' He replied, looking around the room at his team as they stood gingerly in their E.X.O suits.

'There doesn't appear to be any traces of energy left on this level.' She said, lowering her gun.

'Violet Alert. Sixty seconds till self-destruction!'

The room started to flash purple lights as the warning continued to run in the background.

'Can you override it?' Cody asked. A hint of panic twanged his voice.

'No! It's an auto defence procedure. The energy is still active on the lower floors. We must evacuate now!' Serena spun the nano band on her arm. Materialising a small orange marble, she threw it at the blast doors. The marble dissolved, dispensing a viscous orange liquid that quickly spread, melting the doors before them providing access to the stairwell.

'Everybody out now!' she shouted, heading directly to the exit.

As she ran, she hit what felt like a brick wall, falling back; she looked up to see the Black-ops team running up the stairwell to the top floor.

'Ms Myers, what are you still doing here?' Leo said, pulling her up from the floor.

'Not now. Get moving.' She replied, her sharp tone implying haste.

The Black-ops commandos, followed by Serena and the Omega team, made their way up to the top of the roof. As the door burst open, the heat of the summer sun bore down on them as they evacuated in single file.

'There, the evac pods.' Serena said, spinning her nano-band.

A set of oval-shaped pods materialised at the west wing of the roof as the camouflage was deactivated.

As they ran towards the pods, the ground began to shake. The earthquakes could mean only one thing. The detonations had begun.

'Quickly, we assemble at the rendezvous point!' Serena said, bundling herself and others into one of the evac pods.

'Jax, get in the pod!' Leo shouted as the roof began to cave.

A fire had started to spring from the cracks in the steel roof, the smell of electric fire filling the air. Leo pushed Jax into the pod. The doors slammed shut behind them as Caspian hit the jettison button. Then with a bang, the pods shot out from their containers.

The Black-ops base grew smaller with each passing second. Now wreathed in fire and ash, they watched as their base melted, collapsing into the roaring waters below.

Finally, the pods landed on the ground with a tremendous thud. The doors boomed as they blasted away from the carriage.

'Not the best landing, but a landing nonetheless.' Commander Cody said as he stepped out from one of the pods.

'Agreed, We need to report this to the General ASAP!' Caspian said, climbing out of a second pod, his feet sinking into the grassy field as he walked towards the others.

'Was it contained, Commander?' Oren asked, helping his fellow agents climb out of the pods.

'No!' Serena replied, materialising her holo-screen, 'It got out last minute, see it launched off the roof at the last second.' She said, replaying the footage of their hasty escape.

'So it's loose, great!' Leo said, punching the nearest tree.

'Serena, where is the nearest military base to London?' Oren asked.

'Berlin, but they have neither the technology nor the clearance for something like this.' She replied, scanning a list of Nova bases from her holo dex.

'Tokyo.' She said abruptly.

'Tokyo it is, Caspian make them aware of our arrival, Jax we need transport, Tak, Oren, Zyair, get everyone moving.' Leo said, making himself the next leader.

The transports arrived moments after receiving the alert from Jax, the survivors of the attack hastily boarded their rescue ships.

'Ms Myers, are you ok?' Cody asked her, sitting in the chair next to her on board the Yellowhammer.

'Yes, Commander, why do you ask?' she replied.

'You look as though you have seen a ghost?'

'No ghost, Commander but something else entirely!' Serena said.

Staring at the holo-board on her wrist, the images of the destruction flashed in sequence.

First, Serena paused the playback on the appearance of a shadowy black figure. Then, enlarging the screen, she clarified the picture, continuing the playback.

A woman dressed in black, her outfit seemed to show the moon and the stars as they moved around space. Her eyes were as white as bone. Her lips were as black as night. Her hair shimmered in radiant light as it swayed gently in the breeze. She was no human.

'Who is that?' Commander Cody asked as he narrowed his eyes to get a better view

'The Executioner!'

— CHAPTER TEN —

TROUBLE IN TOKYO

The Yellowhammer completed its docking sequence, landing in the ship bay of the east Nova base. The remaining crew of the Black-ops division assembled at the lowering doors of the cargo hold.

'Sequence complete, Commander.'

'Thank you, Captain.' Leo said as the crew left the ship.

Greeted by a familiar face, the Black-ops team stood to attention, saluting at his presence.

'General, it's good to see you.' Serena said, leading the way.

'I can say the same to you, Ms Myers. You appear to be doing well, in light of the circumstances.' He said, removing his cap, nodding at the assembled team.

'Do we have confirmation of the hostile escape?' Serena asked.

'Negative, we are still working on location. We tracked it heading westbound, but it's gone. The energy signal disappeared shortly after escaping.'

'So it could have dissipated? Perhaps, burning out?' Serena asked.

'Maybe, either way, B.I.O.N.A will detect any spikes, rest assured, Ms Myers, we will be there to intercept when needed.' Hill said, leading the team into the central command room.

Walking through the open glass doors into an octagonal room, the Black-ops team took their place at the empty glass desks. There they waited for the General's orders as he strode into the room, with Serena not far behind.

The walls lined end to end with display screens monitoring the old London base, whilst blue and white lights illuminated the vast open space. Then, from the top of the Tokyo tower, they began their debrief.

'Gentlemen, in place of Major Villin, you will bring me your plans of action. What is your plan for when that energy spikes.' The General said, puffing his chest as he scanned the Black-ops team.

'*If* the energy spikes.' Caspian said, taking a seat at one of the many empty desks.

'Meaning?' General Hill asked, turning his head in confusion towards Caspian.

'B.I.O.N.A's tracking sequence only looks for the girl and her unique energy output, not whatever manifestations she can conjure up. These things are wholly unique in their biological makeup.'

'How?' Leo interrupted, forgetting this was no ordinary meeting.

The General burnt his eyes on Leo's face as he cowered in fear.

'The energy she emits has a specific quality to it, hence the burns,' Caspian said, holding up his hands, 'However, the shadow figures she manifests are, well, effectively crude re-creations of herself. They don't burn to the touch nor emit the same energy sequence. We are assuming that anything she outputs is the same.'

'Fine, then upload the energy sequence from her "creations" as you put it and find this damn thing!' The General said, his face turning a slight blush of beetroot.

'The problem we face is if we upload the new data to B.I.O.N.A, it will wipe the pre-existing data on the girl. B.I.O.N.A is advanced but not that advanced. Can we take that risk?' Serena interrupted, causing the room to turn in her direction. 'Listen, we have two choices: keep our tracer on the girl, or track an insignificant energy source that could be making its way back to its creator. My choice is the obvious one.' She continued, the room falling deafly silent.

'Agreed, Ms Myers.' Caspian said, turning back towards the General.

'Well, that solves that.' General Hill said, rubbing his temples to relieve the tension building in his head.

'General?' Leo said, gingerly holding his hand in the air.

'This isn't school, Leo. Ask your question.' The General said, continuing to rub his temples.

'You were in Washington. How is the Major?'

'She's fine, Leo, resting for now.'

'With that attack, she should be dead!' Leo replied in shock.

'She's made of strong stuff, that girl. I'm sure she will be back in action in no time.'

The room fell silent as the Black-ops team set to work on locating the girl in grey.

'General, can I borrow you for a moment?' Serena said, standing from her desk to leave the room.

The General nodded his head as the two of them left the central command room.

'We have had the breakthrough you were looking for.' She said.

'Outstanding work Ms Myers. Bring the weapon; we can begin mass production immediately.' He said, walking down the all-white corridor towards the weapons bay.

'Ah, well, I don't have it.' Serena said, remaining still at the doors of the command post.

'Where is it then?'

'Back at the Black-ops base, or what's left of it. We need to retrieve it; it could be the only thing that will stop her.'

'I will assemble a strike team! Elektra, Gamma and Omega teams will escort you back to the base, retrieve the weapon and bring it back here for production.' He said, pressing buttons on his nano-screen that emitted from his nano-chip.

'I think the smaller, the better, General. I don't think now is the time to bring in the army for one inconspicuous silver ball. The smaller we are, the less noticed we will be.'

'Or the easier you are to take out! No, it's my way, Ms Myers or no way, you are too valuable for me to lose.' He said, turning to walk away.

'General, one more thing. On the footage of the evacuation, a woman was standing on the building as it fell.'

'Woman, you say! And just who is this woman?' he said, turning back in intrigue.

'In my meetings with Aster, we began several procedures to reclaim his lost memories. Within one of these sessions, he described a woman with dark hair. Her eyes would flash with the image of the moon and stars. He called her "The Executioner"!'

'The Executioner, you say? So, we are being watched!' he said, sinking into deep thought.

Pausing for a moment, the General folded his arms, glancing a look back at Serena; he pressed the call button on his holo-screen.

'Retrieve the orb Ms Myers, by any means necessary.' He said, walking towards the landing platform.

*

The Black-ops team continued their work quietly as they scoured the globe for any sign of the energy matching the one in Manhattan.

'I'm picking up a signal from the west quadrant of the city, it's faint, but it's a match.' Oren said, swiping the map onto the wall of screens illuminating the room.

'The Magunafōsu tower.' Caspian said, clarifying the energy concentration.

'Assemble a strike team. We cannot hope to tackle this thing alone!' Leo said.

'We have Sigma team on standby.' Jax replied, looking up from the screen towards Leo.

'Perfect! We end this tonight.'

Leo took the lead as he ran down the corridor towards the Yellowhammer, followed by the Black-ops and Sigma team.

'Quickly, we won't have much time. Battle plans are now live on your nano-chips.' Caspian said, pressing a few buttons on his holo-screen.

The jet raised from the ground as it locked onto the target location.

As it turned mid-air, the engines engaged with a low hum. Then in a sudden blast, the Yellowhammer sped towards the tower.

'ETA ten seconds!'

'Thank you, Captain. Gentleman, please review battle plans on route!' Leo shouted over the roaring sound of the high powered engines.

'The energy is spiking. We don't have much time.' Caspian said as the jet pulled to a stop hovering just above the tower.

The Black-ops team assembled at the jump-off point, attaching their Zip wires to the roof of the Yellowhammer. Then, kicking off from the ground, they slid silently towards the top of the imposing tower.

Landing in unison, they detached their lines and headed towards the entry point.

'Commander, we will meet you at the rendezvous point.' Leo said as the doors to the jet began to close.

Descending fast, the Yellowhammer dropped to the ground floor. Leo watched on as the Sigma team made their way in through the main entrance.

Flicking his wrist, Leo's pupils changed from black to neon red.

'Gentlemen, your chips have been updated with the pre-emptive combat simulators. Give it a try.' He said with a wink.

Activating their chips, each member of the Black-ops eyes changed from black to red. Then, swiftly entering the building, they began their hunt for their prey.

Silently they hunted in the dark, making their way towards the energy spike.

'It's here.' Caspian said, signalling towards the office door.

'Level two-hundred, Commander, do you copy?' Leo said through the comm-link

'Roger that, we are on route to your location.'

'On your order!' Caspian said, staring Leo down as they awaited his signal.

'Keep your guns on MAGNA rounds, don't give her the chance to move.' Leo motioned his arms, signalling the all-clear.

As he did, Takeshi kicked the door square in the centre, forcing it to fly open, revealing a room completely void of anything.

'Room clear, Commander.' Takeshi relayed as they piled in through the single person door.

'Something isn't right,' Leo mumbled to himself, as the Black-ops team moved about the room, 'Caspian, the signal, what happened to it?' Leo asked in confusion.

'It's gaining in strength, directly where we're standing. It makes no se—' as the words left Caspian's mouth, the room went black. Immediately it filled with dark energy.

'EVERYBODY DOWN!' Caspian shouted as the Black-ops team leapt to the floor.

The office erupted in a sea of black flames, deep purple thunderbolts shot from a single point in the centre of the room, striking at the Black-ops team as they moved to dodge each passing bolt.

'This is it, don't give her any chance to attack.' Leo said, producing a black marble from his nano-chip.

Aiming, he threw it directly at the energy source.

Shattering into a sea of black dust, it formed the same jell-glass that Violet had once used. Then, moulding itself around the energy, it sealed it shut, stopping the bolts of electricity.

'Caspian, I need an update. Did it work?' Leo said, slowly standing from the ground.

'It appears to be stable. The spike is lowering at a rapid pace.' Caspian said, daring to break the tiniest of smiles.

'Erm, guys, you might want to take a look at this.' Zyair said as he glared out of the window,

The black mist began to descend quickly towards the ground heading straight towards the Sigma team.

'Shit! Commander, come in, get your men out of there!' Leo shouted into the comm-link, there was no response.

Zyair looked down towards the ground below the mist now dissipated.

'It's gone!' he said in bemusement.

'Caspian?' Leo said, shooting a confused look in his direction.

'I can't explain it, no spike and no half-life energy reading, something isn't right.'

The sounds of screams and gunshots filled the comm-link. Then, the sound of a shrill whistle rang through their ears.

'Commander, what's happening?' Leo said in a panic.

'Get out of there, proceed back to—' The comm-link fell eerily silent.

Leo flicked his wrist to activate the holo-pad, throwing a small steel marble from the window to the ground. Then as it sprouted tiny wings, a small lens appeared upon the surface.

As the marble began its mission, zipping from side to side, it scoped out the lower levels of the building. Finally, images of the Sigma team came into focus. They lay upon the ground completely lifeless, the halls filled with a dark black mist.

The drone continued weaving around the bodies of their fallen comrades until a young girl dressed in grey appeared in view. Her white-blond hair trailed to her waist. Her black eyes stared down the drone as it whizzed around.

'She's here.' Leo said, alerting the rest of his team.

The camera went dark as the girl struck the marble with her black spear.

'Caspian, you said—'

'I know what I said. None of this makes any sense.' He replied, pressing buttons in vain, unsure of how to explain their current events.

'She is learning.' Oren said from the corner of the room.

'What?' Leo sneered, turning in his direction.

'It makes sense, even in Paris, the energy levels lowered before she appeared, now they don't even show at all. She's concealing herself.'

'We need to get out and fast!' Leo said, bringing up the building's blueprint on his nano-chip.

'We could always take the scenic route.' Zyair said, turning to point towards the windows.

'But we don't have anything that—' Caspian trailed off as Leo rushed past him.

'Out we go!' he said, crashing through the glass pane.

Falling from the two hundredth floor, Leo flicked his wrist, producing a green marble, throwing it at the ground, it burst into a sea of green foam. Plunging into the foam, Leo slowed to a gradual stop before he reached the concrete floor.

'Well, that works.' Zyair said, leaping through the Leo shaped hole in the wall, shortly followed by Oren, Takeshi and Jax.

'*Merde*!' Caspian uttered as he ran towards the window.

The sound of screams filled the air as Leo looked up towards the tower. The windows began to spray with blood as the dark mist slowly scaled the building.

Glimpses of the girl in grey flashed by each window as she swiftly made her way through each floor, killing all who stood in her way.

'Commander, what's the plan?' Caspian said, now landing next to Leo, his nano-screen flashing with each death.
'We take it out head on.'

'How? we need more than a simple command!' Caspian shouted.

'Now is not the time!' Takeshi said, pulling himself out of the green foam, pointing towards the top of the tower.

The cries for help had stopped. Standing atop the tower, the girl in grey stared down at the Black-ops team. Her dark eyes glistened in the moonlight.

Then, gathering the dark mist to herself, she formed it into a black ball, suspending it in mid-air.

Then, with a single tap of her finger, she sent it flying towards them.

'Take cover!' Leo shouted as the team jumped out of the way.

The dark energy hit the ground, incinerating the concrete upon contact.

'Commander, we must—' Caspian stopped abruptly.

There floating before him was the girl in grey, her maniacal smile tattooed across her face.

'How did you—?'

Swiping at him, she released a single bolt of purple thunder connecting with his chest. The shock reverberated through his body whilst pinning him to the spot. The smell of burnt flesh flowed in the air as Caspian's skin began to sizzle. He lay clutching himself in pain as the burns started to spread.

'CASPIAN!' Leo shouted as he turned towards the girl. Then, brandishing his guns, he opened fire upon his target.

The girl vanished into a cloud of black mist, reappearing directly behind Leo faster than the eye could see. With a swipe of her arm, she thrust her black spear forward, piercing Leo in the back and pushing through to his chest. Then, snapping her arm back, the spear flew on, leaving Leo's body and a blood-filled hole from where it came.

Tears welled up in Leo's eyes as he fell to his knees, hopelessly clutching to his chest as the river of claret poured to the ground.

Next, the girl turned her attention to the rest of the Black-ops team. She waved her hand, re-gathering her dark energy. Then, once she had enough, she fired it upon the ground. Thunderbolts protruded from the earth, striking at the rest of the operatives sending them into multiple directions.

Leo looked around, his team in complete disarray. The Magunafōsu stood tall, void of life. Tokyo's once pristine streets were now ablaze with black fire. Leo dropped back, still clutching at his chest. He felt himself burning from the inside out, crying out in pain. He slowly began to blackout.

The girl returned from a cloud of dark mist. Slowly, she walked towards Leo, spinning her malefic weapon in the air. Suddenly it froze on the spot. Twisting her hand, she moved the pike a few inches, lining it up perfectly to his head. Then, clenching her fist, the spear shot from the sky, aiming towards Leo's face.

The sound of steel on steel rang out in the air, the chime so loud it echoed across the city. Leo opened his eyes. The spear did not meet its mark.

'Aster?' Leo mumbled as his eyes closed, blacking out from the world around him.

'Major, you are clear!' Aster said, his black blade holding her dark spear in place.

'Roger that, keep her busy.'

Violet dropped from the sky as she dismounted the M.K.One speeder. Falling smoothly to the ground, she landed directly next to the girl in grey.

'Surprise.' Aster said, his mouth forming a sinister grin.

Black flames shot from Aster's sword as he forced the blade up, cleaving the spear in two.

Violet flicked her wrist, activating her nano-band. Then, grasping at the newly formed blue marble, she crushed it in the palm of her hand. Instantly the jell-glass began to multiply. Then, before it had time to solidify, Violet swung her fist, landing a hit on the girl's face, the jell-glass now transferring, moulded its way around the girl in grey.

As she struggled to remove it, black energy began to gather around her.

'Aster now.' Violet said, jumping back from her target.

Swinging his sword arm back, Aster lunged at the girl, twisting his body to the left, then slashing up with his arm, the tip of the sword now facing towards the sky. The girl let out a scream so loud it shattered the glass in all the buildings surrounding the fourth quadrant.

Her arm fell to the ground, blood splattering across the surface as it landed with a lifeless thud.

Spinning on his heel, Aster swung the blade around his body, slashing the girl across her stomach. She fell to her knees, blood draining from her body.

As she knelt perfectly still, black tears dropped from her face. Violet walked towards the girl, activating her nano-bands. She produced a single M-eight, clicking it once, the gun began to illuminate a neon red glow.

'Who are you?' Violet said, grabbing the girl's face with her hand.

The girl ignored Violet, a sinister grin forming across her face as she stared into Violet's eyes.

'Answer me!' Violet said, pressing her gun on the girl's forehead.

'Soon, he will come to collect me, and when he does, your fate shall be sealed.' She replied in a soft and calm voice.

'Who? Who is coming to collect you?'

'The Angel of Death!' She said, chuckling as she finished.

She was soon hysterical, her maniacal laugh growing louder with each passing second, then screaming uncontrollably as the black energy began to form around her. Her face warped as the screams grew to ear-piercing levels.

'Major!' Aster shouted through the vortex of black energy.

Violet squared her eyes, taking a step back from the girl as she continued to scream her shrill cry as the ferocious energy raged around them.

'Fine!' Violet extended her arm, aiming the gun at the girl's head. She fired a single shot, a bright red neon bullet discharged from the barrel, piercing the girl's forehead. The dark energy stopped. The girl fell silent, dropping to the ground into a pool of her own blood.

— CHAPTER ELEVEN —

THE COUNCIL OF PETARIA

The golden sun sat ablaze in the cerulean sky. The willows whistled in the wind as many golden feathered birds landed upon the vast purple lakes of Petaria.

As the birds chirped their sweet songs, their voices carried along with the winds. High they rose into the mountains towards the throne of the divine ruler Solus.

The grand throne of Solus was a marvel to the eyes. Its solid gold pillars soared high into the sky, standing many meters tall. The pure crystal throne rested atop the grandiose pillars glistening in the sun as the circular room remained open to the elements.

Solus sat upon his throne. Clad in his solid gold armour, he breathed in the fresh Petarian air. His gold beard stretched to his chest; his gold hair lay silken straight to his waist; his golden eyes bore down upon the splendorous world below.

At his feet stood a woman, clad from neck to toe in silver silk, her platinum hair shining so bright it blurred her stunning face, her aqua blue eyes casting light upon the ground as she stood motionless, listening in on the sounds of Petaria.

'The birds sing once again, your most divine Solus!' She said, moving glacially towards the edge of the mountain.

'To what end, my dear Parminx?'

'It is too early to tell, perhaps a stroll in the gardens to clear our thoughts?' she turned from the cliff facing towards the giant on his throne.

'I concur. It has been too long.' He said, rising from his crystal throne.

The world shook beneath his feet as he stomped forward from his throne, now shrinking with each passing step until he stood but a few inches higher than his female companion.

As they walked towards the lavender fields below the mountains, a mild breeze grew, gathering force as it whistled a fell screech into the grass below.

'Tell me, my dear, what do the souls say?' Solus asked, watching as the grand willows recoiled in fear, fleeing into the hills.

'They speak of her, once again. She brings ruin to your stunning creation.' She said, her words catching the wind, the fell voices calling her name.

The clouds gathered in the sky, darkening the lavender lands. But then, the golden birds took flight. Their feathers turned to steel as they landed upon the fell grounds.

'What of her? She waned from her great defeat. How now is she meddling in my affairs once more!'

'No, my lord, the spirits are in envy. She has returned once more. Her exile is over!' Parminx's eyes grew dark, her hair turned grey, the light of Petaria faded from her body as the chilling wind thrashed about the darkening land.

'Enough!' Solus boomed.

His voice shook Petaria to the core. The wind, banished from his presence, fled from the lands. The darkness turned to light as the golden sun crept back into view from behind the gathering clouds.

Parminx dropped to the ground, her body now limp and lifeless, her eyes cold and grey, her hair tangled in the long grass and lavender flowers.

Solus looked upon her lifeless body. Then, with pity in his heart, he motioned a single arm into the sky. As he twisted his hand, the sun's light moved until it shone directly upon her. Slowly lifting her body into the atmosphere, the golden light rejuvenated her skin. Her eyes regained their glow. Her hair shone brightly as it flowed freely in the soft breeze.

'My dear, the souls are quite greedy, do not be so quick to give them your life in exchange for words!' Solus said, taking her hand guiding her down from the sky above.

'Thank you, my lord. The voices of the dead have grown plenty. She must not be allowed to disrupt the balance any longer.' She said, bending down upon one knee.

Then she clasped at the air above her, producing a long silver sword, its handle bejewelled in the most glorious of white gemstones, the steel blade so thin it was barely visible from the side.

'I shall bring her in, once again in your name, divine lord.' She finished bowing her head, awaiting Solus's judgment.

'My dear, too many times you have stepped into matters far below your worth. You are the creation of peace. Allow yourself the pleasure of your namesake!'

Solus said, swiping his hand in the air, dematerialising the blade from her hand.

'Summon the firstborn! We shall decide her fate as one.' Solus boomed, clapping his hands together.

Dust from the ground shot into the air. They both disappeared from the gardens in a flash of golden light, only to reappear moments later in the council chambers atop the magnificent throne bearing mountains.

Placing her arms across her chest in a cross, Parminx began to glow, a faint aqua light.

'The divine lord summons you as a matter of the most urgent, proceed to the council chambers. Heed to my call for the creator of all.' She said out loud, her voice ringing across every inch of Petaria.

As she finished her speech, her faint glow began to fade as the council light returned to its normal state. Parminx stood by her seat, waiting for Solus to rest in the solid gold chair atop the round table of polished stone.

Suddenly a shower of pink rose petals fell from the sky, blowing in many directions as the wind carried them wherever they desired until the chamber became overrun in soft pink petals.

A sickly sweet scent drifted through the council chambers as the petals gathered in their numbers forming around one of the smooth stone chairs. The wind whipped the petals into the air then flushed them away. All that remained behind was a tall woman dressed in soft pink robes. Her dark skin glistened in the golden sun. Her white eyes shimmered as they reflected the light of Solus. Her pale pink hair tumbled to the floor in bundles of curls and gentle sweeping flicks. Her smile lit up the room as she rested upon the polished stone chair.

Then placing one hand over the top of the other, her soft pink nails clicked on the stone as she scanned the room.

'Father, might I say, your golden hair is looking lustfully gracious today.' She said, her soft raspy voice filling the room.

'Roma, my heart, my love. I have missed you!' Solus said, his face softening with each word.

'Agreed, your most benevolent, less has your time in the fields been of late, tell me you're not ill of my land.' She said, waving her hands over the stone slabs producing flowers of pure light upon the surface of the chamber walls, filling the room as she weaved her fingers through the air.

'Never could I be sick of your beauty. My heart is yours, my sweet Roma.' Solus said, plucking a single rose from the surface of the table as it bloomed before his eyes.

The sky grew dark as the clouds began to form into a cluster above the open roof of the council chamber, tiny water droplets formed in the sky. They froze mid-air before they landed upon the ground, showering the room in a sheen of smooth frost.

'Oops, did I just kill your flowers, my sweet, sweet sister?'

Dropping from the sky, a man dressed in all black landed hard upon the stone floor. His blood-red hair trailed along the floor as he walked. His red skin glowed menacingly in the dark. His deep red eyes began to melt the ice, burning the flowers as he passed them by.

Roma sat upon her chair, her once soft face now turned to stone as her eyes fixed to her cruel brother.

'Let me guess, daddy this, my love that, pathetic! Sweet sister, must you display your fallacies in public ever so cheaply, as a low-cost whore begging for her coin?' he said with a smirk.

With a flick of her wrist, Roma sent forth a mist of pink haze, sealing the man's mouth shut.

His red eyes began to bulge from his skull as rose thorns protruded from his skin, his blood pooling on the floor around his chair.

'Elbordium, your words to me mean less than nothing. All the worlds would be a better place should you no longer exist.' Roma said.

Then she closed her hand into a fist, crushing the man's skull, his blood splattered across the council chambers.

'My dear, perhaps this is a conversation best left till after we have concluded our meeting.' Solus said, motioning his hand across the room. It instantly cleared of Elbordiums blood as his face returned to normal.

The room began to glow brightly as the faint smell of lilies filled the air. A small yellow orb floated down from the sky towards the centre of the council chamber. With a flash of sudden light, it morphed into a petite woman dressed in all yellow robes. Her pale skin glimmered in the yellow light as her auburn hair swished in the sky.

The glow began to recede, retracting in towards her eyes.

'Father, not that I question your rule, but must we do this now I have many planets in which to breathe life into. This…meeting will just slow me down.

'Vivata, please, if you will take a seat, the sooner we begin, the sooner it will end.' Solus said, unmoved from his golden chair.

'Fine.' She said in defiance, gliding down towards her chair.

'I take it your brother will not be joining us?' Solus asked with a slight twitch of his beard.

'Who can say of Casus and his ways? I believe Parminx was the last to leash him back from his insolence!' she said as she sat upon her chair checking her nails.

'My call was clear, Vivata of life, he is to be here, regardless of his personal beliefs.'

'I am not my brother Parminx, do not tarnish me with your silver tongue!' she hissed.

Suddenly the ground began to shake as the sky turned dark once again. The chair next to Roma set ablaze in an uncontrollable fire as the Gods turned their attention to the burning stone.

A man in gold armour appeared through the flames. His red eyes glowed like fireballs in the black void, his hair the purest white, his deep skin glistening in the heat of the fire wreathed chair.

'Bellium, dearest brother, perhaps we stop the melodramatics until after the council.'

'My dear sister, we can't all be sticks in the mud. So tell me, Parminx have you smiled at all today?'

Bellium boomed, his menacing grin tattooed across his face.

'Discarding Casus, are we all present?' Parminx said as she remained standing, casting her eyes around the room.

'Good, then I shall begin,' Solus said, standing from his golden chair, casting a shadow around everyone sitting at the council table, 'She has returned. As these words escape me, I now understand the reason for Casus's betrayal of this council. Once again, I must ask of you, my most divine children, to aid me in bringing her under control.'

'Forgive me, father, but she cannot be stopped!. As the tales once told, she is the antithesis to creation.' Parminx said, now taking her seat.

'It is clear her intentions are the same as before. Casus has moved to protect her, as he once did, forgoing this council and his family. It is clear the route we must take, bring Casus back for judgment and kill the vessel that is Noxis.' Bellium replied, his note of seriousness did not go amiss in the room of God's.

'It is but a simple task, your most gracious,' Parminx said, turning to face Solus, 'I will travel to the far reaches of the void, locate Casus and bring him in for divine judgment!'

'My dear Parminx, yet again, you have outdone yourself in utter devotion. But no, it is clear to me now he can break free from your justice. It is inevitable that should you locate him, he will only defy you once again.'

'If the God of peace is unable to do said simple task, allow me! I will fill his heart with hatred, bend his mind until all he knows is the sweet embrace of death.'

'My most vengeful child, Elbordium, to twist the soul of death is near impossible and far beyond that of your power. You will be no match for him! The

God of death knows only that, and that is why he fails in his responsibility!' Solus replied.

The sound of playful laughter filled the air as Roma stood from her chair, the room slowly filled with flower petals as she giggled loudly.

'So the God of peace sits on her divine privilege, unable to assist, and the God of hate is nothing but a pathetic waste of space,' She said, her face twisting into a sinister grin, 'Father, allow me to face the God of death, if hate cannot penetrate a soul, then I will show him nothing but love, open his heart to the truth of life, he will know only his duty!' She said, showering the occupant Gods with plumes of flowers.

'My most beautiful daughter. I could never allow you from my sight, especially not on something as dangerous as this. My precious flower, you carry the beauty of Petaria. Should you perish, I will never forgive myself.'

The council looked over to the ever-growing yellow light, now overpowering the room.

'Roma, God of love, you have no understanding of Casus, only your lust of the unknown. Father send me, there are none in existence who understands my brother better than I.' Vivata said, the glow fading back towards her piercing eyes.

'I agree, the balance between life and death must be restored. You and your brother were once one in the vast void until I granted you the gifts untold. It is decided! Bring me your brother. My judgment shall be swift and absolute.' Solus said, standing from his throne in preparation to dismiss the council.

'So, the God of life sets out on another mission, tell me, father, do you think it the wisest decision? After all, her missions of the past have taken far longer than they ever should. The one-hundred-year search, the many thousands of years it took you to repopulate Luxaria, to briefly name a few. Yet, they were all simple tasks and one's you failed to understand the importance of.' Roma said, snapping back at Vivata.

'Pathetic! So this is how you are Roma, run to daddy when you don't get your way. You know, if it were not for that pretty face, I would have crushed you a long time ago, when you were nothing but a sickly flower in the shit strewn meadows of Petaria!' Vivata said, her eyes shot a bolt of yellow lightning directly towards Roma.

'ENOUGH!' Solus shouted, clapping his hands together. The lightning faded before it could reach its mark.

The air turned cold, the sky darkened as the clouds turned grey, and the golden sun disappeared, cowering behind a shield of bilious clouds.

The Gods sat back down in their chairs, shook from the sudden outbreak of Solus.

'I gave you all the divine light of creation, and for what? So you can bicker at each other like adolescent children! No! this will not do!' Solus boomed, shaking the ground with each spoken word.

'Your most benevolent, what is your wish?' Parminx said as she stood to greet his gaze.

Solus sat back in his golden chair, contemplating his next words. The council looked on eagerly, awaiting his decision.

'Bring me the Executioner.' He said in a low growl.

As the day faded into the night, the light of the moon and stars illuminated the council chambers. The ghost-like glow cast grim shadows upon the walls. The God's sat in their stone seats unphased by the rapidly changing light. The moon grew brighter, slowly growing in size in the black night sky. Then, finally, the light reflecting its surface began to reach its peak until the council chamber was nothing but a ball of pure white light.

As the light slowly faded, the figure of a woman appeared in the centre of the room. Her dress moved with lights flickering in constant motion. It reflected the image of the moon and stars in the night sky.

Her eyes twinkled like diamonds in a vast black ocean. Her dark silken smooth hair flowed freely in the gathering winds framing her maroon tinted lips plumped to perfection.

'Lunerios, my light in the dark. I must entrust you with the most important of tasks.' Solus said, his soft voice dancing about the moonlight walls.

The woman gazed upon Solus, her dazzling eyes bearing down upon him. She nodded her head in solitary silence. The contract was unspoken but as clear as the morning sun.

Then, extending her arm into the sky, she clicked her fingers once. The sound reverberated through the council hall, bouncing from wall to wall growing in volume with each collision, the faint traces of impact marked the stone as the soundwave crashed about the circular room. Then, turning in mid-air, the sound wave changed its course, now aiming back in Lunerios's direction, striking her in the chest, it burst into a pale blue light, then as the light faded, she was gone, and the unnatural night returned to the day.

— CHAPTER TWELVE —

THE TRAITOR LIVES

Lunerios landed upon the surface of the earth. The yellow sun continued to burn down as it radiated its astonishing heat.

'Strange?' she said to herself, curious as to why the light had not faded in her presence.

Lunerios extended her arm out in front of her body. A black mist began to form into a perfect sphere in the centre of her palm.

'So this is where you've been hiding.' She said as she lowered her arm.

The black energy ball remained in the air. It rippled as it swiftly moved from side to side, then up and down, almost as though it was scanning the area.

'Bring me to her.' She said to the sphere, her starlight eyes glimmered in the bright earth sun.

With that, the ball sped through the air dispersing into smaller dots of black energy that shot off in multiple directions.

'Always in a rush! When will you ever take the time to look at what's directly in front of you?'

'Why are you here?' Lunerios asked, turning her attention to the man clad in crimson red armour standing next to her.

'Bellium sent me. He cares of your... existence, must be nice!' the man sneered, flashing his blood-red eyes in her direction.

'I know nothing of what you speak, Dente.' She said, turning away from the short and slightly portly man.

'Careful, my dear, even you are not exempt from the truth, the power of the moon and stars will only get you so far, just remember that next time you lie to my face!' the man said, his voice turning cold as he continued to stare her down.

'I care not for whatever magical power you possess, Dente. I have a mission to accomplish. Trading meaningless words with a low ranked fool such as yourself will not assist me. So be gone. You will only slow me down.' She said with a swish of her arm, conjuring a sudden and sharp blast of wind, sending Dente high into the air.

A single black energy ball returned from a distance, zipping around her like a buzzing bee returning to the hive.

'Show me what you have learnt.' Lunerios said, clasping the ball in her hand squeezing it firmly in her hand.

The black mist dispersed, seeping into her skin, travelling through her veins up towards her eyes, turning them a soulless pitch black.

As the energy flowed through Lunerios, it began to show images of the girl in grey and the many deaths she had caused.

'Well, my good woman, what is it? What have you found?' Dente asked, glacially floating back down to earth.

'She has been busy. It is clear now why she chose this planet to resurface on. It's teeming with life, more than enough for her to get her fix.' Lunerios said, her eyes returning to the sparkling gems they once were.

'So you have found her then?'

'No, but the destruction she has left holds a slight trail of unmistakable dark energy.'

'Well then, my dear girl, we must travel to them. If there is even a shred of live energy left, we can track her down.' Dente said, moving closer towards Lunerios.

'There are multiple places, London, Brazil, Manhattan, Paris, all in the past few days.' She said, reading the names as they drifted into her mind.

'And the death toll, has she had her fill?'

'Ten million and rising, her energy is growing at an exponential rate. The more deaths she claims, the stronger she becomes.' Lunerios said, contemplating her next move.

'Your plan, Executioner.' Dente said, straightening out his crimson cloak.

Lunerios paused, taking in a deep breath. She sighed. It was clear that Dente would not leave and could come in some form of use.

'We split up. I am sending you to Paris. I will make my way to London. These appear to be the closest and most recent. Now listen to me carefully, old man! You are to signal me immediately should she be there! Do not try to tackle her on your own! Am I making myself clear!'

'Naturally your most frightful. After all, we don't all have the pleasure of being second-born.' Dente snorted as he began to shimmer like light reflecting off the water's surface until he faded away from sight.

Lunerios turned her body towards the exact location of London, bending her knees the ground below her began to split and sink, then with one heavy jump, she blasted into the air, rivalling the thrust of the Yellowhammer.

*

Dente appeared in the burning wreckage of Paris, the sea of black flames still burnt across the scorched lands, the putrefied air was stagnant with the smell of molten steel and charred flesh. The once-proud Eiffel Tower creaked in the soundless barren lands where Paris once stood.

'My my, such outstanding power and not a soul in sight.' Dente said to himself, admiring the hellscape of the once beautiful city.

'I wonder?' he whispered to himself.

With a snap of his fingers, a red glow began to emit from the palms of his hand.

'Surely she wouldn't be so sloppy?' he said to himself as the red glow began to engulf the landscape.

Suddenly the air cleared from its black smog to bright blue skies. The black fires extinguished, leaving nothing but molten steel and the scattered bodies of the Parisian inhabitants.

Dente's hands began to shift to a deep shade of red as the black mist slowly receded into his palms.

'So you are that stupid!' he grinned, watching on as his hands turned black.

'My dear, you clearly had no intention of covering your tracks? Silly girl!' he said, twisting his hands in a circular motion, the black energy gathered into a ball as it left his body, the dark matter reflected in Dente's blood-red eyes as he watched on in sheer intrigue.

*

Lunerios flew through the light blue sky, taking in the sights and sounds of the world below. The waters crashed as the sounds of sea animals filled her ears. The birds passed her by as they flew in their flock. Then, kicking her heels, Lunerios gathered speed, spotting in the distance plumes of dark smoke erupting from the ground, muddying the pale blue sky.

'Dente, the target has been located. Move-in on my location to intercept.' She said, narrowing her eyes on the vast cylindrical city that is London.

'Certainly Executioner, there's not much left here anyway.' he snorted in response.

Suddenly a shadowy black figure appeared before her, travelling at tremendous speed. Lunerios paused in the air, adjusting her sight to focus on the shadow man. She smiled a wicked grin, knowing all too well of the shadow man's creator. Then, with a slight swipe of her hand, she sent a gust of wind soaring towards her target. The razor-sharp blast passed through, slicing the shadow man in half.

But it was not enough. Slowly reforming, the shadow man regained its full form. Lunging at Lunerios with its dark blade, it moved in to attack.

'So not just residual energy?' Lunerios said to herself, watching as the shadow man raised its blade, readying himself to attack.

Meeting her enemy head-on, Lunerios flung her arm back into the air. Her hand instantly formed into a malevolent claw. As she swung her arm in front of herself, she snagged the shadow man. Then grasping at the shadow man, her razor-sharp talons securing him in place, her arm began to glow a soft pale white, like the reflection of the moon. It overwhelmed the shadow man, encasing him in a sphere of shimmering white.

'Dente, it would appear she has learned from her past. She is now able to produce energy replications of her natural power. I have managed to immobilise one. However, it will need transporting back to Petaria. Where are you, and why is it taking you so long?'

'My apologies, Executioner. I have located something quite unusual. There are markings across the scorched land, her weapon of choice no doubt.'

'Your point, Dente?' Lunerios said, her patience running thin.

'She was attacked. Someone fought back! The residual energy left behind shows a person with great power offering resistance to her onslaught. These are not the signs of a mere mortal. These humans don't possess that type of power.'

'Continue your research as you wish, Dente. I will require proof of your hypothesis.' She said, ending the conversation.

Lunerios clasped her hand shut, the white sphere closed on the shadow man, condensing it to a single point. Then with a motion of her arm, the white orb flowed into the air towards the vast reaches of space.

Narrowing her starlight eyes, she focused back on the black clouds of smoke.

'Let's see what destruction you have managed to cause.' She said to herself, now flying in the direction of London.

Lunerios landed upon the steel ground. The smell of molten metal filled the air as she surveyed the damaged building. Then, taking a single step forward, the sound of pistons fired from across the base platform. Turning her head in time, she caught sight of the escape pods jettisoning from the sinking base.

'Fascinating, so you were unable to contain even one per cent of her power.' she said out loud, smirking at the escape pods.

The sound of metal crushing below her grew louder. The steel surface now bent to her weight as it began to melt at her feet.

'Dente, I require your location!'

'48.8566° North, 2.3522° East, by earth measurements!' he said.

Lunerios shot from the base faster than a speeding bullet, heading straight towards the coordinates Dente had relayed.

'What time should I expect you here?' Dente asked in his usual snarky voice.

'Not long! I am approaching your location now, do not touch anything until I arrive!' she commanded, gathering speed. Then, she passed out of visible sight, travelling faster than any ship made in Nova.

'As you wish, Executioner!'

As Dente walked through the carnage of Paris, looking for any clues as to who the girl had been battling, he heard the sound of a high pitch whistle fill the air, landing with an almighty crash, cratering the land around her. Lunerios emerged from the hole in the ground, the charred dust now thrust into the air.

'Never one to do anything subtly,' Dente said, shaking his head, 'I suppose my thoughts don't count for much in the eyes of a second-born. Would you care to hear the "proof"?'

'Talk fast, and leave the attitude behind. You may be the arbiter of truth but remember Dente, you are far from needed!' she said, her eyes burning into his as he cowered from her icy stare.

'Right, well, then let us begin. The metal pyramid-like tower seemed to be the point of entry. It's now all but destroyed. However, I think the metal would have acted as some form of conductor or power amplifier! Her electric attacks would bounce off that thing rather spectacularly. I'm sure it would have been a horrendous sight to behold.' he smiled, imagining the scenes in his mind, enjoying every moment.

'So this was the inception point?' Lunerios asked, scanning her eyes over the barren lands of Paris.

'Yes, but it would appear she was caught off guard! Look, over by that ridge a mass of mortals all dead. They must have been visitors to this monument, forced out by her intrusion to the grounds below. Isn't it crazy that these people put themselves in a lightning rod and wonder why they get shocked!' he laughed in his most bigoted fashion.

'So they escaped, how? She is silent. Mere mortals wouldn't stand a chance.'

'I would assume this planet's defenders drew them from the building, look at the bodies, all dead from residual energy. This work is not directly hers.

She is far too precise. These cuts appear to have been made in haste!' Dente said, lowering himself to examine the dead scattered across the field.

'So she was otherwise preoccupied?' Lunerios asked as the pictures of the event slowly unfolded in her mind.

'Look here, my dear girl. Marks upon the ground! Wouldn't you say they were from a spear, maybe a black sphere, the one she possesses?' he said, stroking his chin scanning the ground as he continued his inspection.

'Considering that is her weapon, I'm not that shocked. But, so far, you have yet to show me where this supernatural force, fighting on behalf of the mortals you have hypothesised comes into question!'

'My farsighted girl, these are marks of a battle, one of great strength and powerful action. No human could last this long, not against her!'

'Humans have come a long way since we last visited Dente. Are you so blind that you are unable to picture their advancements! Or perhaps you have more information you're slowly building too?'

'My good girl, you catch on quick. Maybe, your most gracious, we could use the power of the moon of stars. After all, it is at your complete disposal. Why guess when we can know. After all, the truth will set us free.' He said, winking as a sly smile spread across his face.

'What novel ideas you come up with Dente, however, as you saw upon landing, that power seems to diminish upon this planet, the night has not drawn upon my presence as it usually does.' She said, crossing her arms whilst continuing her survey of the broken lands.

'Oh, how the mighty have fallen, what grace bestowed upon thee has now waned in the vast yellow sun. But, tell me, second-born, how does it feel to be amongst the common folk?' Dente mocked as he spewed his vitriolic speech.

Lunerios grew with rage, extending her hand, her fingers began to glow a pale white. Then, swiping them towards Dente, a beam of pure white light emitted from her fingertips, striking him in the chest. He exploded into thousands of tiny stars, each one spraying off in different directions.

'Finally, some peace and quiet!' she said to herself, closing her eyes for a few moments as she gathered her thoughts.

Lunerios sat upon the ground, holding herself perfectly still. She began to glow a faint white light.

Slowly the clouds formed into a thick mass, encasing the light blue sky. The lands grew darker with each passing second as the clouds gathered in abundance, blocking out all light across the world.

The darker the lands grew, the brighter she became, until all lands covered in an unnatural dark night.

Lunerios stood from the ground, raising her arms she levitated from the floor, rising slowly she reached the sky towards the clouds of her creation. Then plunging her hands into the cloud, a gust of wind gathered to her person. Now swirling around her body in a rapid spin, the winds picked up momentum.

Once the time was right, Lunerios parted her arms, pushing the clouds away. The gathering winds shot into the sky, whipping what remained of the dark clouds into nothing as they dissipated, leaving behind a clear dark sky, the full moon shining ethereally in the sky, surrounded by the twinkling of starlight.

Beams of pure moonlight filled the scorched lands. Twinkling lights began to form in places around the once-proud city, forming into people and buildings as they relayed the events of the Paris attack.

'Day into night, yours has always been the most dramatic of gifts.' Dente said, his eyes fixed on Lunerios.

'Why won't you die?' she said, now floating back to the ground.

'Ahh, my clever girl. Truth can never die.' He said with a wink.

Lunerios formed her hands into fists, slamming them onto the ground. A sonic boom shot from where she stood, flooding the moonlit land. As the boom reverberated, it began to mimic the sounds of the day in question.

'Keep your ears and eyes open, Dente. This battle will be over faster than it begins!'

Both floating into the air, Lunerios and Dente watched on as the events unfolded with the starlit people replaying every attack, every death, every cry for help until the sound of a speeder filled the skies.

'What is that?' Lunerios said, her eyes sharpened on the speeder as it rushed into view.

Lunerios watched on as the moon figure jumped from the jet. Lunerios opened her hands wide, the moonlit figures paused.

As they floated down to the starry image, her rage began to build. It was undeniably him.

'General Voss,' Lunerios said, clenching her fists, her eyes beaming in the night sky, 'Enough!' she boomed.

As she clicked her fingers, the moonlit figures burst into a sea of twinkling lights, the moon diminished as the sky rapidly returned to daylight, the image of Paris quickly faded back to the smouldering wreck.

'So, the traitor lives!' Dente said too afraid to address Lunerios directly.

'It would appear so! We must head back to Petaria. The divine lord must be informed.'

'Yes, yes, quite right, my dear. It would appear we are no longer dealing with just a rogue killer, but the God slayer himself!'

— CHAPTER THIRTEEN —

THE GOD OF WAR

Solus sat proudly upon his crystal throne, the golden light of Petaria bathed the grounds around him as a soft breeze cut through the still air. The golden birds flew towards the ground, nestling themselves at the foot of the divine lord.

A solitary cloud drifted through the pristine sky, slowly making its way towards the unblemished sun. The lands of Petaria whistled with a chime of unrest, vibrating through the planet towards the ears of Solus as he watched the grounds gradually darken.

'So it has begun.' He said to himself, breathing a heavy sigh.

The sun started to set on Petaria. The sound of the bird song faded as they grounded themselves in preparation for their long sleep. The chimes grew harsh as the world turned dark. Then, finally, the sun disappeared behind the dark veil of night.

The world turned cold as the warmth of the golden sun escaped from the land. Suddenly dots of twinkling stars blinked in the night sky. Their pearly lights began to glow upon the surface of Petaria, reflecting their ethereal glow.

'The moon is late. It is unlike her to be so late!' the voice of concern came from the distance.

'Yes, but her mission takes president, my son!' Solus said, turning towards the man as he approached.

'And yet, father, you offer her no assistance!' the man wandered into view. His dark skin glistened in the starlight as he walked. His eyes shone a blood-red like two fireballs in the void.

'Bellium, my son. I should imagine that your envoy will be more than enough support for her. After all, she never did take too kindly to help, well from most.' Solus said with a sly wink.

'You assume too much old man. She is not as powerful as we. Vivata should have been sent in her place!' he boomed, unable to control his anger.

'You dare question me!' Solus said, emitting a powerful golden light, knocking Bellium back towards the ground.

Solus grew with each passing second. His golden stare pinned Bellium in place, forcing him to yield under the supreme force.

'Since time began, there have been none who question my rule, save but one, and she was banished long before you were born. So who are you to defy my logic?' Solus said. His voice shook the mountains and cracked the floor as he stood motionless, awaiting a response.

Bellium broke the golden stare, with a sudden burst of red flames, he flew from the ground towards Solus, his divine hammer in hand. He swung it towards the giant with all the force he could muster.

Solus laughed. Raising his arm, he curled his finger, securing it under his thumb. With a flick, he struck Bellium in the chest. Flying back, the force of Solus sent him at high speed towards the ground. The earth crumbled with an ear-shattering crash as Bellium smashed through its hard stone surface, the pressure of Solus's attack still sending him deeper into the planet.

'My foolish boy, not even with the power of all the firstborn would you stand a chance!' Solus laughed as he shrank back down to his more comfortable size.

'I have to commend you, my son. You truly live up to your name's sake!' he said in a jaunty fashion.

Solus waved his hand over the crater where Bellium had fallen through. The lands began to shift as small bits of rock and stone flew up from the deep dark hole, the air filled with chipped pieces of rock and stone as Bellium floated from the hole into the sky. Then, with a swift jolt to his hand Solus patched up the grounds, and the land returned to what it once was.

'You see, my boy. It is futile to believe you even stood a chance!' he boomed as he released his grip, allowing Bellium to drop to the floor.

Bellium shook his head as he slowly pulled himself up from the floor. The dizzy spell rushed over him as he tried to regain his composure.

'If she dies—'

'She will not! I have sent her on far more dangerous of a mission in the past, and you have remained neutral. Your feelings for her cloud your better judgment. Since her birth, I named her the Executioner, and that she shall remain!' Solus said, extending his arm out as a sign of peace.

As the two walked from the council grounds towards the viewing ledge upon the highest mountain of Petaria, Solus waved his arms, clearing the clouds from the night sky. The ridge towered above all in Petaria, Solus's favourite place in all the land. It gave him unencumbered views of the meadows and the deep lake down below. Even in the dark of night, the water still shone. Its amethyst tone illuminated the sky.

'Do you remember the last mission I sent you on?' Solus asked, casting his gaze over the God of War.

'How could I forget, Eco!'

'How are you feeling? now that your wounds of that planet are fully healed?' Solus asked.

'Some wounds never heal!'

'Pride is not of your immortal state, just what you hold close, cast aside your indigent persona, it is in power that you will find your solace!'

Bellium looked out onto the purple waters. The thoughts of his past failure gripped his mind.

'Speak your truth. If you seek atonement, I shall gift you what you wish.'

'It is not the God of Chaos that I fear. She is but an ant underfoot. No! It is in the tenacity of the mortals that my trust is misplaced. Perhaps, father, we are not as all-powerful as you have led us to believe?'

'Mortals are but a passing blip in the grand structure of life. I should know; they are of my creation. Your fear is needless. Do not allow this sickness of the mind to darken your thoughts any longer!' Solus said as he gazed over the lands below his mountain.

The two stood in silence for some time as the waters swished below. Suddenly a faint light appeared in the sky. Its ghostly white glow stood out from the sparkling specks dotted around the darkness of space.

'Ahh! She has returned.' Solus said, casting his eyes into the night sky.

The light grew brighter and larger with each passing moment until finally, it became the size of the moon.

'Lunerios, my most precious star. Tell me, child, what news do you bring from your adventure?' Solus said as his voice echoed through the lands of Petaria.

Lunerios landed on the ground with tremendous force. The earth shook in fear at her terrifying presence.

'My lord, we have tracked the God of Chaos. She resides on the planet known as the earth!'

'The dirt planet?' Solus said in confusion.

'Yes, she is growing stronger. She must have reached maturity sooner than the last time. Her abilities are truly devastating.'

'And what of her current status?' Solus said impatiently.

'Alive. We were unable to determine her exact location; however, there are far more pressing matters to attend to.'

'And what pray tell, may that be?'

'My lord, it would appear a native Econian has managed to infiltrate the planet.'

'You mean?' Solus said, his eyes widening slightly

'Yes, my lord, the traitor lives!' Lunerios said, now turning her attention to Bellium, whose eyes lit up brighter than ever before stared back at Lunerios. His silence spoke a thousand words.

Solus flashed his golden gaze towards Bellium, extending his arms and placing his hands on his shoulders. This movement was rare from the creator, so much so it was shocking for both Lunerios and Bellium to see.

'My son, do you think ill of me to have failed you so deeply?' he said, dropping his head in shame as his voice boomed through the air.

'No, father, I do not!' he lied, masking his anger-filled words.

'We shall correct this travesty for you, my son!' Solus said as a golden tear dropped from his eye.

Taking the solid gold tear that dropped into his hand, Solus placed it on the fascinator of Bellium's blood-red cape.

'The tear of God, may it provide to you my divine protection, a gift as much as an apology.' he said, a soft smile brandishing across his face.

Solus raised his hand into the sky, extending his index finger. A flash of golden lightning shot down from the sky connecting with his finger. The light-emitted was blinding. Even to the Gods, the power of Solus was something to fear. With this flash of light, they were gone, whisked away towards the council chambers.

Suddenly they appeared in the oval room. The gold light filled the unoccupied chairs, forming into the firstborn Gods.

'I wish you wouldn't do that father, what would you do had I not been decent?' Roma said, shaking off the remnants of the golden light, returning to her usual soft pink glow.

'My love, it was I who gave you form, do not discredit your beauty with indecency!'

'Why are we here?' Elbordium said, slamming his fist into the stone desk, creating a slight crack in the polished surface.

'Calm yourself, my son. I have assembled you all once again to discuss the revelations found by Lunerios. My dear, if you may.' he said, waving his arms to the podium in the centre of the round council hall.

Lunerios strode to the podium, placing herself in the centre. She addressed the council as one.

'From my recent investigation into the location of the God of Chaos—'

'Silly girl, where you have not meant to be searching for Casus? You see, father, sending inferior beings to do the work of a God is pointless.'

'Hold your tongue Roma, before I cut it out!' Bellium snapped as his fierce red glow began to pulsate.

'I see I have touched a nerve, tell me, Bellium! When will you stop your feelings for this cheap whore from clouding your judgment!' Roma laughed, clacking her nails on the smooth stone surface.

An intense wave of rage washed over Bellium. The sky grew to a blood-red as he clenched his hand. Lightning struck the council hall towards Bellium, leaving behind his divine hammer, with a swing of the jewel-encrusted weapon he struck at Roma, giving in to his hatred.

'ENOUGH!' Solus shouted with a click of his finger. The Gods were pushed back towards the council walls, their body's pinned in place by the omnipotent force of Solus.

'This is not why I brought you here, calm yourselves and open your ears, take heed of Lunerios, for she has worked to my plan,' he said, releasing his grip on the firstborn, 'Continue!' He ordered as he sat back down in his chair.

'I have discovered the traitor from Eco. The one who led the revolution against the Gods. He now resides on earth.' Lunerios said, standing proud in the centre of the room.

'He must be brought to me for judgment, immediately!' Parminx said as she approached her chair.

'And just how do we know what you say is the truth? It may be that what you saw is not the vile General. After all, the moon and stars can only see one side of the planet.' Roma said, continuing to click her nails against the stone desk.

'You dare to call me a liar. What would the God of Love know of truth?' Lunerios said, turning to face Roma, her icy stare burning down on the God of Love as she clenched her fists in preparation for a fight.

'No, not a liar, just…misguided.' She said, flicking her nail as she relaxed into the council chair.

'Then we call upon the emissary I sent to earth.' Bellium said, snapping his fingers.

Dente shot from the sky, landing hard upon the ground next to Lunerios.

'My lord, perhaps a bit more warning next time!' he said, clambering to his feet.

'Dente of truth, speak now your words of Virtue, and make it quick.' Parminx commanded.

'Naturally, your grace. Gods and Goddesses, your most divine lord Solus, we stand upon the grand council of Petaria to uncover the t—'

'In short, Dente!' Parminx said, rising from her seat, her formidable stare shaking him to his core.

'Right, naturally, the lady Lunerios speaks only the truth. We have discovered the traitor galavanting about the land of dirt. He fought hand to hand with the God of Chaos, successfully, one might add.' He said, facing Roma's direction.

'Fine! So we have your word. I will see for myself.' Roma said, summoning a mass of rose petals towards the council chambers,

'No!' Solus boomed, shaking the ground, stopping the petals in their tracks. 'You think I would risk the love of all to this so-called God slayer, my dear, he is not worth your time. Lunerios, my Executioner. Can I trust that you bring him back alive? Then I will deliver justice to this insolent waste of life!'.

'My lord, consider it already done!' Lunerios said, crouching into a low bow.

The light of the moon shone upon the podium as the air began to sweep around the room. As the wind formed an almost tornado-like appearance, Lunerios jumped, dispersing the wind across the lands. It shook the ground and blustered through the trees waking the planet from its slumber. Then, taking flight into the sky, she headed at full speed towards the earth.

'This meeting is adjourned!' Solus said. Then in a flash of golden light, the council chamber was clear. The room was now empty of all Gods except for Solus and Parminx.

'My lord! Do you remember the events of Eco and what led you to the planet all those years ago?

'Your question is of none of my concern, my dear, be gone from my sight and rest your mind.' Solus said, leaving the chambers heading towards his crystal throne.

'I do not ask to challenge your memory, but we must remain vigilant in these times of uncertainty if the General of Eco lives, so must the passion of Xelios!'

'Do not speak to me of that pathetic fool. Xelios is dead. Their planet laid to waste. This General is nothing more than an ant that broke away from the colony!' he said, growing in size until he dwarfed the lands below.

'But my lord, has he not already felled one of us before? History is in danger of repeating itself. Surely you can see this?' she asked, her soft voice growing in concern.

'The God of War fell, and in my light, he grew again, you fail to understand, I see all! Now be gone. I do not require council!'

'We cannot be blind to the potentials of the humans. They were, after all, made in your image.

Tell me, my lord, did you ever find the weapon he used to slay Bellium?'

'Yes, not only was it found, but it was also destroyed. So, now your concerns are laid to rest!'

'So the God slayer is gone?'

'Enough of your questions, Parminx,' He said, sitting upon his crystal throne, 'By my words of divine providence, these mortals shall hold no part to play in the future of my grand plan.'

Parminx looked upon Solus as he rested upon his throne. The world grew quiet as all things living settled in for the one hundred years of the dark. Parminx made her way towards the edge of the mountains. Casting her eyes over the dark lands, she placed her hands upon the stone ridge. Breathing deeply, she began to glow her faint silver glow, her eyes clouded over as the crisp wind encased her body.

'My lord, I must now confess to you the vision that has fallen upon me! You do not wish for my council, but you must.' She said as a single silver tear fell upon the ground.

— CHAPTER FOURTEEN —

THE LUNAR ASSAULT

As the dust began to clear in the dark Tokyo sky, the girl in grey lay motionless upon the ground. The sound of sirens accompanied by flashing lights filled the sky as the cleanup team worked swiftly through the night to clear the destruction of the Magunafōsu tower. Finally, Violet and the Black-ops team safely returned to the U.N.N base aboard the Yellowhammer.

'How is he doing?' Violet asked as she loomed over Zyair as he inspected Leo's body.

'He's alive, just!' Zyair said, continuing his work on Leo.

'Caspian, how are you holding up?' Violet shouted over to the second medivac bed.

'Fine, just waiting for the skin grafter to finish!' he said as a small nanobot worked its way around his body, gradually replacing his burnt flesh.

'We are approaching the base. Any preference in the landing bay, Major?'

'Yes, Commander, entrance bay four, please?' Violet said as the Yellowhammer began to lower towards the four-hundredth floor.

Landing in the centre of the bay, the Black-ops team dismounted the jet. Then, accompanied by the floating medivac beds, they made their way towards the main doors of the landing platform, the girl in grey's body slowly following behind them.

'Do you need me to stay, Major?'

'No, Commander, you may head back to your base.' Violet said as their comm-link rang through.

'Major Villin. You sure know how to make an entrance. I just thought I would drop by on my way to the President's office. Make sure you're alive and well!'

'General Hill! Thank you for your assist—'

'Don't mention it, V!' he said with a wink as he boarded the Yellowhammer, swiftly passing the Black-ops team.

'Zyair, go with Leo to the medical bay. Keep me informed of any developments!' she said, quickening her pace towards the central command room.

'Right away, Major!' He replied, moving towards the elevator with Leo slowly following behind.

The doors to the central command room opened with a hiss. There they lead into a perfectly square room with each wall covered from floor to ceiling in vast panes of glass. The centre of the room held an extensive array of tables and chairs; each one pointed towards a glowing orb floating above a solid steel block. The room lit up with a mixed mash of neon colours as the twinkling lights of Tokyo glistened in the far off distance.

'Gentleman if you please!' Violet said, flicking her wrist activating the orb in the centre of the room. It began to emit the images of their mission at hand.

'The target has been eliminated. She will be taken to bunker one. She will be kept under heavy guard whilst we run diagnostics. The answers to many questions lie within her.

'What of General Hill?' Caspian asked as the nanobot replacing his skin finished working, dematerialising back into his nanochip.

'He will be relaying the information to the President. The initial threat is finally over.' Aster said as he moved across the room, positioning himself next to Violet.

'So we are in the clear?' Jax sighed a heavy relief.

'Not quite, gentleman, we have but scratched the surface of this case. We will now be moving into phase two of our operations!'

'Phase two?' Jax said, taking a seat next to Caspian.

'No, I think I get it. You mean where is she from, who she is, when is the next attack, what's the bigger picture?'

'Thank you, Oren, once again, you have proved yourself more advanced than most,' Violet said, moving towards her newly assigned desk,

'Caspian! I need a favour. All the raw data on the anti-matter shield she was able to generate has been collected in this,' she said, tossing a black marble through the air, 'Its fourth-gen jell-glass, the same one I used in Paris. It has her specific genetic sequence on it. The code for her protective shield. Before Aster and I made it to Tokyo, we were able to replicate the genetic structure, using it in the live rounds.'

'So that's how you managed to shoot her?' Caspian said, catching the marble.

'Yes, in a mass form, this could prove to be useful, decode it, reassemble the sequence so that we can use it against the next one.'

'Next one?'

'Yes, and one more thing! I need you to gather as much intelligence on the deaths of all victims. The kill sequence, the pattern of death, why there, why then. She must have had a choice and chose these people for a reason.'

'But that doesn't explain what you mean when you say "Next one",' Oren said, stepping forward into the glow of the holo-display

'We have reason to believe this attack was not an isolated incident. The intel provided by Commander Voss has shown that a second attack could be imminent, potentially from the same girl! I need you to find her origins, no more estimations, no more guesses or theories, Oren, give me hard facts!'

'Yes, Major.' He said, backing away back to his desk.

Violet flicked her wrist, activating her nano band, a small screen materialised in front of her face.

'Zyair, I require your assistance, is Leo stable?' she asked. A slight tone of concern came from the back of her throat.

'As he will ever be, we have patched him up, just waiting for him to wake up.'

'Good, then make your way to bunker one. We need more information on the girl, more than just her physical DNA sequence. Her body will need to be examined. Look for how she attacks, her muscle tone, her vision, what does she have that made her so powerful?'

'I'll make my way down immediately!' he responded as the screen shut down upon his last word.

'Tak, take this. It's a re-play recording from data probe four. We have mapped most of her movements and assault style, but more work is needed to develop the tactical approach. We need to understand everything about her, predict her movements before making them. Remember, she is unpredictable. I don't expect a machine to understand nuance.' she said, throwing a small data chip in Takeshi's direction.

'Right away, Major.' He replied, moving towards his station

'Jax, have you managed to work on what I asked of you?' Violet asked cryptically.

'Yes, but I have hit a roadblock. I believe the only way to move past this is with the help of Ms Myers!'

'Fine, send out a call. I understand she is on her way back to this base?' she asked, unsure of Serena's actual location.

'Yes, Major, the General sent her back to London, but we have received information that a jet is back on route.'

'Why did she go to London!' Violet said sternly.

'I'm not sure the G—' Violet held her hand up, cutting Jax off mid-sentence.

'Aster, with me!' she said, standing from her desk as she made her way towards the command room doors. 'I need yo—'

'WARNING RED ALERT!'

Violet spun on the spot, the room illuminated with flashing red lights as the wall of screens disconnected, displaying their evacuation sequence.

'WARNING RED ALERT, EVACUATE THE BUILDING IMMEDIATELY.'

The siren continued to alert as people left their desks heading for the emergency evac pods.

'Caspian, identify now!' Violet shouted from across the room.

'We're picking up a UFO. It's moving fast, against the wind, and heading in this direction, ETA in five minutes!'

'WARNING AMBER ALERT!'

'Capsian!' Violet shouted, now running to the window,

'Its picked up speed, ETA sixty seconds

'Brace for impact!' Violet shouted as she lunged onto the floor.

'WARNING GREEN AL—'

The UFO flew straight into the tower, the windows on all floors shattered as the soundwave ricocheted across the building. The impact's force was so strong that occupants on all levels found themselves forcibly ejected from the building.

Now soaring through the sky, Violet looked behind herself, catching a glimpse of the woman who stood alone in the empty building.

'The Executioner.' She whispered to herself as she began to free fall towards the ground.

'Major!' Caspian shouted as they sped towards the ground.

Twisting mid-air, Violet flicked her wrist, producing a small flat silver disk. Throwing it to the ground, it shot past all the Nova guards landing on the floor below, sinking itself into the ground. The disk clicked once, emitting a burst of radial energy, slowing each person as they reached the first-floor height, allowing them to land in perfect safety.

'Evacuate to the safe zone, all black-ops with me; maintain formation!' Violet said as she landed, immediately materialising her M-eights.

'I'm not picking up an energy signal, Caspian said, forcing his way through the crowds of scrambling people.

'This is next level Casp, don't expect much intel!' Aster said, rushing to Violet's side.

Violet looked up into the night sky, drawing her attention to the female figure now floating in the air. Her silhouette cast a shadow over the moon as it glowed brighter than it ever had glowed before. The sharp beams of starlight began to scorch the ground as she slowly lowered to the concrete floor.

'Do not give her a single moment. Shoot to kill!' Violet said as her guns glowed green, the explosive rounds charged and ready to fire.

Lunerios lingered in the air as she slowly lowered till she hovered just a foot above the ground.

'Mortals, heed my words. Hand over the traitor, any sign of resistance will be taken as a direct threat. You will be exterminated should you resist!' she said, now landing on the floor.

Violet opened fire. Relentlessly striking at Lunerios, joined by immense firepower of the Black-ops team. Vivid green clouds began to form as each bullet met its mark, exploding upon impact. The heat from each round caused a small light to filter through the thick bilious clouds.

The sound of hissing slowly crept in as the guns stopped firing. Then, having exhausted their explosive rounds, Violet flicked her wrist. The guns changed from green to blue as the U.V. rounds began to fill the clips. Slowly Violet took a cautious step forward.

'Stay on guard! I doubt we have even landed a single hit.'

Just as the words left her mouth, the smoke cleared with a single rush of air, revealing Lunerios, who stood in the same spot with not a mark in sight.

'Impossible!' Caspian said, his hands shaking with fear.

'Pathetic, so this is what you abandoned Eco for General Voss, some silly girl with purple hair four stations lower than your own. I will ever understand you, mortals!' Lunerios quipped.

Aster clasped his hands together. Mysterious black energy formed around his arms, moving to his hands. As he pulled one hand away from the other, he produced a black sword, the same as his fight with the girl in grey.

'Your fight is with me, Executioner! Unless you prefer to pick on beings far below your calibre?' Aster mocked as he inched closer towards her.

'How...foolish, you will pay for your sins, General Voss. I will see to that!' she said, producing a single-handed axe of pure pearl.

The offset axe looked bigger than her. It was so big that it completely blocked out the moon's light when she held it to the sky.

Violet turned to her teammates, signalling for them to stand down, moving back from the battlefield.

'We need to find a way of getting her off this planet!' Violet whispered into the comm-link as they fled from the scene.

'We could—' Just as Caspian began to speak, a chunk of brick and mortar landed directly next to him, forcing Caspian to jump out of the way.

Aster had begun his attack on Lunerios, his blade making contact with the shimmering axe, his hit with such force it sent her back into the Nova building, firing chunks of brick and steel flying in multiple directions.

'If we stay out here, we're all gonna end up dead!' Jax said, leading the group out of the immediate danger zone.

'Over there to the safe zone, we need to regroup!' Violet said.

'What about Aster?'

'Leave him. He is more capable than you know.' Violet said, focusing all her attention on the evacuation.

The sound of jet engines ploughed through the cries and screams. Then, as people scrambled to safety, the buildings began to crack and fall as the battle between Aster and Lunerios raged.

'Major, incoming message!' Jax said as he looked down at his nano screen.

'Violet?'

'Serena!'

'Thank god you're ok. We're circling the base now!'

'Land at the safe zone, next quadrant across!' Violet shouted through the comm-link.

The jet made a complete turn doubling back on itself, then began to fly in the direction of the safe zone. Just as the engines kicked in, Lunerios sprung into the air from the ground. With a swipe of her axe, the jet hewed in two.

'SERENA!' Violet shouted, dropping to her knees as the jet split in two, erratically spinning in the air towards the ground.

Now rushing towards the jet as it crashed upon the ground, Violet readied herself to jump into the wreckage.

'No, Major!' Caspian said as he gripped Violet by the waist pulling her back onto the ground.

'Let me g—' the jet let out a terrible shriek followed by a magnificent explosion as it erupted in flames of green and blue.

Violet crawled to the jet, trying as she might to peer through the wicked flames in hopes that Serena was not there.

Her eyes filled with tears as the butterflies in her stomach jumped. The world began to turn upside down as Violet felt a wave of nausea wash over her.

'Vi..lt.'

The comm-link crackled, the volume was faint, but it was enough.

'Serena?' She shouted into the comm-link, wiping the tears from her face.

Looking around frantically, there she saw her, standing at the base of the safe zone.

'Violet, we're here.' The shout was faint but audible.

Violet rushed towards the safe zone, her black-ops team followed at her heels, sweeping past the ongoing destruction of Tokyo.

'Serena!' Violet shouted back, running into her arms, 'Your safe, thank god!' Violet said, breathing a sigh of relief. She held her tighter than ever before, her force just a little too much.

'I thought I lost you?'

'Not to worry, Ma'am, I had it covered!' Cody said, beaming a smile from his dirt-filled face.

'Thank you, Commander.' Violet said, keeping her grip on Serena.

'Major, we have a plan.'

'What is it, Caspian?' Violet said, finally releasing her strong embrace.

'If we can get close enough to her, we should be able to send her back from where she came!' Caspian said, flicking his wrist to show a holo-projection of the Nexus portal.

'You mean you plan on purging her via the Nexus?' Serena said, staring straight into Caspian's eyes.

'It's not enough. This thing is a God and far stronger than you can imagine. It may provide us a moment of relief, but she will return!' Violet said

'Not if we can send her back incapacitated!' Serena said.

'So, what's the plan?' Violet asked, not seeing any other solution.

'We use the nexus to push her through and close the portal right after. We can set the Nexus to an open distance. Once she's through, the portal closes, and she lands where she lands.' Caspian replied.

'Ok, but how do we go about incapacitating her?'

'With this!' Serena said, holding out a single bullet.

'A single round, they didn't fare too well last time.' Violet said.

'This is an antimatter bullet, the same type you used against the girl.' Serena replied

'How do you know this will work?' Violet asked, her eyes widening at the sight of the bullet

'In short, we don't, but that anti-matter is unlike anything we have ever seen. If Aster's story is true, then it will work.' Serena said, handing the bullet to Violet.

'Now, all we need to do is lure her to the Nexus.' Caspian said.

'Not quite,' Serena replied, producing a black and purple disk. 'This is a first trial phase mobile nexus transporter.

Violet shifted her gaze towards Jax.

'She's more like you than you think, Major.' Jax said unapologetically.

'And how do we know *this* will work?' Violet said, less than pleased about the idea.

'Again, we don't. V this is all experimental, but it's our only shot!' Serena said, clasping the disk firmly in her hand.

'No, you're not part of this!' Violet said in defiance.

'And who's going to stop me, you?' Serena said, placing her hands on Violet's cheeks, her bright smile beaming down upon her.

'Fine, stick close to me. Commander Cody, you will provide a defence!'

'Major, what should we do?' Caspian said.

'Stay here, guard the doors; if this goes wrong, you will be the last defence.'

Violet, Serena and Cody made their way back to Tokyo's Nova building. The sound of steel on steel rang through the air. Glass smashed as they witnessed one dark figure land a strike on the other glowing white figure.

'Looks like Aster has her on the ropes.' Cody said as they made their way towards the battle.

'Don't be too sure, commander!' Violet muttered as she hopped over an upturned transport pod.

Violet crept into position, observing both the battle and Serena, assisted by Commander Cody to intercept Lunerios.

'Aster, I need you to break away. We have a plan.' Violet said via the comm-link.

'Sure think Maj—' the comlink went dead as Violet witnessed a shadowy figure flying directly at her, jumping out of the way into a backflip. She dodged the incoming body, turning just in time she noticed Aster land hard on the ground. The strike from Lunerios was mighty.

Violet loaded the single M-eight with the glowing red bullet, her gun began to vibrate.

'HEY!' Violet shouted, hoping to attract the attention of Lunerios,

'You dare beckon to me, mortal!' Lunerios said, floating to the ground, her axe still in hand.

'How about a real opponent!' Violet jeered, hoping to catch her enemy off guard.

'Fool! Entire army's stronger than you have fallen at my feet!' she said, raising the axe into the sky.

It began to glow with the light of the moon. The white heat radiating was so intense that it started to melt the steel structures around her. Raising her arm Violet pointed her weapon directly at Lunerios, her aim steady and true.

'You think a bullet is enough to stop a God? You will die in vain!' Lunerios jeered.

Violet pressed once on the trigger, firing the bright red bullet directly onto her target, striking her in the chest. Stunned, Lunerios stumbled back. She had never felt pain quite like this. The bullet pierced her skin; the sensation burned her from the inside out. Dropping to her knees, she let out a scream of tremendous pain.

'Now!' Violet shouted as loud as she could.

Serena sprung from the side of a building, jumping onto the back of Lunerios.

'See you in hell bitch!' Serena said directly into her ear, slapping the disk onto Lunerios's chest.

Black sparks emitted from the disk as purple thunderbolts shot out in various directions. Lunerios gripped Serina by the neck, flinging her towards the closest wall.

Her head hit the brick, the sound of a deep crack echoed across the street as her head ricocheted off the wall.

The purple volts encased Lunerios forming an impenetrable seal. As she let out another ear-splitting scream, the disk erupted in a cloud of smoke, sending Lunerios into the void, sealing shut as she passed.

— CHAPTER FIFTEEN —

RETURN TO ECO

Violet sunk to the floor. Her knees scraped across the cracked concrete as she breathed a heavy sigh of relief. The plan had worked.

'Violet!'

Her name rang across the battlefield. Turning her head, she noticed Serina lay on the ground. The sight of her lifeless body sent a spike of pain through her unlike any she had felt before.

'She's still breathing, but it's faint. We need to get her to a medical bay immediately. She's losing a lot of blood!' the sound of Cody's voice drifted in and out.

The sound of the ocean filled Violet's ears as she swayed on the spot, the world slowly darkening from her view.

'Major, MAJOR!' Cody shouted as he shook Violet by her shoulders, trying to rouse her from her unusual silence.

'Commander, we have her; grab Serena, the closest medical bay is quadrant two, one mile east!' Jax said, flicking his wrist to activate the call button.

Moments later, the Yellowhammer flew into view directly above Commander Cody. Lowering at a rapid pace, it landed in the only free space it could find.

'Which base?' Cody asked, grabbing Serena in his arms as he ran to board the Jet.

Caspian flicked his wrist, moving his hand in rapid motion. A board of red dots illuminated the screen.

'Leo was sent to Washington during the evacuation. We will meet you there!' he replied, snapping the screen shut, turning his attention to Violet, who now lay across the ground.

'Still breathing!' Jax said as he lifted Violet onto his shoulders.

'Tak, assemble a jet. We need to get moving!' Caspian said, signalling the cleanup crew.

*

Violet opened her eyes to the sight of all her black-ops team sitting in silence. Their beady eyes fixed on her, twinkling with each passing blink.

'What happened?' she asked, still in a slight daze.

'You passed out, Major. Caused by shock,' Zyair said, pressing buttons on his holo screen as he moved to scan Violet, 'However, all vitals are fine; you're as good as new.' He said with a warming smile.

'You know, Major, you have to stop ending up like this! I know healthcare is free and all, but this is pushing it!' Aster joked, spinning in his chair.

'Not to push you too far, but we need answers; what happened to you after Paris? The last time we saw you, you had multiple puncture wounds, a spear sticking out your hand, and enough dark energy in your veins to kill an entire army. Not that I'm displeased to see you're ok, but, how!' Zyair asked.

Violet paused, her thoughts returned to the mission at hand.

'First things first, how is Serena?'

'Fine, she's perfectly fine. She is in the lower med bay. Her vitals are strong, just resting for the moment.' Zyair said, relaying the information on his holo-pad.

'Good, patch me through once she is awake!' Violet said, sitting up in her bed, 'On to the next order of business, we need a base, Tak! Find me the closest ops base to wherever we are.' She said, snapping her nano bands back onto her wrist.

'I'm fine to Major. I can see you are concerned!' Leo replied, standing from his chair.

Violet rolled her eyes as she pulled the covers off the bed.

'Never doubted you for a second, Leo. Now, if you don't mind, gents, I need to get changed.' She said, swinging her legs from the bed.

As she placed her feet upon the ground, lifting herself from the bed, she stumbled, falling forward into the arms of Leo.

'Yea, I don't think you're going anywhere for a little while!' Leo said, pushing her back on the bed.

'Fine!' she mumbled in defeat.

'Looks like you have some time to answer my question.' Zyair said, sitting on the chair next to her bed.

Violet looked around the room at her black-ops team, who gawked at her in anticipation.

'We don't have time for this!'

'Come on, Major, it is rare we get to hear anything about you, open up a little!' Aster said, putting his feet up on Leo's shoulder, only for them to be slapped back down by a rather angry Leo.

'If I must,' She said, taking in a deep breath, 'I don't fully know what happened straight after the battle in Paris, but I will do my best to explain.' She said, crossing her legs and cracking her neck. 'I woke to find the President in my room, just as before she felt it her duty to tell me of her vision of the future, her premonition of things to come if you will.'

'So the President of Nova is a psychic.' Leo mocked, holding back his laughter.

'Yes! There are far more strange things in this tiny universe that you would barely comprehend, Leo. You would do well to open your mind to them!' she said sternly.

'So what was her vision?' Caspian asked, trying to move the conversation forward.

'That if I lived, all would die, to which she then proceeded to clasp her hands around my neck and try her hardest to kill me, again!'

The rest of the Black-ops team fell silent, stunned by the revelation they had just heard.

'So the President's a murderer too?' Leo said, overseeing his words.

'No, she would only be a murderer had she been successful, as you can see she was not,' Violet said, flashing her eyes at Aster,

The rest of the team turned to face Aster, seeing the cold shot sent from Violet.

'So what happened, Aster?' Caspian inquired,

'I stopped her, chased her down, had the General not grabbed me when he did, she would be dead.'

'So how is it your not dead?' Leo asked in amazement.

'Murder can't predicate murder Leo, can you imagine the court ruling, "He stopped me from murdering my ex-girlfriend and then tried to kill me... lock him away"!' Aster said, putting on his best Presidential voice.

'So she's just wandering around, carefree and all murdery!' he said, a slight quiver in his voice.

'Calm yourself. The President isn't after you, just those she deems threatening. Besides Leo, if she truly wished me dead, do you not think I would be by now?'

The room fell silent as each person contemplated their following words. Soft beeps of electrical machinery filled the room as they sat in thought.

'Well, actually, Major, you still haven't told us how you managed to live through the assault in Paris?' Zyair said, his intrigue getting the best of him.

Violet let out a sigh as she stretched her arms, swinging them from side to side.

'Genetics.' She said abruptly.

'We're gonna need more than that!' Leo said, leaning in from his chair.

'Fine! I can explain much but, I have a rare genetic mutation, one that is still in the process of being studied. But, from what we know, I am the only one who has it.'

'What is this mutation?' Caspian asked.

'It was named gene-V. From the outset, you only see two examples, Violet eyes and Violet hair; this is not a mod!' she said, waving her hand over her face and hair.

'Cool, I always thought you did it to match your name.' Leo said, pressing his face up to Violet's as he stared into her eyes.

The sound of a crack bounced across the room as Leo returned to his chair, his hand covering his blood-red face and the distinctive hand imprint left indented from one furious Major.

'The effects of the gene mutation are both a blessing and curse. I have been gifted with the ability to heal quicker than any other human. Run faster, hit harder, think smarter. But the effects leave a mark. Like sealing a hole in the wall. You can make it look brand new, but it will forever be damaged.' Violet said, daring to test her strength standing from the bed.

'What do you mean?' Zyair asked.

'It means I can't keep up this momentum for much longer!' Violet said, her voice returning to its confident tone.

'Simple solution. There are many Bio mods Nova tech has developed. I'm sure we can kit you out with a few upgrades, boss.' Leo said, also rising from his chair.

'If only it were that simple, Leo. You see, the other downside to this is that my body cannot handle any form of intrusion. It would see the mod as a threat, expelling it before it had the chance to implant.'

'Well, never know unless we try!' he said, tapping wildly at his holo-screen.

'That's just it, I have tried. The nano-chip was the first test, then the biometric in eye scanner, each one rejected. Hence this.' She said, spinning the nano-band on her wrist.

'So what's the upshot then?' Aster said drily.

'Super strength, speed, sight, you name it. But against a God, it's not enough.' She said gingerly, making her way to the opposite side of the room.

'God?' Leo said, looking around the room at the other shocked faces staring back at him.

'Yes Leo, God, Gods, Immortals, whatever you want to call them, the only one who stands any chance of actually facing up to those things is Aster!' she said, turning back to face the men.

'Yea, and look where that got me!' Aster laughed, waving his arm bound in a nano sling.

The room fell silent, each member of the Black-ops team stunned as they tried to digest what Violet said.

'So, we're facing off against God's?' Oren said, daring to be first to speak.

'Yes, and I have no plan on how we even begin to develop a plan.' Violet said, stretching her legs in a bid to loosen her tightened muscles.

'Aster, you said you fled when your homeworld came under attack, right?' Oren said, the cogs ticking away in his mind.

'Correct, what's your point?'

'How did you escape?'

'Via pod Oren, you still have it in the weapons-teq yards. How is this important?'

'Something had to of distracted them long enough for you to get away, right?'

'Yes, the girl, she appeared in grey, killing an entire army. That was more than enough time to get away!'

Oren paused, mulling over the brief conversation.

'Well! that was pointless!' Leo said, swishing towards the hospital doors.

'No wait, I think I understand,' Caspian said, shaking his finger in thought. 'Something had to happen for her to appear. I mean, she only appeared during heightened electromagnetism in the atmosphere.'

'That was her effect. She caused it.' Aster said

'No, it was a natural event. She just manipulated it, using it as some sort of gateway. That's how she managed to disappear and reappear at will, using the natural energy source!' Caspian said

'Aster, had there been any other deaths on Eco caused by her before or during the war?' Oren asked.

'No, just that one time.'

Caspian shot a look directly at Violet. His eyes spoke more than words.

'Aster, what happened before she arrived!' Violet said, catching on quick.

'The man in gold appeared; he began his judgment, summoning the Executioner.' Aster said his words slow and steady as he recalled the events.

'Further back Aster, what happened before the man in gold? How were you captured!'

'I was celebrating. The invading army began to flee in full retreat.' he said, his eyes glazing over. 'We ran back to the citadel to secure the city. He was there waiting!'

'The man in gold?' Violet asked as she inched closer to Aster.

'He bound us, held us in chains, he cried, his golden tears as they shattered upon the ground!'

'Who, Aster, who was the man in gold?'

'The one above all else, he had come, come to mourn his son!'

Violet walked closer to Aster, leaning down until she was close enough to whisper, her voice piercing his ears.

'How did his son die?'

'I am the God slayer!' Aster said, his eyes turned milky white, his face drained of all its colour, the sounds faded in Aster's mind as he collapsed onto the floor, his body convulsing as he foamed from the mouth.

'Zyair, I need some help!' She said, grabbing Aster, trying to stop his convulsions.

'Quickly get him on the bed!' Zyair said, clearing the chairs as the rest of the Black-ops team stepped away. Violet grabbed Caspian's arm, dragging him out of the room.

'What the hell was that!' Caspian said in shock.

'There was a connection, however small. We just tapped into his mind. It's part of their gift.'

'What gift?'

'No time to explain, tell me Caspian, what did you see when he spoke, what vision came into your mind? Violet said, grabbing at Caspian's shoulders, her piercing stare burning into him. Caspian stuttered, trying to arrange the images floating around in his head.

'I saw a man!' he began closing his eyes, his words short and stilted as the images flashed in rapid-fire.

'Describe him!'

'He has white hair, he wore gold armour, and his eyes are red.'

'What's happening around him, Caspian?'

'A battle!'

'Then what?'

'A black bolt, it hit him. He fell to the ground.'

'And?'

Caspian suddenly opened his eyes to see Violet's face inches away from his own, breathing heavily in anticipation.

'Nothing, it's gone!' Caspian said, slumping to the ground in defeat.

'Dam it!' she said, running her hands through her hair, letting out a heavy sigh.

They both fell silent, listening to the mild commotion coming from the hospital wing as Zyair fought to stabilise Aster.

'What was that?' Caspian asked, still visibly shaken.

'You were given a glimpse into the past. Aster has a gift. Supposedly all Egonens have it. This could have been our chance to get the complete picture.'

Caspian remained quiet. His heart still beating a mile a minute, his head thumping from the painful images that once invaded his mind.

'The man in gold.' Violet mumbled, pacing the empty hallway. 'God slayer....' She continued as she relayed the past week of events in her mind.

The lights in the empty halfway flickered as she paced up and down, passing Caspian as he sat on the floor nursing his throbbing head, the sounds in the room next to them had quietened, the commotion had stopped, and Violet continued to think.

'Traitor...., The God of War.... Eco.... Eco, that's it!' She said with a click of her finger, 'Caspian on your feet!' She demanded, pulling him up from the floor.

Turning on the spot, she pushed the doors to the hospital wing with a mighty force, slamming them against the wall as she stormed the room. Startling each of the Balck-ops members in the process.

'Gentleman, I have a plan. First, suit up, next stop, Eco!'

— CHAPTER SIXTEEN —

THE THREE RINGS OF NOVA

The Yellowhammer slowed to a stop hovering just above the ground at the base of the Washington guard. The afternoon sun shone brightly in the cloudless sky. A gentle breeze fluttered by as the jet finally grounded.

'Why have we landed here and not the landing zone?' Violet asked the Commander of the Yellowhammer in a short and fiery tone.

'Clearance ma'am, we have been rejected!'

'What!' She said, storming to the back of the jet as pistons hissed, slowly lowering the doors.

Violet bounded towards the entrance doors of the Washington guard. Just as she arrived, a small black lens formed in the centre of the doorway.

'Present identification.'

'Major Villin, Black-ops!' She said out loud as the lens scanned her eye.

'Access denied!'

The lens dematerialised as two roof-mounted guns suddenly spun into action, aiming directly at Violet, following her as she moved.

'Woah Woah Woah, hold up, do you even know who this is?' Leo said, approaching the door kicking the base to rematerialise the glass lens. 'Put me through to General Wies!' He said, turning back to face Violet. 'Don't worry, Major, I'll sort it.' He said with a wink.

'You have two minutes till mandatory intruder protocol activates. Please evacuate as instructed!' The mechanised voice said as the guns loaded, the second gun now focusing on Leo.

'I get the feeling we're not welcome, Major.' Aster shouted from the Yellowhammer.

'With three bases destroyed in four days. I would say they have a good reason to not want us in there.' Caspian said,

'Fine, Come on, Leo. There are more ways to enter a building than through the front doors!' She said, storming back towards the Yellowhammer.

'Where to now, Major?' the Commander asked.

'Top floor, enable the EMP's!' she said as the door closed.

The jet took flight hovering above the ground. Then in a sudden bolt, it shot up towards the top floor of the six hundred story building.

'Are the EMP's ready?'

'Yes, Major, but I can't fire upon that building. Need I remind you this will be taken as an act of war!' The Commander said, his voice shaking in anticipation.

'Commander, may I remind you that you are black-ops personnel. I am your Major, need I say more!'

The Commander flicked a flashing switch on the dashboard, one rocket spun underneath the base of the Yellowhammer.

'Gentlemen, prepare for ground descent. We go in via the roof once the EMP has disabled the defence system, any questions?'

'Are we really about to storm the U.N.N capital base?' Leo asked

'Enough questions! Commander, on my mark!' Violet said, pressing the emergency door open button.

The doors to the Yellowhammer opened, revealing the roof of the capital base. With a wave of her hand, the Yellowhammer ejected its EMP, sending it soaring through the air towards the signal mast atop the tower. The shell exploded, emitting a wave of blue energy, frying the signal mast. The lights that scattered the roof of the building faded as the droning sound of electric motors faded. Now was the time to strike. Hooking her zipline to the top of the Yellowhammer, Violet jumped from the Jet hotly, followed by her black-ops team as they zipped towards the landing platform of the Washington base. Landing in a roll, Violet sprung from the floor, unclipping herself from the safety cord. A single grey marble materialised in her hand with a flick of her wrist. Smashing it in her hand, it turned to putty that she moulded to the door handle.

'Get back!' She shouted, pressing a single button on her holo-screen.

The door sizzled at first as the putty melted the handle, suddenly a bang shot through the sky as the putty exploded, sending the door back over the ledge of the building.

'The command post is one floor down, on my lead!' she said, equipping her H.U.D. and swiftly entering the building. Violet stormed the hallway towards the central command post, slamming open the entrance doors to floor six hundred.

'Please present identification.' The glass lens said as Violet approached the reinforced command post doors.

Violet flicked her wrists, materialising her M-eights. Then, with a single shot of a glowing green bullet, she pierced the lens, wedging the shell in the joint of the door. Then, with a single tick, the round exploded in a cloud of vivid green smoke.

'I think you may need something a little more heavy-duty.' Leo said, activating his nano-chip.

A burst of nano-bots flood from the chip, materialising into a handheld cannon-like device. The tip began to glow a dark green as the buttons littered the weapon flashed in random patterns.

'Cover your ears!' Leo said, nodding his head. A full helmet materialised over him, covering his entire head. As Leo pressed a single button on the weapon's base, a single shell jettisoned from the barrel. The force pushed Leo back as he ploughed into the Black-ops team, the rocket connected with the reinforced doors exploding upon contact. The doors dislodged from their hinges sent flying into the command room by the power of Leo's weapon.

Violet glided into the square room in full combat gear, her purple hair flowing loose as it caught the wind in her stride.

'Under section three of the U.N.N defence proclamation act of 4997, I Major Villin am commandeering this base, all those designated to the black-ops division are to remain, if not leave!' She barked as she made her way towards the command post.

The room fell silent as the multiple military men and women stared vacantly at Violet, who by this point had made her way to the top of the command post.

'Major Villin, one does not simply storm into my base and demand—!'

'General Weis, it would be in your best interest to take my lead. Or, should you prefer, I can have you escorted from my command post. The choice is yours!' Violet said, turning her back on him as she wiped the screens clear of their current work.

'Who do you think you are?'

'That's quite enough, Weis. I'll take it from here!'

'General Hill! Am I to assume disciplinary actions are in order against this woman?' he said in shock.

'She is well within her rights General, now if you please.' Hill said, gesturing towards the still smouldering door.

'Fine! But you have a real problem with that one!' he shouted, pointing his finger directly at Violet as he stomped out the room.

General Hill looked around the room catching eyes with the Black-ops team, who stood quietly in the corner. Then, shaking his head, he strolled towards the central command post where Violet stood making her preparations.

'I understand it to be a national emergency, V, but as the sayin goes, you catch more bees with sugar than shit!'

'Please, General Weis can nurse his sore pride another day!' she said, swiping at her nano-band, bringing the screens to life.

Images of their current mission, case files, and video clips filled the room as her team took their place at the tables just below the post.

'Gentleman, it's time we got on with it!' She said, turning on the spot. Her violet hair glistened in the reflection of the bright LED screens.

'It has been less than twenty-four hours since the attack on Tokyo Major. Some of us are still a little bruised.' Aster said, grumbling as he dropped to his seat

'That's quite enough, Aster. There is a mission at hand.', she said, cracking a smile from the corner of her mouth.

'So, what's the plan?' Leo said, sitting forward in his chair.

'We must head back to Eco!'

'Why? What's the point? We're being attacked here, not there! What do they have that we don't?' Leo asked, shuffling his feet on the floor.

'A weapon, one that could ensure the protection of Nova for many years to come!'

'What weapon?' Leo asked, his ears pricking up at the thought of new technology

'Aster, do you care to explain?' Violet asked, stepping down from the podium.

Aster slowly walked towards the central command post. All eyes fixed on him as he took each careful step. Then, taking a deep breath, he readied himself for the questions he knew he would face.

'The once-great King Xelios set up a defence against the Gods, knowing that his greed would not come without repercussion. In his fit of rage, he created a weapon, strong enough to stop any God, rivalling the power of the firstborn.'

'Wait a minute. I thought you were the weapon? So you said, "I am the God slayer" in the hospital wing?' Caspian said.

'No. We sort of, I'm only part of the weapon. The complete weapon was a gun, infused with a mystical essence, strong enough to claim the life of an immortal.'

'So what part in all this did you have to play?' Caspian asked.

'My job was to bring him in line, secure him in range of the weapon. Once it fired, the bullet was unstoppable!'

'So, you're telling me a single shot took down a God?' Leo asked, 'Bullshit!'

Violet rolled her eyes, slapping Leo over the back of his head.

'Continue Aster.' She said, taking a seat next to Leo.

'To dum it down, by earth standards, it is an antimatter weapon, similar to Ms Myers current weapon production, or the back bullet we used against the girl in grey, only far more powerful and less clumsy.'

The room fell silent as each person absorbed the information Aster had just given. Then, finally, the light tapping of a foot against the floor came as Aster focused on Oren.

'So, your plan is to go back to Eco, reclaim this lost technology, and bring it back here to earth?'

'Yes!' Violet replied

'One question, how do we get there?' Jax asked

'That's where you come in.' Violet said, staring back intently.

'Ok, to the three rings it is!' Jax said as the rest of the Black-ops team stood from their seats.

*

The sky elevator was one of three elevators in Nova that led to the three orbital rings. Each ring encased the globe hovering just above the earth in the beginning boundaries of space. Moving swiftly through the glass tube, the pod carrying Violet and her Black-ops crew made its way towards the central landing bay of the first ring.

'Major, we are coming up to the bridge.' Caspian said

'Thank you, do we have confirmation from the Admiral?'

'Yes, he will be there to assist.' Caspian said as the pod slowed to a halt.

The doors slid open to reveal an all-glass room, the black void of space before them glinted sporadically with starlight in the distance, the perma-steel slabs extended across the floor, making their footsteps rattle as they walked towards the observation deck.

'Admiral, I hear you have a ship for us?' Violet asked

At the vast glass panel stood a short, slightly portly man dressed in royal blue. Solid silver medals hung proudly from his chest as they reflected their freshly polished glow. The man smiled as he turned to face Violet. His thick bushy beard rested neatly upon his chest as his well-groomed moustache grazed the tip of his nose.

'Violet, a pleasure to see you again. What has it been?'

'Seven years, to the day.' Violet said, a soft smile swept across her face as she embraced the man in the longest hug she could get.

'My dear girl, you've grown since we last met.' The Admiral said with a laugh in his voice.

'Not at all, still the same height as I've always been.' She said, releasing him from her embrace.

'I must be shrinking!' He said with a roaring laugh slapping Leo in the stomach as he walked past, 'Now what's all this I hear about you needing a ship?' he asked as they walked towards the docking yards.

'We need to reach the planet, Eco. Do you know its location?' Violet asked, smiling with each passing word, a sight rarely seen by her comrades.

'Eco, you say... never heard of it. Do you have the launch coordinates?' he asked, materialising his holo-chip.

'We have traced the planet's rough location to quadrant four of the Andromeda galaxy, but the exact location is unknown!' Oren said, typing on his holo-pad, flicking it on screen in front of the Admiral.

'Andromeda, you say. It's a big place, my boy!' he said with a chuckle whilst stroking his moustache, 'Without the full location co-coordinates, you'd be flying round in space, without a hope in hell of finding this place.' He continued to chuckle whilst shaking his head.

'Once we reach the quadrant, I am more than satisfied that we will find what we need.' Violet said, with a sly wink to the Admiral.

'Well, if you're sure, the X-two intergalactic is the fastest ship in the fleet!' he said, typing the details onto his holo-pad, bringing the image of the ship on screen. In a flash of light, the spacecraft materialised in the docking bay within a matter of seconds.

'It'll get you there in about six months, that is if you use the Hyperloop. But you will have to adjust for re-animation. Wouldn't want you catching space sickness!' He said, jabbing Leo in the ribs.

'Six months!' Leo said, 'There may be no earth left by that time!'

'Technology is good, my boy, but not good enough eh, it's the best I can do.' the Admiral said as he strolled towards the ship admiring its imposing beauty.

Violet turned to look out of the windows of the orbital ring. Her thoughts drifted off into space as she stared into the sparkling void.

'Well, that's that then!' Leo said as he walked towards the orbital lift, followed by the rest of the Black-ops team.

'Something I said?' Violet turned round to see the Admiral staring back at her. His rosy glowing face never failed to put a smile on her face.

'No, never, it's just. We need to be there as soon a possible. The mission demands it. The world counts on it.' She said in defeat.

'Well, a little thing like time has never stopped you before. Why I remember a time when we sent you on the U.N.Tritant to Mars. Do you remember?' he said, chuckling to himself, 'It was a two-month mission. You were back in two weeks; mission completed an all!' He said, shaking his head.

'That was different.'

'How so, because you want it to be? No, no, that's not the Violet I know.' He said with a wink as he strolled towards his quarters.

Violet paused, laughing to herself. She shook her head. It was not often that someone made her laugh, but it would be the Admiral if anyone were going to. Then, as she turned to face the void, a thought struck her mind like a pinprick to the finger.

'That's it!' She said, pressing the button on her holo screen, 'Gentlemen, assemble the Yellowhammer. We need to pay a little visit to the shipping yards!'

— CHAPTER SEVENTEEN —

THE NEXUS

The sky pod plummeted towards the ground at breakneck speed as the Yellowhammer flew into view, landing upon the ground just outside of the elevator shaft.
Boarding the jet, Violet made her way towards the cockpit, taking place in her usual seat.

'Where to Major?'

'U.N.N. trade sector, please, Commander, make it swift. We are in a bit of a rush!' she said, looking out of the passenger window.

The jet sprung into action, reaching top speed as it flew towards the intended destination.

'You know this whole area was once the battleground for the U.S. on their final assault of Russia. As the great story goes, General—'

'Thank you, Commander. I'm pretty familiar with the story.' Violet said, rolling her eyes.

As the Yellowhammer reached the MAGNA. security wall, it stopped abruptly. The engines powered down, causing the passengers to jolt forward in their chairs.

'What's the hold-up?' Violet asked.

'We are not permitted to enter. All Black-ops credentials are in lockdown!'

'I have a code.' Jax said, rushing to the cockpit.

'U.N.N-T.J.X, four four seven six.' The Commander said, reading the code aloud.

'Welcome special agent Jackson Rush, docking permitted. Bay two only!'

'Special agent!' Violet said with a snicker.
Jax re-took his seat, now blushing from Violet's jab. The Yellowhammer lowered to the snow caped ground, securing itself in bay two.

'Do you need us to wait, Major?'

'No, Captain, I should imagine we won't be back for some time!' Violet said, making a hasty exit from the jet.

As they approached the Perma-steel doors, Violet held back, allowing Jax to walk ahead. Then, pressing his hand upon the black screen, the doors to dockyard two slowly creaked open. The lights to the connecting corridor illuminated a path towards the main chamber. Stacks of steel cabins lined the walls stretching at least forty containers high, leaving the room's centre entirely open.

'The main Nexus portal is up ahead!' Jax said, still in the lead as they walked down the vast corridor, then down the winding staircase towards the centre of the room.

'Can I be the first to say that this is a terrible idea, and at best, you may all end up dead!' Serena said, her arms crossed as the Black-ops team came into view.

'Nice to see you too!' Leo replied.

'The portal has not been properly fleshed out yet. As the head of the office of science and technology, I must impose. In all good conscience, I cannot allow you to do this! Travel across the globe has its issues, but interstellar travel, it's insane!' Serena said, unbudged from her defensive position.

Violet glared at Jax, her face flush, holding back as much of her anger as possible.

'Alright then, so what grand plan do you have?' Violet hissed, turning back to face Serena.

Serena remained still, her face unchanged, her arms crossed as she continued her death stare at Violet and her team.

'You think I don't know of the secret tests, V?' Violet shot another glare at Jax, unable to meet his eyes as he remained perfectly still, staring intensely at the ground.

'Then it would appear we are at an impasse!' Violet said, ordering her men to stand down.

The Black-ops team split off, taking their places on the nearest chairs encircling the Nexus portal. As they sat, engaging in small conversation, trying as they might to listen into the heated discussion of Violet and Serena as they engaged in their negotiation.

A short, forty something-year-old man walked into the room. His crimson cape flapped and swished in the airy room as he strolled towards the Black-ops team, clad in silver-plated armour that glistened under the fluorescent light.

'Good afternoon humans, would you mind telling me your plans? My... Ohh, let's just call him boss! He is somewhat interested in finding out.'

Violet sprung to her feet, flicking her wrists. She activated her M-Eights, glowing a vibrant green. She shot a single bullet towards the crimson caped man. He evaded the shot, disappearing from sight only to reappear in the centre of the inactive Nexus.

'So this is what you intend to use. One can only assume it's to pass over to the next planet. What a crude instrument. I suppose it's not much of a shock!' He said, inspecting the Nexus, 'But where, and why, questions I have yet to ask, yet to attain answer!' He continued, turning on the spot to face Aster, 'Ahh, you've already told them, smart boy!

Well, that's fine. I don't need you to speak to get the truth!', He said as he levitated from the floor.

'Dente of truth, I thought you were dead? It matters not. Your questions will go unanswered!' Aster said with a sly grin.

'Good show, my boy, only fools rush in! And, I am no fool. So, tell me, what do you hope to find on Eco? A weapon, perhaps? One to fell the Gods of old!' Dente said, clenching his fists. Then slamming his fist onto the ground, particles of red dust flew up into the air.

'You see, my boy. I am a coward by nature, so all I need is to hear the words, either by mouth or by thought. The latter is excruciatingly painful, but I'm sure you were already aware of that. Now for one last time, What do you intend to find on Eco?'

Aster sank to the floor. His head felt like a thousand knives had struck him all at once. The pain mulled in his head as he felt a warm stream of blood trickle from his nose. Letting out an ear curtailing scream of pain, the rest of the Black-ops team stood motionless, unable to move, their bodies pinned to the spot.

'Fine! You can fight against it all you want, Aster, but you will not win!' he said, turning to face Violet.

'You!' he said, glaring into Violet's eyes. 'You have the heart of a dragon, my dear. You will be a fun one to break!' he said. A menacing smile cracked across his face as he flicked a single finger in her direction.

"*We are using the portal to go to Eco and retrieve the God slayer!*" the words fell into Dente's mind, his eyes opened wide.

'So you give me this information freely?' he said. His face shifted, furrowing his brow in distaste.

Violet smiled. She lifted her guns free from Dente's curse, firing green bullets at her target round after round. Disappearing and reappearing with each passing shot, Dente soon found himself at the top of the viewing deck.

'It's been a pleasure, but I must dash. I bid you *adieu*!' he said with a bow, then suddenly he was gone, evaporating into a cloud of red smoke.

'Why did you tell him!' Aster said as he punched the concrete floor, his pain gradually subsiding.

'He would have killed us all to get that answer. This way was easier.' She said, turning to face Serena, 'The time for negotiations is over. We pass through the portal!'

'Fine, then I'm coming with you, Serena said as she turned to face the Nexus.

*

Dente crash-landed on Petaria, the soft ground yielding below him. As he tumbled forward, his body slammed hard against the glorious golden throne of the divine lord Solus.

'Dente! Explain your actions!' Parminx said, pulling him up off the floor.

'Supreme Goddess. Dare I look upon the silver maiden to explain a tale of grandeur. I have returned fro—'

'To the point! Dente!'

'The traitor and his mortal friends are planning to return to Eco, your most redoubtable!' he said with a bow.

'My lord, we must meet them head-on, stop this insurrection before it has the chance to sprout wings!' Parminx turned her glowing gaze towards Solus, still sitting upon his crystal throne.

'Calm yourself. Many manners of actions can obtain peace. War is the great equaliser that through which can bring about eternal peace!'

'As you wish!' she said, clapping her hands together.

The world around them grew light as she began to glow brighter with each passing moment. Until, at last, she released a final flash of blinding light. A man in gold armour appeared before her. His white hair rustled in the breeze, his blazing red eyes burnt like two fireballs in the void.

'Bellium, God of War! It is up to you to stop the rising insurrection of the traitor and mortal planet earth. I trust we shall not experience the same failure as your last assault?' she said, casting a shameful look down upon Bellium.

'Your lack of faith is tiresome, Parminx. Need I remind you that under my assault, the Econians fell, stopping any kind of rebellion. Or has your mind lost all sense of memory?' he said, folding his arms as he turned towards Solus, still sitting upon his crystal throne.

'My most vengeful son, your sister is only trying to aid in your eventual conquest, do not pass her assistance off as a mere insult, but rather, embrace that what was and what will be!' Solus said, now rising from his seat, shrinking to meet the eyes of Bellium.

'Divine lord, I will ensure the Econian is brought to justice. The mortals will fall like ants underfoot,' Bellium said, bowing down before the golden light.

'Then to Eco, you go, Dente's news of their plan will surely come to pass sooner rather than later!'

Parminx raised her hands, gathering clouds in the clear night sky. Tightly they formed as she swirled her arms, blocking out all signs of the sky.

'Lunerios. I call upon you to aid the God of War!' she said, her faint voice echoing across the dim lands of Petaria.

As the words left her mouth, the clouds broke. Revealing the sky, dotted with millions of stars and the shimmering white of the moon of Petaria, now growing in size as it approached the planet. As she jumped from the moon's surface, Lunerios landed upon the ground before the God of War.

'You are injured. Tell me how?' Bellium asked, clasping hold of Lunerios and pulling her closer as he inspected the injuries she had sustained.

'Earthlings, and their bothersome ways. They are a tricksy people!' she said, releasing herself from his grip, turning from his view to hide her battle scars.

'The traitor, did he do this to you?' Bellium asked, clasping her hand, laying it upon his chest.

'Yes!' She replied, hiding her face in shame.

'Consider him dead!' Bellum's eyes glowed fiercer than they had ever before.

A faint red glow illuminated around him as the heat began to scorch the ground. Then, they were gone, fading from view in a burst of red fire.

'Hell hath no fury than the God of War!' Solus said, cracking a wicked smile as the sky above him cleared of the moon and stars, returning to the black void it once was.

*

Serena sat on the table surface in the hanger of the Nexus portal. Her eyes gazed upon the Nexus as it remained motionless, shrouded in spotlights.

'I thought you said the time for negotiation was over. Well, this feels to me like a non-negotiable!' she said, tying up her short hair.

'That was when it was just us, but you, you're not a fighter!' Violet replied, sitting on the chair, her legs resting on the table surface.

'Ohh so, what? Because I'm not a man, or you or "Black-ops" means I cannot defend myself? Need I remind you, V, whilst you were recovering in a hospital, I was facing an enemy in the base, or had you forgotten?'

'That's my point! Enemy. Singular, this will be an army. The person we head into battle with is a God. Literal God, with an army, how useful do you think you will be?'

'Same question V, what army are you taking with you? It's just you, six men, and one Aster!' Serena said, standing from the desk. 'No, I'm coming with, regardless of anything you have to say!'

The door to the hanger opened as Leo walked in. Numerous floating cloth filled boards floated behind him as he made his way towards the Nexus.

'Ladies and gentlemen, with me, are the latest in Nova guard weapons technology, lovingly handcrafted by my faithful hands, and like me, they are soft, smooth and hard in all the right places!' he said. Throwing a wink in Violet's direction as she walked towards him.

'Get on with it, or the live testing of said weapons will be on you!' she said, leaning in, her face centimetres away from his.

'Right, as you wish, Major. Presenting the all-new. M-ten, lighter than the eight, sturdier, and comes with over twenty customisable round charges!' he said, handing Violet the single gun, 'Including the new MAGNA rounds and single antimatter charges, this baby packs quite the punch!'

Violet flicked the gun, watching as the lights on the side and hilt changed from blue to green, white, red, violet and countless other colours.

'Impressive Leo, so no more manual rounds to load?'

'Nope, leaving a lot of space in your nano-bands for these!', he said, revealing the following table, 'Fourth-gen marble tech, in all the flavours.'

The floating table housed different coloured marbles, each displaying a greek letter in the centre of its highly polished surface.

'Full lists of applications suitable to each marble can be found on your nano-bands, along with countless, practical solutions these babies can provide,' Leo said, grinning from ear to ear. 'Gentlemen, your Chips have been updated already.' he finished taking a bow as he backed away.

Serena walked towards the remaining floating boards unveiling each one.

'After much research, we have developed the next-gen upgrades based on standard performance: unique combat style and threat level. Major, for you!' she said, handing her a small square violet box, 'To replace your H.U.D, this is the visual B.I.O.N.A contact, or VBC for short. When placed over your eye, it can present up to a thousand pre-directed outcomes a second. Scan through any type of wall or blockade, including lead allowing for a full three-sixty unimpaired vision. The data analysis will allow for resolution at the moment, providing you with consistent and constant feedback. The perfect thing for when the future is so... unknown.' she said, smiling at Violet.

'And what presents do we get?' Leo said, stepping directly in front of Violet, blocking her returning smile.

'Leo, who could forget!' Serena pulled out eight badges, each with the words E.X.O in different coloured letters, matching their specialist armour, 'For you, Leo.' Serena said with a smile, handing him a red E.X.O badge.

'Cool, but what does it do?' he said, holding it towards his face.

'It is the new External Xi Operations Armour, perfectly lightweight, unbelievably durable.' she said, folding her arms, pleased with her work.

'How does it work?' Leo asked, flipping the badge in his hand frantically.

'You will need to take off your current Ar—' Serena trailed off as she witnessed Leo unclip his chest plate and armour faster than light, now standing in nothing but his underwear.

'Hold it in your hand, firmly!' she said 'now squeeze!'

As Leo squeezed on the Badge, he felt a rush of nano-bots swarm his skin, forming into a chest plate, combat pants, and moulding around his feet to create boots, solidifying in place with a clunk.

'Wow, feels like I'm wearing nothing at all!' Leo said, jumping on the spot, then lunging whilst flapping his arms in the air to show off the suit's stretchy nature, 'Hold on a second, you said durable, just how durable are we talking?'

Serena lifted her brow, flashing a smile at Violet, who had already raided her M-ten; taking a single shot of a non charged round, the bullet struck Leo on the back. Falling to the ground, he let out a cry of pain.

'You're fine! The bullet didn't even scratch the surface.' Violet said, shaking her head, lifting Leo from the floor.

'You knew that was going to happen, right Major?' Leo moaned through gritted teeth.

'No, not really!' she said, brandishing a wicked smile as she collected her E.X.O badge from Serena.

'One more thing!' Serena said, picking up a small hand size chrome pole, 'Handheld Melee weapons, for when things get a little too close for comfort!'

She gripped the bar in her hand, shooting forwards. The pole extended about a metre from her hand. The edge sharpened as thin as a sheet of paper. A glowing red line grew from the free edge as she swished the blade in the air.

'Lazer blades!' Leo said in excitement, jumping up and down on the spot.

'Yes, in the event the laser edge is unresponsive, the blade is still sharp enough to cut through permasteel!' She threw a smooth steel ball in the air and swung with the chrome sword, cleaving the ball in two. 'It is person-specific. Only you can activate it!' she said, handing out the bars to their respective owners.

'What is that?' Violet pointed towards the silver ball, emitting a faint blue pulse.

'I don't yet have a name for it. I thought of calling it the nullifier, but it's not catchy enough.' she said as she spun the ball in her hand.

'So what's the use?' Caspian asked intently.

'It uses a distinct antimatter pulse to eliminate almost all types of energy compositions. I used it during our escape from the Black-ops base.

'So that's what you went back for?' Caspian said from across the room.

'How will that come in handy? The girl in grey is dead. The energy signal was specific to her.' Oren asked, now standing from his chair.

'All living things produce or run on an energy source. This device will give us some insights into their weakness!' She said, turning the ball slowly in her hand. 'Ultimately, you can believe they are Gods, or not. But whatever they are, there is an explanation rooted in science, and I intend to find the answers!'

— CHAPTER EIGHTEEN —

TRAVEL THROUGH TIME AND SPACE

The Black-ops team, accompanied by Serena, assembled at the Nexus portal. Suited in their new E.X.O suits and fully equipped for any eventuality, they stood motionless, staring into the emptiness of the portal.

'We have to go at some point!' Caspian said, his stomach rumbling as he spoke.

'Nervous Casp,' Leo said, digging his elbow into his side.

'Yes, and you should be too. This type of thing is unheard of.' He said, pushing Leo away, 'We are the test subjects on highly illegal use of untested technology!'

'Right.' Leo said, staring blankly back at Caspian.

'Look, Caspian's right, this portal has the opportunity to inflict a pain worse than death. We could come out the other side dead or crazy or even merged into one. Or not come out at all. Please tell me; you have all considered the risk!' Serena said, stepping out from the line formation to face the rest of the team.

'Yes, all possibilities have been considered. Extensively, I might add. But if we are to get to Eco in any amount of reasonable time, there is no other option. I would not be doing this if there were any other way!' Violet said, clasping Serena's hand in hers, 'Trust me, please!' she smiled, warming Serena's heart.

'Fine, then let's get on with it!' She said with a heavy sigh, dropping her hunched shoulders in defeat.

The Black-opts team assembled in the centre of the Nexus portal as Serena moved to the side, accessing the control pad.

'Do you know the coordinates?'

Everyone looked towards Aster, who stood scratching his head facing the wall.

'Aster, please tell me you remember the coordinates?' Violet said in disbelief.

'It's still fuzzy, plus who knows that information? If I asked you, would you know earth's coordinates?'

'Zero, Zero, Zero.' Violet said dryly.

'You earth people and your smart ass atti…' Aster said, mumbling to himself as he stepped off the raised platform. Then, walking towards the nearest computer, he typed in the coordinates for the Andromeda galaxy.

'It is located in the fourth quadrant of Andromeda, the central ring from the core!'

'That leaves about two million planets then!' Oren said, jumping off the platform towards Aster.

'Hold on! you said you were tracking energy spikes from the girl in Manhattan, right?'

'Yes, your point?'

'What planet did you get the first burst from?'

'A.C54100, also in the fourth quadrant!' Oren replied, turning back to face Violet.

'It's as good as any.' She replied

'Hold on; we don't know if the planet we're heading to is the correct one? Major, please, you must call this off.' Caspian said in a panic.

'No, now is not the time to lose your nerve, have faith Caspian. Sometimes when everything around you makes no sense, trust in your gut!' she said, standing proud as the Nexus made an almighty clang.

The frame began to rotate as bolts of deep purple lightning shot from within the portal. Then, the lights that dotted the portal frame began to flash their red warnings as the room filled with a mist of purple haze.

'It feels different from last time!' Aster shouted, rushing back towards the portal with Oren in pursuit.

'Bigger portal, Further distance!' Serena shouted over the crashing sounds of thunder striking against metal.

Jumping back in line, the Black-ops team stood waiting for the portal to form. As the purple mist began to gather in the void of the circular frame, it condensed down to a thick cloud of viscous smoke.

'We must walk in. The main transporter is more stable than the access point you had in the base!' Serena shouted as bolts of purple thunder flooded the room, lashing at the steel crates.

'Then in we go!' Violet said, closing her eyes, taking the first step into the deep purple fog, then she was gone in the blink of an eye.

'How do we know it worked?' Caspian shouted.

'We don't. The comms won't work at that level of distance!' Serena replied, looking back in concern.

'Into the unknown, we go.' he said to himself, taking a step forward, allowing the purple haze to envelop him entirely, followed by the rest of the Black-ops team.

*

Violet opened her eyes. The sight of desolate buildings and scorched grounds filled her vision as she breathed in the chalky air. The muddy grey clouds whirled above the sky, blocking out the sun. The dead grass remained still in the chilling breeze. The sound of dust and debris rattling against one another filled Violet's ears as she awaited the arrival of her comrades.

'So this is Eco?' she said to herself, thoroughly unimpressed.

Looking around her, the bodies of her comrades appeared from a cloud of purple smoke, all except for one.

'Where is Serena?' Violet said, addressing her team.

'She went in before me.' Aster said, looking around the desolate land, tears forming in his eyes as a rush of memories filled his head.

Aster dropped to his knees as the horrifying events began to replay repeatedly in his mind, the final days of Eco and the destruction of his homeworld.

'SERENA!' Violet shouted as loud as she could, her stomach turned to knots, she could feel the tears well in her eyes, her breath quickening, each second felt like a lifetime as she frantically searched the field.

'CASPIAN RADIAL ENERGY SCAN NOW!' She snapped, grabbing Caspian by the collar, shaking him violently as he panicked, activating his Nano-chip.

Just then, the sky turned dark. The clouds gathered in mass, blocking the sky from view, then in a sudden break, the clouds parted as Serena fell through a haze of purple mist, her lifeless body now hurtling towards the ground.

Leo Activated his M.O.D, jumping high into the air. Grabbing Serena, he pulled her close to him. He activated his nano-chip with a flick of his wrist, producing a light blue marble, throwing it towards the ground, exploding on impact. The marble shot blue sound rays up from the floor, encasing Leo and Serena as they fell, slowing their descent until they landed safely upon the ground.

Violet rushed towards Leo, still holding Serena, wiping tears from her face. Finally, she plucked up the courage to ask him the question.

'Leo, is she—?'

'She's alive Major. It's ok.' Leo said, placing Serena on the ground. The slow movement of her chest rising and falling comforted Violet. Then, knowing she was still alive, letting out a gasp of relief, she turned to face Caspian.

'Cas—'

'No need, Major, I understand,' he replied, smiling at her.

Violet turned to face Aster, who still knelt upon the ground. His body remained motionless as his head hung low from his shoulders.

'Aster?'

'I'm fine, just give me a moment!' He replied, his low voice holding back the tears.

The darkness faded as the clouds returned. The Black-ops team sat in silence on the scorched ground of Eco, waiting for Aster to return from his grief.

Standing suddenly, Aster turned to the rest of the group.

'My apologies. It is unlike my people to show this much emotion, especially of past matters.' he said, nodding his head towards Violet.

'It's fine, Aster. We understand.' She replied, running her hands through her hair as she stood from the ground.

The group fell silent as they looked around the charred lands of Eco, taking in the desolation caused by the God of War and the battles once fought all that time ago.

'Well, that was an intense five minutes. So what's next on the plan?' Leo said, rocking back and forth on his feet, his arms supporting the back of his head.

'Not now, Leo?' Violet returned to her usual short sharp tone, 'Caspian, I need an energy scan of the planet. Check for any intruders; we may not be alone. Zyair, I need you to keep an eye on Serena, Tak, you scout out the local area Aster, follow Tak. Everyone else stays put. We make no moves until safe to do so!'

'There doesn't appear to be any energy spikes. The planet seems stable. Not even a solar disturbance.'

'Zyair, how is she doing?'

'Fine Major, Heart rate is normal, her vitals all check out. Vision seems normal, but she remains unresponsive.'

'Can we attach an adrenaline stim?'

'In my history, there is a reason if a person is out cold, but everything is fine. If we pull her out now, her mind could be at risk. Remember her statement "go crazy", no it's best we let her be for now.'

Violet turned from Zyair, knowing what he was saying was true but fighting back the urge to force him to do as she asked.

'The path ahead is clear Major!'

'Good work Tak, Aster whereabouts are we?'

'East sector, the weapons division. Eco had an entire city dedicated to defence. And this was the headquarters.' he said, making his way back to the rest of the Black-ops team.

'Perfect, so the God slayer is here?' she asked

'No, the other side of the world. Xelios knew if he kept it with the rest of the armoury, that would be the first place they would come looking.' Aster said as they began to walk towards the half-destroyed buildings.

'So what's here then?' Leo asked.

'That!' Aster pointed towards a large steel slab in the centre of the town, encased in the earth it stretched across the land for miles, further than the human eye could see.

'I don't understand?' Violet said, glancing towards Aster.

'It's what's underneath it. I hope!' he said, gleefully running towards the entrance bay.

'Aster, I need an explanation!' Violet shouted, slowly walking behind him.

'We had a ship big enough for us to use on interstellar missions. Xelios had many plans for it. But, unfortunately, it was never used!'

'How do you know it will still be there?'

'The destruction looks superficial. Like they only focused on ground level. Eco was much more than that! We dug into the ground. There was just as much life under the surface as above!' he said, kicking away the stone and rubble that gathered around a square steel sheet.

'This is the manual entrance. I have a feeling the main energy source was damaged during the war. But we have a backup generator at bedrock level.'

'Bedrock, would that not be thousands of levels deep?' Caspian said, rushing towards the entrance.

'Yes!' Aster said, staring blankly back at Caspian.

'Right, so we won't have the time. We didn't come here to re-activate your planet. We came to save ours.'

'We have auto transit modules. They don't require electricity to get where you need to be, just in case the power cut when you were underground!' Aster said, lifting the hatch to reveal a deep dark hole that seemed to stretch on with no end in sight. Aster gripped the ladder just below the entrance, then slid down the poles, ending his conversation.

'Zyair, stay here with Serena, Tak, you stand guard!' Violet said, grabbing the poles attached to the ladders and sliding down to meet up with Aster, followed by the remaining Black-ops team.

The tunnel seemed to go on for miles. Violet had lost count of the floors she had passed as she followed Aster on his descent.

'Here we are.' Aster said as he activated a light from his nano-chip whilst dusting off a skeletal frame of what appeared to be a wheeless motorcycle.

'How does it work?' Violet said, grasping the bike in her hand.

'Simple, most things on Eco are BIO functioning, just place your hand on the reader, and you're away.' Aster placed his hand on the small black pad attached to the bike's centre console. His eyes turned jet black as the bike sprung into action. Spotlights embedded into the bike began to glow a deep blue as the bike hovered from the floor.

'Fascinating!' Jax said, looking closer to inspect the alien technology, 'So how long does it last?'

'That all depends.'

'Depends on what?' Jax replied.

'If you're alive or not.' Aster said with a cheeky wink.

Aster twisted the handle as the bike sped into action, zipping down the dark path ahead. The blue light faded from view as he reached the end of the tunnel.

'I guess we'll just wait here!' Leo said, slumping to the ground.

Violet walked towards the edge of the path. The wind whistling through the tunnel caught her attention.

'Major!' Caspian shouted as he ran to catch up. 'Where are we heading?'

'The wind, it's passing through, which means this leads to an open space!' she said as the nano-band emitted a powerful beam of white light, illuminating the ground.

'What makes you so sure?' Caspian asked.

Winking, Violet pointed towards her left eye, what once was violet now a neon red.

Reaching the end of the path, they encountered a sheer drop where the tunnel finished, followed by nothing but a vast black space that seemed to stretch on for miles.

'Who's going to be the first to tell Aster there's no ship!' Caspian said,

Just as the words left his mouth, the corridor lit up in a flash of blinding white light, the vast empty chasm now filled with spotlights shining down, their light bounced from wall to wall illuminating the pure white space.

'Energy's back on!' Caspian said, holding his hand towards his face trying to block the harsh light.

Just before Violet had the chance to speak, she could hear the sound of Asters speeder in the distance. Looking into the empty room, she could see him travelling towards the ridge at high speed across the ground. The slight blue blur suddenly darted upright as it scaled the wall faster than any mode of transport she had seen on Nova.

'I'm back!' He said, pulling to a halt floating in the air at the end of the tunnel.

'Apparently so, just one thing, where is the ship?' she said,

'Cloaking field.', Aster replied, pressing a button on the speeder.

The ship began to reappear, fragmented and distorted, it slowly materialising out of what looked like thin air.

'Clever. No wonder you fit in so well on earth.', Caspian said.

'Technology is a bit more advanced here, but the similarities are rather striking.' Aster finished his sentence turning in mid-air to face the ship that had now finished materialising.

Before them, in the vast open chasm, stood a megastructure, unlike anything Violet had ever seen before. It stood over a five-hundred metres tall, stretching on for many miles unseen. The long ovalish ship stood proud, with many glass panes coated in black reflective metal. It reflected the light twinkling like stars in the expansive void of space.

'The Hellbourne. Isn't she a beauty? Originally it was designed to carry the population of the falling moon to ECO, but after the elevator's completion, we didn't need it. My guess was Xelios would have used it. Had his plans of galactic conquest come to pass!' Aster said.

'It is magnificent!' Jax said as he and Leo finally caught up with Violet and Caspian.

'I knew you'd like it. Shall we take a look?' he replied, pressing a button on the spreader.

Steps sprung from the threshold of the tunnel end, lowering towards the ground below. The white bricks suspended in mid-air evaporated as they passed over each one. Finally, reaching the bottom of the stairs, the boarding doors of the Hellbourne began to lower.

'It's fully automatic, made to travel great distances, and fully weaponised, just in case!' Aster said as they made their way through the ship.

'That way to the cockpit!' he said, pointing left at the entrance bay as he tried to gather his bearings.

'So we can use this to get home?' Violet said, entering the flight deck.

'I don't know. It's been out of use for some time; we never actually used it!'

'So we're hedging our bets on a glorified people carrier?' Leo said, kicking at a side panel of the ship.

'Yes, but it's the only thing we have. It will have to do! Jax, are you able to fly this thing?' Violet said

'Errrm, yes, I think!' Jax said, glaring at the vast control panel, the words above buttons in the native Econian language.

'The system will guide you. As long as you have some understanding of thermodynamics!' Aster said, pressing a single button on the Hellbourne control pad.

The doors to the mega-ship began to close as the solid steel roof began to retract back. Jax placed his hand on the transparent black pad in the centre of the control panel. The lights around the cockpit lit up as the engineer kicked into action. Jax's eyes turned jet black as he kept his hand on the control pad.

'Jax... Jackson!' Violet said, waving her hand in front of his face.

'Just give him a minute. This type of ship has a lot of instructions. It takes a few moments to get to grips with it fully.' Aster said, smiling at Violet from across the cockpit.

Jax let go of the pad, his eyes returning to their dark brown as he stumbled, steadying himself against the main control panel.

'Jax!' Violet said, now holding him upright 'Aster, what's going on?' Violet said, her temper short.

'Econian technology is different. First, it has to tell you how to fly. Jax just received a crash course. It's intensive, but he will be fine.' Aster said, taking control of the panel as Jax weighed himself.

'Welcome to Eco!' Caspian jeered, assisting Violet in moving Jax to the Captain's seat.

Aster took control as the ship began to lift from the floor. The solid steel roof had finally opened, allowing the carrier to ascend towards the ground level.

'Zyair, Tak, climb aboard!' Violet said via the comm-link as they reached the ground level.

'Lifting Serena, Zyair and Takeshi sprinted towards the vast open space, slowly being filled by the mega-ship, jumping from the ground towards the doors that now dangled just next to them.

'We have boarded Major.' Takeshi said, remaining in the boarding room.

'Good assemble in the cockpit, follow the lights.' She replied as a series of arrows illuminated the way towards the rest of the Black-ops team.

'So what's the weapons spec on this beast?' Leo said, swinging on one of the chairs in the cockpit centre.

'Light auto rails, multi missile defence, orbital bombardment, it's designed for defence, not much of an offence beast, but it can dig you out of many problems when needed.', Aster replied, tapping on the control panel.

'Major!' Zyair said, walking through the doors to the cockpit, carefully placing Serena onto the closest chair.

'Good, you're all here. Now, this vessel will be our escape, and carrier of the God slayer weapon, Jax and Serena, will remain on the ship until we board.'

'How do we get back down, Major?' Takeshi asked.

'Aster has provided some us with some speeders.'

'They work in space, ground, air, whatever you can think of.' He said, smiling from the control panel.

'So, what's the plan?' Leo said, stretching his legs as he walked towards Violet and the rest of the Black-ops team.

'So far, we have the advantage. Using this map as a guide, we will begin at the weapons facility, then make our way towards the golden citadel.' She said, pressing a flashing button on the cockpit roof, a holo-map of the planet Eco projected into the centre of the room. Moving it with her hands, she enlarged it to their location, 'Once the weapon is secure, we head back towards the Hellbourne. Jax, remain vigilant. We don't know who long this will take. You must be prepared for any eventuality!'

'Yes, Major!' Jax said, rising to his feet, the effects of the training now fading away.

'Sounds good to me, let's do this!' Aster said, switching the Hellbourne to autopilot.

As they assembled at the drop-off point, the ship's doors lowered. The remaining black-ops team mounted the Eco speeders, placing their hands on the sensor pads, the bikes started to glow blue.

'Aster, Lead the way!' Violet said, awaiting his instruction.

'Once you kick-off, meet back at the weapons facility, the steel door is still open, head towards the lower facilities level, zero-ten, this level has something we will need.'

Then with a push, Aster dropped from the ship, free falling on his speeder through the air, shortly followed by the rest of the Black-ops team.

The wind bustled past them as they free-fell through the sky. For a moment, Violet forgot all about the mission as she gripped the handles tightly, both excited and petrified at the same time.

'Major, I'm picking up multiple energy signals, one unregistered, the other matches the energy produced by the Executioner!' Caspian said

'So they have arrived!'

— CHAPTER NINETEEN —

THE A.I ARMY

Free-falling towards the ground, the Black-ops team activated their speeders. Then, jetting off with a dark blue light trailing behind them, they hastily headed down into the deep empty chasm towards floor zero-ten.

'Major, the energy reading is off the charts!' Caspian said, still reading his nano-screen.

'Yes, it's his army. We were in for a rough night!' Violet said, pushing her speeder to the max, zipping past each member of the Black-ops team drawing level with Aster.

'They have arrived. Aster, where are we heading?'

'The grand ruler Xelios always had a backup plan, but it was never fully executed like most of his genius schemes.

'So we are heading towards his contingency plan!' Violet said, a low tremble of doubt in her voice.

Each level looked the same as they flew deeper underground, following Aster as he led them towards the secret bunker. As they approached the magnificent steel doors of level zero-ten, the Black-ops slowed to a halt, looking upon the tall doors in amazement.

'This is it!' Aster said, dismounting his bike. He jogged towards the control panel whilst the rest of the team watched from behind their speeder screens.

'And just what exactly was your leader's plan?' Violet asked, tapping the handle of her speeder.

'You'll see soon enough!' Aster said, placing his hand upon the black screen of the control pad.

Just as the doors began to creak and clatter, the holo-screen on Caspians arm began to flash.

'We have movement. The two main energy signals are amassing in the east quadrant. Also, there is quite the uplift in numbers!'

'Wait, East quadrant, relay the coordinates!' Aster said as he continued to fiddle with the door access pad.

'Upper East, fifty-three degrees north, two degrees east.'

Aster turned from the control pad, grabbing Caspian's arm to view the map.

'Perfect! The golden citadel!' Aster said, pushing Caspian's arm away, rushing back towards the panel.

'So they have come to destroy the God slayer!' Violet said.

'Yes, but they will have a difficult time locating it. Xelios was no fool.'

'How do we even know it's still here and working?' Leo asked

'Why would they come if there was no threat? Trust me on this, they are just as frightened of us as we are of them!' Aster said, now returning towards his speeder.

As the doors scraped across the ground, a blast of wind swept through them, lifting the dirt and rubble into the air. Violet squinted as she tried to look past the swirling clouds of dust.

The room was dark, pitch-black to the human eye. Violet winked, activating her in-eye H.U.D. The room lit up in a sea of red light as the H.U.D revealed rows upon rows of man-shaped objects, each standing perfectly still. Aster pressed a switch on the inside control panel. Lights on the roof sprung into action illuminating the room in a soft, warm glow as the uplights punched their way through rows of human men who stood in perfect formation. Their eyes closed, their arms by their sides, unarmed and unguarded. Violet and her Black-ops team made their way around the men, daring to take a closer look.

'What the?' Leo said, walking towards one of the soldiers.

'This is the A.I. army. Impressive, right?' Aster said, leaning on one of the motionless men.

'They look so... real, lifelike even!' Violet said as she inspected the troops, adorned in their combat uniforms, each identical to the next.

'Is there a particular reason they all look like you?' Takeshi said, motioning his head back and forth from Aster to the A.I. man.

'As the General, the decision that Xelios made was to model them after me. It's not clear why. But knowing Xelios, it would have been some tactical decision!'

'Makes sense. In war, you aim to kill the General! But how do you know which is the real one?' Violet said, still inspecting the A.I. men.

'Well, this is all well and good, but how do we turn you on?' Leo said, slapping Aster on the back with a toothy grin.

'There is a central control panel, there!' Aster said, pointing towards a glass cabin atop the vast room.

'So what, we press the green button and then what?' Leo said, walking towards the metal lift in the centre of the room.

'They do as commanded.'

'By who, though, you?' Leo said, pressing the call button.

'By rank as a military leader. In this case, it's the Major.' Aster said, glancing over towards Violet.

'Ahh right, yes Major, I—'

'Enough, Leo. Don't think I won't let it pass that you just forgot who is in charge here.' Violet said, pushing Leo out of the way of the metal doors.

The lift fell towards the floor, opening its practically new doors with an ear-pleasing swoosh.

'Gentlemen, we do not have all day!' Violet said, holding the door as the rest of the Black-ops team scrambled hastily towards the lift.

Entering the main control panel of the A.I. army, the doors to the steel lift opened to a central command post. The glass box room had multiple screens littered about most randomly. Each screen came fitted with a control board that flashed in various colours.

'Looks like it's up to you, Commander.' Leo said, scanning the compact room.

'Major, I'm picking up a huge force travelling in your direction. They have assembled at the edge of the Hellbourne container.' Jax said, hovering high into the Econin sky.

'What type of force, Jax, be specific?' Violet said, staring over at Aster.

'It looks to be an army. The Hellbourne has gone into defence mode!'

'Caspian, why can Jax see them, but we can't?' she asked.

'I don't know. I'm still only reading energy from the eastern quadrant. Perhaps the Gods have learnt how to keep off our radars!'

'Aster, lock the doors!' Violet said as she stared down the empty doorway leading into the army bunker.

The doors slid shut, locking as they sealed. Aster continued to press buttons on the control pad as reinforced plates slid from the side walls shielding the already heavy steel door.

'That should hold them!' Aster said, continuing to work on the control pad.

'For now!' Violet retorted, keeping her eyes fixed on the doors.

Just as the brief exchange took place, the sound of a thud filled the room, the walls shook, and the floor quaked. Violet and her team watched on as the thunderous sound grew louder. With each passing thud, the steel began to dent as panels fell from the roof and walls, crumbling to dust as they smashed upon the ground.

'We don't have much time. Aster, get these things up and running. They know we are here!' Violet said, rushing towards the lift.

The steel doors continued to bend as each earth-shattering boom echoed through the cavern. Then, reaching the centre of the room, Violet flicked her wrist, enabling her M-Tens. Then, aiming for the centre of the door swiftly followed by her team. She readied herself for battle.

'Whatever comes through that door, you stand your ground. Leave none alive! She said with a wink, activating her in-eye H.U.D.

Aster finished inputting the activation sequence. Suddenly the room lit up with over a thousand pairs of blue blinking lights facing the indented doors.

'It worked. All levels are active!'

'How many in total, Aster?' Violet said, keeping her eyes fixed on the dented door.

'Ten thousand, total!'

Just as the words left Aster's mouth, the doors to the room unhinged, the final strike sent them soaring across the room, colliding with the central command post. The sound of an all mighty crash ricocheted from the walls as showers of glass erupted across the room. The debris fell from the roof, crushing many of the A.I. Army who stood awaiting their orders.

Then, standing amid broken steel and cracked rock, a woman in black. Her dark dress was ever-changing as it glowed, reflecting the moon and stars. Her eyes shimmered like starlight in the night sky;

her dark maroon lips formed a twisted smile as she slowly walked into the room.

'The Executioner!' Violet said as she charged her weapons.

'So, this was what that pathetic old fool had planned!' Lunerios said as the dust cleared, her heels clicked upon the floor as she strolled into the room.

'Executioner! Under U.N.N. Law, you have—'

'Who are you to speak at me mortal! I will crush you, your little friends and the traitor!' Lunerios said, her face twisting into a maniacal glare. 'Kill them all, leave the traitor to me!' She said, motioning her arm towards Violet and her team.

'Open fire, leave none alive!' Violet shouted as she pressed the trigger on her M-ten. Neon green bullets sprayed across the room with a single click, each one erupting upon impact into a cloud of neon green smoke.

The army mobilised, producing various weapons, they proceeded to fire upon the intruders. The battle had begun!

'Major, what's the plan?' Aster shouted as he dropped from the roof, producing his U.N.N. standard adult rifle.

'Stick with me. We lead the Executioner away from the rest of the troops!' Violet said, continuing her fire.

Aster ran towards Violet, lunging through the air. He tackled her to the ground, just in time to avoid the pearl axe that swung above their heads. Violet looked up to see the face of Lunerios beamed down upon them.

'Ready for round two?' Violet said, bearing her teeth.

Lunerios swished her hair in defiance, pulling the axe into the air, then thrusting it upon the ground, narrowly missing them as they rolled across the floor.

'Head to the back. We need to drive her away from the rest of the army. Give them a chance to get out!' Violet said, rolling up onto her feet.

Running as fast as she had ever run before, Violet sprinted towards the main exit of the army base, dodging each bullet as they flew past, her eyes never once faltering from the planned route.

'Get set up. I will stall as much as possible!' Aster said, clapping his hands together.

Shrouding himself in a veil of dark energy, Aster slowly pulled his hands apart to reveal a sword, its black blade coated in a film of black flames. Lunerios moved towards Aster. He knew she would take the bait. Aster swung his sword towards the Executioner, the room filled with the sound of steel on steel as his black blade connected with her pure pear axe.

'Pathetic!' Lunerios said as she pushed with little force knocking Aster back towards the sidewall, 'I thought you were stronger than that, or are your past injuries catching up with you? Either way, you won't last me, traitor!' She said, holding out her hand aiming it towards Aster.

Tiny orbs of pure starlight began to drift towards Lunerioses hand, forming into the size of a basketball. Then slapping the ball with the back of her hand, she sent the light towards Violet.

'No!' Aster said, pushing off the ground, leaping towards the light, reaching it just before it struck Violet in the back. Aster struck the energy with his sword. It exploded upon contact, shattering the black blade and forcing Aster, Violet and the rest of the A.I. Army towards the wall.

'Foolish, to even think you stood a chance!' Lunerios said, swinging her axe from side to side, chopping down any who stood in her way.

Violet lay on the ground as she tried to gather her bearings. The sound of metal cutting through air rang in her ears. She knew the Executioner was close. Springing to her feet, she activated her M-tens, the guns began to glow, pulsating flashes of electric blue. She aimed directly at Lunerios. Opening fire, a sea of blue bullets showered the air striking the Executioner in the chest. Flashes of ultraviolet light burst from each round as plumes of blue dust sprayed across her body, freezing her in place.

'It's working!' Aster said in surprise as he watched Lunerios struggle her way through the wall of freezing powder.

'It's no good. She's breaking through!' Violet said, keeping up her assault.

'Leave her to me!'

'No! we take her down together.' Violet replied.

But it was too late. Producing a black blade, Aster leapt towards the God, slashing at her, his strike aimed directly at her neck.

'Fool!' Lunerios bellowed, flashing her starlight eyes at Aster as he moved swiftly in her direction.

Dropping his sword, it disappeared in a poof of black flames. Aster now found himself frozen to the spot. Unable to move even an eye, his gaze fixed upon Lunerios as she flexed her arms, shattering the frozen powder from her body. The remnants twinkled to the ground like glitter in passing light.

'I will show you the true meaning of repentance, Traitor!' she sneered through gritted teeth.

Violet sprung into action, producing a small black marble. She threw the object directly at the God, landing a perfect hit on her forehead. The marble shattered on impact as blue jell-glass began to form around her face. Loading her M-tens, Violet activated the new antimatter rounds.

With the barrels of her guns glowing a startling blood-red, she aimed at the distracted Lunerios, homing in on her chest.

'Wait, we don't have enough. We need the rest for Bellium!' Aster shouted as he willed his limbs from entropy.

The jell-glass finished forming around Lunerios, encasing her whole body, pinning her in place. Then, the room fell silent as the A.I. army purged the room of what remained of Lunerios's army.

Aster fell to the floor. The invisible force faded from his body.

'What do we do now?' Caspian said as he deactivated his weapon.

'No time for rest, I'm afraid. The transfer of command will go to Takeshi. Lead the army towards the East quadrant. Aster and I will meet you there!' Violet said, pulling Aster up off the ground.

'What about her!' Leo said, pointing his laser blade at the blue figure.

'Leave her to me!' Violet said, de-materialising her M-tens.

Takeshi and the Black-ops team left the room, making their way towards the now heavily scratched spreaders.

'What about the army?' Leo said, prodding Takeshi in the arm.

'They come with rockets, Leo!' Tak said, pointing at the now hovering army that had amassed behind him.

'What do we do about her?' Violet asked, turning back to face Aster as he regained his composure.

'As I said, leave her to me!' He replied, clapping his hands together.

He produced another black blade, writhed in black flames. He lunged at the encased Lunerios, slashing at the clear blue glass. The sword struck, shattering the hardened shell. In a moment, too quick for any eye to see, Aster felt the grip of resistance across his sword.

'How?'

There before him, Lunerios stood free from her bonds. Her hand gripped the black blade as a devilish smile crept across her stern yet soft face. Then, bearing her teeth, she pulled the sword down towards the ground, forcing Aster to bend at the knee.

'Even after all these years, you still think yourself mightier than a God!' She said as she slammed her foot into his chest. The single strike sent Aster flying back through the exit at the end of the room, through the walls on the other side straight into the labyrinth of corridors.

His body connected with the wall in an almighty crunch. He slid to the floor. His body lay still broken and bloodied.

Violet watched on in shock. It all happened so quickly and yet played out in slow motion.

'Mortal, I do not judge you for being taken in by this traitor, but I shall grant you this opportunity to worship me, as your kind so eagerly once did!' Lunerios said, her voice strong and bold, her eyes penetrating deep into Violet's soul.

'Piss off!' Violet said, throwing a small black grenade upon the ground. The shell exploded on impact, erupting into a cloud of vicious black smoke flooding the room and hiding her from sight.

'How the hell am I going to escape!' She said to herself as she ran towards the end of the corridor, frantically searching for Aster.

'Major.' Aster grumbled as he struggled to move.

'Aster, come one, we must get to the surface!' she said, pulling him up from the floor wrapping his arm around her shoulder.

'What about her!' He groaned, trying to find his feet.

'There's only one way to deal with her. We need to get to the God slayer Now!'

— CHAPTER TWENTY —

WAR HAS BEGUN!

Continue east towards the citadel. Remember, the aim is to draw out Bellium's forces!'

'And then what Tak? Wait around?'

'No, we are to follow the Major's instructions only, no winging it this time!' He said, accelerating as fast as he could.

The A.I. army advanced, following suit of the Balck-ops team as they slowly approached the Golden citadel. Suddenly a burst of silver arrows flew into the sky. Aiming towards them, they honed in on each person.

'Take cover!' Takeshi said, pulling down on the handles of his speeder, plunging it towards the ground.

As the speeder fell towards the floor, the arrows suddenly changed direction, darting down, following his exact movement. Then, he produced a violet marble with a flick of his wrist, throwing it in the air.

The marble shattered upon the tip of the closest arrow, bursting into a plume of purple smoke, disintegrating any projectile that came into contact.

'Leo, you were right. There truly is one for everything!' He said as the speeder landed, hovering slightly above the ground.

'Now is not the time. We have two units approaching. A mass has gathered in the air, another across the land, we will need to split up!' Caspian said, his holo screen flashing with multiple red dots.

'Tak, Zyair, Caspian, take the ground assault, Oren and I will deal with the air team!' He said, producing two automatic rifles from his nano-chips. 'Jackson, we will need an aerial map, transmit all data to my nano-chip.' Oren said, pulling his speeder high into the air.

'Sure thing! I am transmitting the data now!' Jax said via the comm-link. 'You have hostiles, incoming from the east.' Jax said as a map sprung to life on Oren's holo screen.

'Mobilise the army, prepare for the attack.' Caspian said, loading his standard-issue U.N.N rifle.

The clouds that hovered above the daylight sky began to break as a low humming sound filled the air, like wasps swarming in for the kill. Then, a dark shadow passed, descending quickly towards the ground.

The beating of wings against the air grew louder into a roar, each one a mighty thunderclap as they struck the ground with incredible force, causing the dirt and debris to plume into the air and space around them. As the cloud of dust began to dissipate, the army of the gods was left behind. There they stood in their gold armour. It glistened in the sun's low light as they remained perfectly still. Their golden eyes burned down upon the A.I. army as Takeshi moved towards the front of the line.

'They appear to be a scout troop. I am picking up more units. They are continuing their approach from the east!' Jax said, relaying information from the Hellbourne.

'Then let us not waste another second!' Takeshi said, flicking his wrist, producing the S.I.N. Automatic rifle.

The golden hoard stood tall flapping their wings in unison. The thunderous drums echoed across the field as they began their war cry. Ear-piercing screeches filled the air as they brandished their vampiric teeth. Then, gripping their gilded bows, they began to un-quiver their golden arrows.

'Their armour is thick, undoubtedly bulletproof. Headshots only, gentlemen!' Takeshi said as he analysed his opponents.

'Ermm guys, something else is on its way! It's big, and it's fast!' Jax said from the safety of the Hellbourne.

'The God of War!' Takeshi said, his eyes widening to the giant man flying towards them at breakneck speed.

Bellium landed upon the ground, the earth beneath him began to crumble, succumbing to the pressure of the giant man. His golden armour glinted with splendour, reflecting the light of Eco across the land. His skin set ablaze as he clenched his fists, smouldering in a heat unlike any other. Punching the ground, the land split in two, erupting into a sea of red flames that soared into the air.

Bellium threw a punch through the fire, his fist coming out the other side now containing a magnificent golden hammer. The long, slender handle stretched far past the giant as he stood one hundred feet in the air, his eyes beaming down upon them like two fireballs in the void.

'Erm Jax! We're gonna need some help here!' Leo said, pulling away from the soaring giant.

'Mortals! I shall give you all the final chance to worship me as you once did. Return to your lands and let this be the end of your petulance!' Bellium said as each word boomed through the air, rattling the trees and crumbling the half-standing buildings, 'Should you choose to face me in battle, I will grant you your wish of death. Now turn to me in repentance. And I shall greet you so!' he finished swinging the hammer above his head, red flames emitted from the hammer face as he proudly stood, waiting for a response.

'Bellium! God of War! We have been awaiting your arrival. These words that you speak are bold, to say the least! Were you not the one Aster slew, right here, on this planet, all those years ago!' Takeshi said, calmly stepping towards Bellium.

'Foolish words, from a foolish being, you humans never learned the virtue of silence, allow me to put you back in your place!' Bellium said with a sneer.

Swinging his hammer from the sky towards Takeshi, a rush of heat swept by as the hammer lowered towards him. Closing his eyes, Takeshi knew there was no time to move away. Standing perfectly still, he waited for the inevitable bone-crushing strike, but nothing happened. Instead, the heat passed as the world around him fell deathly quiet.

Then, daring to open his eyes, a white sheet of light filled the air above, rippling in waves like silk in the wind. He moved his arm up to touch the material. It was soft to the touch and as durable perma-steel. It encashed them in a dome, big enough to cover the entire A.I. army and Leo and Oren as they hovered in the air.

'How is this happening?' Tak asked, looking over to Caspian in shock.

'It appears to be some form of forcefield, look!' Caspian said, pointing towards the softly glowing light emitting from the armies fingertips.

'Fascinating, isn't it?' Caspian said as he watched the light pour into the sky.

With a grip of their hands, the light began to retract, gathering towards the hammer it formed directly underneath the golden weapon. Then, a sudden burst of white flames forced Bellium and his hammer back. The immense power from the explosion flung him into the air as he struggled to maintain his grip on the godly weapon.

'It's like an endothermic reaction followed by a full release of kinetic energy!' Caspian said in amusement.

'In English, please!' Leo said, swooping down towards the ground.

'The energy input is absorbed, then released back onto the provider!' Caspian said, rolling his eyes.

'Enough! Now is the time. Strike whilst the iron is hot!' Takeshi said, motioning his arm towards the army of the Gods.

The A.I. army raised their weapons of war, the barrels of each gun began to glow a distinct red, one they had seen before.

'Do you think....' Caspian said as he loaded his weapon of choice, a single handgun of polished copper.

'Undoubtedly, Caspian!' Takeshi said, flinging his arm down.

A shower of red bullets flew through the air. Then, glinting like rubies in a cave, they soared towards the invading army. Shattering on impact, they burst into clouds of red dust, covering the battlefield, shrouding the enemy from view. Takeshi raised his arm, halting the fire. The smoke slowly cleared in the windless lands, revealing the extent of their assault.

Half the army had fallen, but it was not enough. They were still gravely outmatched. The army of the Gods spun into action, pulling back on their golden bows; a volley of arrows flew across the sky, impaling hundreds of the defenders. Each golden arrow met its mark with deadly precision.

'Press forward!' Takeshi said, now running at pace towards his enemy.

'Hostiles detected, air-bound!' Jax said as the Hellbourne pulled into view.
As they manoeuvred through the sky, a rush of arrows flew at speed towards Leo and Oren.

'Pull up!' Leo shouted just as a single arrow pierced the shell of Oren's speeder.
Oren jumped from his bike, flipping back onto Leo's as he rushed past.

'Close!' Oren said, catching his breath.

'We need air support. Jax, a little help!' Leo barked as he continued to duck and weave the oncoming projectiles.

'Coming up!' Jax said, pressing multiple buttons on the Hellbourne.

The Hellbourne clunked into action. Its base mounted cannons rose as they rapidly searched for their targets. Then, locking on to a member of the golden army, it fired a single blue shot of pulsating energy. Veering to the side, then moving in multiple directions about the sky, it gave chase to the single target. Finally, it struck, freezing the winged man in the air, clipping his wings as he fell towards the ground.

'One down!'

'Yea and about a million more to go, surely that thing has more firepower than that!'

'Cut me some slack, Leo. I don't see you operating this thing!' He said in anger.

The single-shot alerted the rest of the winged army. Focusing their attention to the ship, they darted off, diverting all their power onto the Hellbourne.

'Yea, that'll do it!' Jax watched the entire army take to the sky, heading directly towards him and the ship.

'That's good Jax, keep them busy. Onward, we make for the Golden citadel!' Takeshi said, mounting his speeder and taking off, along with the rest of the A.I. army.

'Wait, Tak, what about the Hellbourne?' Caspian said, awaiting further orders.

'All Black-ops on defence, assist the Hellbourne. I will take the Citadel and flush out the rest of Bellium's army.'

'And what of Bellium?' Leo said, looking around for the God of War.

'I suspect gone to nurse his broken ego. He who presses the advantage will win the war!' Tak said, now too far for them to see.

'Enough of the talk! Can someone help me!' Jax said as the sound of sirens filled the comm-link.

A round of golden arrows flew through the sky, striking at the ship, denting and piercing the solid shell with each strike. Steel plates and shards of metal fell from the sky as the army of the Gods kept up with their relentless attack.

'Shoot them down, Jax!' Leo said as he returned fire, selectively picking off members of the army, with Oren assisting from the back.

Pressing multiple buttons on his control pad, the Hellbourne began to engage as each of its cannons turned to face the army of the Gods. A spray of blue lights shot from each cannon as they gunned down the attacking force.

'They're targeting the weapons!' Jax said, trying to captain the biggest ship he had ever flown.
One by one, the cannons disengaged as each golden arrow found its way into the connecting ports.

'I can't do this alone!' He said unable to focus on each target.

'You're not alone.'

'Serena, you're awake!' He said with the broadest smile he had ever made, forgetting the army for a brief moment.

'Let me help!' She said, pushing him out of the way. 'So that's how it works.' She placed her hand on the black screen in the centre of the ship console.

Her eyes turned black as she stood perfectly still. Seconds seemed to pass like hours as the darkness flowed into her veins, travelling around her body until suddenly she blinked. Then, the darkness faded into the black screen, leaving Serena at the helm, her breath short, her fingers tingling. Gripping the control pad, she looked over in Jax's direction.

'I need you to man the second bench. When I tell you to press the green and red sequence buttons, then slowly pull the lever at the base of the bench towards you. After that, I will do the rest!'

Jax nodded, then ran to the second bench listening intently for Serena's signal.

'Right, activate homing missiles, enable ION shift, transfer all power to central body defence, and prepare the radial orbital cannon!' She muttered as her hands grazed the surface of the control panel.

The Hellbourne sprung to life, firing hundreds of rockets from many secret compartments, each one landing hit onto its target. Then a burst of sound, like a balloon popping, filled the air as a soft blue forcefield surrounded the ship's main hull. Finally, a cranking sound ticked as the ship's base began to open, purging from its body a cannon unlike any found on Nova.

'Jax, now!' She said

Jax did as instructed, pressing the green, then the red button. The sound of the roaring engines cut out only to be replaced by a low, dull drone that grew louder with each passing second. Then, pulling the lever towards him as instructed, the ship began to rattle, the floor trembling beneath their feet.

'Slowly, Jax! Too fast, and the orbital cannon will auto-fire!' Serena said, her eyes focusing on the army below. Slowly the base cannon on the Hellbourne glowed a faint red light, growing in brightness with each pass of the main lever Jax controlled.

Bellium lay upon the ground. His ego bruised more than his body. The sound of the battle waged in the distance as he shrunk down to his usual size.

'My lord, you are required on the battlefield, the mortals, they have activated an orbital cannon, our forces will surely be depleted, should they be successful!' The General of Bellium's army said as he landed on the ground.

'Leave them to me, amass your soldiers with the rest at the citadel. There you shall await my orders!' He said, turning his attention to the ship.

Bellium knelt upon the ground. A raging wind swept around him, carrying dirt and debris clanked and shattered as it spun wildly into the air. Then with a powerful jump, Bellium leapt towards the ship.

'Stop him!' Takeshi shouted, pointing his arm in Bellium's direction.

The A.I. army changed its direction, flying now towards the God as he soared through the air. Loading the S.I.N rifle with the antimatter bullets, Takeshi aimed, locking onto the target, firmly pressing the trigger. Multiple rounds of red bullets struck Bellium, forcing him back towards the ground.

'Fool, you have landed a single hit, but it will be your last!' He said as he swung his golden hammer over his head, then forced it down. A wave of super-powered energy shattered the earth as it made its way towards Takeshi's position.

'MOVE MOVE MOVE!' he shouted, pushing up on the handles of his speeder, forcing himself into the air.

The burst of energy was too quick, shattering the bike and disintegrating thousands of the A.I. army. Takeshi fell to the ground. His limp body flapped in the air without slowing down.

'He's not responsive!' Caspian said, trying to move to intercept.

'I got him!' Leo said as Oren caught Takeshi, the speeder now dropping towards the ground.

'We're a little heavy, Commander!' Oren said as he gripped Takeshi tightly.

The speeder crashed into the ground, throwing Leo, Oren and Takeshi across the grassy knoll.

'We're fine!' Leo said, groaning in pain.

'Not for long, mortal!' Bellium said as he thrust his hammer towards them.

'Lever is down, now what?'

'Now we fire!' Serena said, pressing the red flashing button to the console's left.

The Hellbourne jolted, knocking both Serena and Jax to the floor. The room plunged into darkness as the blast shields slid across the windows. The cannon gathered the air around it, letting loose a single bolt of blood-red energy. It moved fast towards the God of War, encasing him in a prison of red walls, letting out a scream of intense pain, Bellium sunk to the floor as the ground began to crack and crater under the pressure of the supercharged weapon.

'Come in, Black-ops, this thing is radial, get the hell out of there!' Serena said via the comm-link

'We only have three speeders left!. Leo, take Tak, Oren, get on Zyair's!' Caspian said, pulling up in the handles he shot into the air, hastily followed by Zyair and Leo.

The ground split in multiple directions. Fire protruded from the gaps as the world plates started to shift, the red beam suddenly stopped, then in a burst, radial energy soared through the land of Eco, vaporising anything in its way. Dozens of army members turned to dust as they became trapped in the red waves of pulsating energy.

'Gentlemen, we have neutralised the army and the God of War. We are heading towards the citadel!' Serena said as the Hellbourne's rear thrusters kicked into action, moving them steadily across the sky.

The ground continued to smoke as plumes of lava shot from the gaps in the world. Then, finally, the ground began to dent and cave as the fire spread through what remained of the grassy knoll.

'Major, Commander Voss, do you copy!' Caspian said into the comm-link.

The line fell silent, not even a flicker as they hovered in the air, awaiting any sort of response.

'What's going on? you don't suppose…!' Leo pointed down towards the heavy flowing lava that now found its way into the aircraft hanger.

'No, I suspect something else entirely!'

— CHAPTER TWENTY-ONE —

INTO THE CAVES

Violet dropped another level, going deeper into the network of hidden tunnels. The sound of footsteps in the distance kept her on her toes.

'Aster! Come on. We have to keep moving!' She said, heading towards the end of the next tunnel towards another steel hatch.

'These health stims are not what they used to be!' he said, jabbing his arm with another glass canister. The vivid pink gel sank into his arm with a crisp hiss as he lagged behind, trying his best to keep up. 'You should have just let me shoot her. Then we wouldn't be in this mess!'

'She is just the distraction. Believe me! I've faced them before!'

Violet looked Aster up and down as he limped towards the hatch. Her eyes judged him more than they ever did.

'What?'

'Have you faced them before? I have to say, Aster, you're not faring too well against them!' She quipped, pulling the hatch revealing another dark tunnel.

'Out of practice!' he said, stabbing himself with another pink vial.

Violet rolled her eyes, waiting for Aster to climb down the hole. Then, following him in, she closed the hatch, locking it in place.

'Where are we? she asked, flicking her wrist to activate her nano bands. A small orange marble materialised in her hand. It began to levitate into the air, pulsating as it flew about the tunnel.

'The caves! My people built them long ago, for events such as this!' He said as the pink goo began to work its magic.

'I'm not getting a signal!'

'No, you won't. It's built that way!'

Violet and Aster continued to walk through the tunnels. They stretched on for what felt like miles, with no end in sight.

Violet suddenly paused, grabbing Aster by the scruff of his neck. She stood perfectly still.

'Do you feel that?'

'Yes, your grip is rather strong!' Aster said, slapping Violet's hands away from him.

'Shhh!' She said as she felt the wall of the deep dark tunnel.

The ground shook, rattling them from side to side. The walls began to rattle and shatter, with metal shards falling from the roof.

'Earthquakes are not a thing on Eco!' Aster said, steadying himself as the rumbling subsided.

'Then what was that?' Violet asked, pressing buttons on her nano band, turning it on, off, and then back on.

'What are you doing?'

'Trying to get some form of reading, something doesn't feel right.'

Just as the words left her mouth, the sound of footsteps crunching on the ground came vividly from behind them. Violet leant back just in time as a pearly white axe swung over her head. Aster met the axe with his black blade wreathed in fire. He held Lunerios in place as Violet produced her M-tens.

'This time, we do it my way!' she said; with a single click of her gun, the barrels began to glow red.

Lunerios pushed down on her axe, shattering Aster's blade. Then, swiping back up, she sliced the side of his face. Then, spinning on the spot, she back kicked him in the chest, sending him soaring down the tunnel out of eyesight.

'What a disappointment!' she said, looking over to Violet. 'Men, they can never be trusted. How about a round or two, just us girls!' she finished with a menacing smile.

Taking a shot, Violet sent a single red bullet towards Lunerios. Her shimmering axe deflected this. Crouching to the ground, Violet pounced towards the Executioner, gripping onto her head with her legs.

'Please!' Lunerios said, griping Violet by the head, pulling her off, holding her in the air, 'You thought that was going to work. I guess you're just as pathetic as he is!' she pulled her axe back. Then with a strike from the back of her axe, she sent Violet through the air deep into the tunnel.

Lunerios walked towards the dark of the tunnel. Her white pearl axe lit the way as she stopped at the foot of Aster's head.

'Any last words, traitor?' she said as she gripped his hair, lifting him and dangling him in the air.

'Say hi to Solus for me!' he said, a wide grin across his face.

Suddenly dropping from the roof, Violet landed on Lunerioses back, slapping a small purple disk between her shoulder blades. Lunerios grabbed Violet by the hair, throwing her to the ground.

Violet pressed a button on her nano-band, the purple disk began to glow, erupting into a cloud of purple dust. Flicking her wrist, she emptied her nano band of black marbles. Crushing them in her hand, she threw the dark blue dust at her enemy.

The dust began to intertwine with the violet cloud, solidifying and pulsating with purple energy each passing second. With a swing of her laser sword, she cut Aster from the Executioner's grip. Finally, she pressed the button on her nano-screen. The purple disk emitted a bolt of violet thunder, encasing Luneriose's body and freezing the blue powder instantly.

Then in one final flash, she was gone.

*

Bellium rose from the lava, his skin untouched by the heat and fire of the desolate hellscape surrounding him. What remained of the earth crumbled below his feet as he trudged through the Lava.

'Lunerios, my love. I no longer feel your presence. Tell me of your location!' He said out loud into the smoke-filled sky.

The faintest glimmer of moonlight shone through the daylight sky. Bellium was comforted by this sign. Then making a fist in the air, Bellium's golden hammer appeared in a burst of red flame. Gripping it firmly, he spun it once, forming a portal-like hole

Into The Caves

in the air next to him. The castle walls filled the transparent circle from both sides. Passing through the portal, he found himself inside the golden hall surrounded by many of his military Commander's, who searched frantically in and amongst the grandest positions of the once divine ruler, Xelios.

'Tacky!' Bellium said, holding a diamond crown as his army searched the castle for the elusive God slayer weapon.

'My lord, there is no possession this castle holds of a weapon you seek. Perhaps you are misguided!'

'I did not ask for your thoughts. Keep looking, Commander!' He said, turning his back on the army as he wandered down the halls of the golden citadel.

'One more thing, my lord. The mortals! They have made their way towards the kingdom. Our forces are weak. We have not the strength to stand up to another attack from their ship. What is thy bidding?'

'Send in the Seraphim, leave none alive!' He commanded, dismissing himself to venture alone into the labyrinth of caves below the city.

*

Caspian clung to the handles of the Eco speeder as though his life depended on it, flying high above the ground faster than he had ever travelled before the golden citadel lay ahead.

'Can anyone else see that!' Caspian said via the comm-link.

'You mean the thousands of soldiers. Yea, we were outnumbered from the start!' Zyair said as he pulled ahead of Caspian.

'Commander, what's the plan!' Oren asked as Leo held back, analysing the situation.

'I don't know. The tactician is still sleeping like a baby!' he said as he prodded Takeshi in the ribs, trying to wake him. 'Zyair, how many health stims did you give him?'

'Don't look at me. I have a doctorate in medical —'

'Now is not the time. We're coming up on the castle, Leo, your lead, we follow you!' Caspian said as they lowered towards the outpost outside the golden citadel.

The castle walls loomed over them as they landed at the main entrance. The Hellbourne continued making its way towards the army of the Gods. Slowly it descended, keeping its distance from the now grounded Black-ops team.

'Jax, we need you to keep the army busy, draw them away from the citadel, or at the very least clear a path!'

'Roger Commander, we are approaching the target now!' Jax said as he and Serena manned the control pads, preparing themselves for battle.

The ship began to bank in the air moving now to the crowd of gold armoured soldiers, who started to beat their wings, filling the air with the ominous sound of dull thuds. The cannons spun into action, firing blue energy bolts upon the winged soldiers, dispatching them one by one.

'Good work, keep up the fire! Now we move in.'

'Just one thing Leo!' Caspian said, pointing to the still unconscious Takeshi slumped over the speeder.

'Zyair, please tell me you have something a little stronger?'

'This is never a good idea; he needs rest. So I say we move him to the Hellbourne!'

'And I say he's fine. Wake him up!' Leo ordered, taking the rest of the group by surprise.

'Someone's been hanging out with the Major too long!' Zyair said, flicking his wrist. Then, selecting a small green vial, he stabbed it in Takeshi's chest, waking him up immediately. 'There, happy now?' Zyair said, moving back towards his speeder.

Takeshi sat up straight on the speeder. The whites of his eyes shrunk as his pupils swelled. Then, breathing rapidly, he turned to the rest of his team.

'How long was I out?'

'About five minutes. Commander Reed demanded your presence!' Zyair said coldly, re-mounting his speeder.

Into The Caves

'So, what's the plan?' Takeshi said, turning back to face Leo.

Before Leo could speak, a high-pitched whistle filled the air, the sound so harsh it brought tears to their eyes. The Black-ops team were blind to where the noise came from; the grey clouds were unblemished by anything but the Hellbourne. The lands around them remained barren and scarred.

'Caspian, what's that sound and what's making it?' Leo said, covering his ears as it grew in intensity.

'I have nothing, Commander! I can—!' just as Caspian began to explain, a bolt of pure white thunder stuck his speeder, flinging Caspian into the air with a powerful explosion.

The ground began to shake. Suddenly a crater appeared in the not too distant green land. Then another, until seven meteor-sized holes scattered across the land could be seen. The whistle had stopped. The dusty air began to clear, but the craters were empty. Not a rock or stone in sight.

'I don't like the look of this!' Leo said, picking Caspian back up off the ground.

'Agreed, we make for the golden citadel, now!' Oren said, turning towards the castle gates.

There, standing before them, were seven men. Each one stood ten feet tall, draped in pure white robes. Seeing their own faces in the glistening platinum armour, they knew something was different about these men. Their eyes were pure white, matching their long white hair. Each one carried a white bow with platinum arrows in their quiver.

'I think now might be the best time for diplomacy!' Oren said, taking a step towards the seven men. 'Gentleman, allow me to introduce myself and my colleagues.'

A platinum arrow landed at Oren's feet. To the human eye, the men had not moved. They were fast and dangerous.

'Oren, get back. There is no reasoning with them!' Leo said, flicking his wrists. He materialised his two fully automatic rifles, the barrels now glowing a strong neon blue, 'They only know war, so let's show them war!'

'No, wait!'

It was too late. Leo opened a barrage of bullets against the men in white. Each round burst on impact, releasing their fine blue powder, freezing them to the spot. The men in white barely moved as the glass shattered into tiny pieces of glitter.

'Bad move!' Oren said, running back towards his speeder.

One of the men in white clicked his finger. The clouds began to swirl in the sky, moulding into one solid formation. Suddenly bolts of pure white lightning struck the ground around them, lashing at their feet as they dodged out of the way. Each bolt landed a direct hit on the econian speeders, causing them to erupt in an explosion of black and red flames.

'I think it's time we left!' Caspian said, running as fast as he could from the blazing wreckage of the bikes.

'Agreed!' Leo said, turning on his heels to escape the men in white.

A gust of wind passed them by as the men in white appeared, now surrounding them from all angles. Slowly they inched forward, arming the white bows. They aimed at the Black-ops team.

Caspian flicked his wrist, emptying his nano-chip of violet marbles. Then, throwing them upon the ground, they burst into clouds of purple smoke, blocking them from view. Then, moving quickly, he produced a red marble. Launching it into the centre of the field, it burst in a radial blast of red laser, descending into the ground.

'Into the hole.' He said quietly through the comm-link as they each jumped into the hole.

Flicking his wrist again, he produced a white marble, pressing it into the dirt above him. It suddenly grew, taking on the look of the land around it until it patched the hole in the cave roof.

'That—!'

Caspian held his hand over Leo's mouth as they stood in silence, hidden in the murky depths of an unknown tunnel.

Some time passed as the sound of footsteps above began to wain. Caspian motioned his hand for the rest of the team to follow him as he made his way down the tunnel. Walking for what felt like miles, they made their way down the winding tunnel. Finally, they came about a hatch sunk into the ground. Its rusted metal door stuck out like a sore thumb amongst the almost black like dirt.

'Is it safe to talk now?' Leo whispered, looking around the room.

'With you, it's never safe! But I think our "friends" have finally gone!' Caspian scanned the hatch before lifting it up, revealing another deep, dark hole.

'Where do we think it leads?' Oren said, visually checking the hatch pressing down on the ladders.

'Who knows, but anywhere is better than here!' Leo said, gripping the metal ladder and beginning his descent.

'It's not often you'll hear me say it but, agreed!' Caspian said, following behind Leo as the others lined up in front of him.

Through the winding tunnels, they walked. Caspian flicked his wrist activating his nanochip, then deactivating it, only to reactivate it again.

'What are you doing?' Oren asked.

'I can't get a signal. Our comms are dead!'

'Then we keep moving!' Leo said as he led the troupe down the vast dark tunnel.

'Where to exactly?' Zyair asked, lagging behind.

'I don't know. I'll let you know when we find it!' Leo retorted, tripping over a ridge in the dirt.

Leaning down, he brushed the dirt away. The ridge felt solid, like a handle to another latch. Sure enough, he swept it away a copper hatch remained, gleaming like new.

'Interesting, surely this would be rusted by now?' Leo said, banging on the metal door.

'Yea, you would think!' Caspian said as he walked over to inspect.

Suddenly the hatch swung open. Two arms came swiftly from the dark, dragging Leo and Caspian into the hole.

'Commander!' Oren said, loading his U.N.N rifle and jumping down, followed by Takeshi and Zyair, their weapons locked and loaded.

'Freeze—Violet?'

— CHAPTER TWENTY-TWO —

THE GOD SLAYER

'That's Major to you, and drop the weapon!' Violet said, shaking her head.

'How did you end up here? Where are we? What's that? Why's Aster covered in bruises?' Leo said in quick succession.

'One at a time, Leo!' She said, walking into a dimly lit, circular room at the end of the shallow tunnel, 'We're here by sheer luck. Our fight with the Executioner brought us further into the tunnels than I hoped! We are in the deepest and most secure part, according to Aster, that is! This!' she pointed towards a small handgun that lay upon a podium in the centre of the circular room, 'Is the God slayer! And that is what happens when you go face to face with a God!' She finished pointing to Aster as he smiled, hoping to cover up the black and blue bruises from Lunerios's beating.

'It's not as bad as it looks!' Aster replied, stretching his head.

'So this is the God slayer?' Leo said as he walked around the relatively unassuming gun.

Aster took a step forwards, holding his arms out to the side as though to motion everyone to stand back.

'It is dormant. It has a single fire in it. After that, it needs to recharge.'

'And the recharge time is?' Caspian said with a flick of his wrist, producing his holo pad to begin making notes.

'Too long.' Aster said as he crouched to a squat, looming over the weapon.

'Useful, in real terms, Commander.' Caspian retorted. His shortness made Violet snicker.

'About one full cycle in Eco. Roughly three earth days!' Aster said, flashing a bold stare back at Caspian, now was not the time for attitude.

The small room that housed the weapon was covered from floor to ceiling in a thick black coating of a strong-smelling liquid. It clung to the air making it hard to breathe.

'What is this?' Leo said, wiping his finger down the wall

'After effects of the God slayer, discharge, effectively.'

'Gross!' Leo said, wiping his finger across his crimson armour smudging its pristine sheen.

'More concerning, is it toxic?' Zyair asked.

'Not to humans, but it can have a strong burning sensation to our godly friends!'
Aster placed his hands upon a stone slab at the podium's base that housed the handgun. As the slab began to glow, a holographic screen ran across the platform, displaying the sequence needed to activate the weapon.

'What does it say?' Violet asked as the econian words flashed about the screen.
Aster paused, reading the words carefully as though it was his first time.

'Aster?' Violet said, taking a step forward.

'I don't know!' He replied, turning back in hopeless bemusement.

'What do you mean you "don't know"!' Violet said, clenching her fists in a brief moment of anger.

'I never used the weapon the first time around. I was the distraction; it was fired by…'

'By who?' Violet said, unclenching her hands, watching as Aster's face changed from confused to sad, his face dropping in pain.

'Aster?' Violet said, placing her hand on his shoulder.

'Never mind who, long story short. I don't know how to activate it!' He said, stepping back into the corridor.

Violet followed him as he made his way towards the copper hatch.

'Aster, wait! Surely the instructions mean something to you?' Violet said.

'That's not how language works here on Eco! You are born with your voice. No others will ever understand your voice unless you allow them to. She kept hers a secret. Even from me!' he said, a pool of shallow tears formed within his Blood red eyes as he sunk to the floor.

'Who was she?' Violet asked, lowering herself towards the ground, sitting next to him, her back firmly placed against the wall.

'I guess you could call her my Serena of Echo', He said with a low chuckle as he fought back the tears.

'I see!' She said, the emotional conversation never was her strong suit, 'So she made the weapon?' Violet asked, shuffling her feet on the floor as she stretched her neck.

'Yes, and many other things, she is… was… will forever be known as the best scientist Eco ever had!'

'What happened?'

Aster looked up at the copper hatch as he began to recall the last day of Eco.

'In the final war of Eco, we were successful in our mission. We had managed to bring Bellium down. I lured him to the citadel as planned, and she fired the weapon. It couldn't have gone any smoother. Hindsight is a terrible mistress!' He said, turning to face Violet, 'We didn't account for Solus. Just when we thought victory was ours, he appeared before us in a flash of gold lightning, claiming the citadel as his own. The God slayer was no use. It needed time to recharge! Solus learnt quickly of our weapon, striking the tower with his golden spear. I can still hear her as she fell. Her scream still haunts me to this day!' Aster said, placing his head in his hands.

Violet looked into the room across the corridor, the gun still lying motionless upon the podium.

'So he missed the weapon!' She said, keeping her mind on the task at hand.

'To a fashion, yes. The gun shrinks after it fires. It's a defence mechanism. And now I can't use it. You know it's just like her. She always thought she was invincible.'

Violet remained by his side, knowing her words of comfort would fall flat should she try to understand, instead opting to stay still, hoping her presence was enough.

*

Leo kicked the slab, the holo-screen flickered, temporarily disconnecting before returning to life.

'What the hell do you think you're doing?' Caspian said, grabbing Leo forcing him back away from the weapon.

'Percussive maintenance!' Leo said, flinging his arms into the air

'Can both of you stop? The last thing we need is to be arguing amongst ourselves and potentially setting this thing off. From what the Commander described, we only have a single shot or three days waiting. We don't have that much time!' Oren said, positioning himself between Caspian and Leo.

'In my history of weapons tech, there is nothing that a light tap or jolt can't fix.' Leo said in defence.

'Right, but this is alien, and you're an idiot!' Caspian retorted.

'Enough!' Takeshi boomed. His unusual outburst stunned the crowded room. 'The Commander and the Major will be back momentarily. This behaviour is not what she expects from her "elites"!' He said, his stern words casting a blanket of shame amongst each soldier.

'Does anyone have any suggestions?' Zyair said, breaking the cold silence.

'I will work on the weapon with the aid of Zyair.' Leo said, dropping his usual mischievous voice.

'No, how about a more senior member of the team, Oren?' Caspian said

'Leo is right. At this moment, none of us matches up to his weapons knowledge!' Oren replied

Leo pushed past Caspian as he made his way towards the God slayer. With the weapon still motionless, he glared over it, his eyes penetrating every aspect of its existence.

An ear-piercing alarm sounded as lights built into the floor lit up the room and the surrounding corridors. All eyes turned towards Caspian as he fumbled with his holo-pad

'We have visitors!'

As he finished his words, Violet and Aster burst into the room.

'Catch me up!' she said in a rush.

'Intruders! Unknown location. Leo will work on the weapon, Zyair will remain on guard. Major, we are at your disposal!'

'Good, then it's just us five, remain close, we will draw them out to the battlefield. Leo, on my mark, be ready with that cannon!' she said, rushing from the room.

'We need to get to the surface!' Violet said as she gripped the stairs to the only evacuation tunnel.

'No! I have a better idea!' Aster said with a wicked smile, 'We lure them further down. If we're lucky, there may just be a way to take out the whole army.'

Just as Aster finished his sentence, a platinum arrow grazed his face, implanting itself on the wall next to where he stood. 'It's not the army. Quick run!' he said, taking off down the empty corridor, followed by Violet and the rest of the Black-ops team.

'What is it then?' Violet asked, catching up to Aster.

'The Seraphim. Elite warriors! Solus's personal bodyguards!'

'So tough then?'

'I haven't met anyone yet who has managed to kill one!' Aster finished his breath getting short.

A flurry of arrows whistled down the tunnel, penetrating the ground close to their feet as they continued to run, evading the Seraphim as long as they could. The tunnel opened to a vast expanse, housing a large metal cylinder in the centre of the room.

'What is that?' Oren asked, pointing towards the rusted canister that stood thousands of feet tall.

'Fuel supply, it's used to power all of Eco!' Aster said as they approached the tunnel cliff.

'There, speeders!' Caspian said as he pointed down to the bottom level.

'That's over twenty floors down!' Violet said, turning back to see the Seraphim hot on their heels. 'Too late! Jump!' She shouted as they leapt from the edge, freefalling towards the ground.

Flicking her wrist, she produced a neon green marble, then threw it as hard as towards the ground. It shattered, exploding onto a sea of neon green foam. In unison, they landed upon the soft green cushion.

'To the bikes, Major, follow my lead!' Aster said as the sound of beating wings thundered in the cavern.

Mounting the speeders, they ascended with lightning-fast speed.

'Prepare for attack!' Takeshi said, materialising his S.I.N. Automatic rifle.

'No, Your guns are of no use here!' Aster said, pulling away from everyone else as he veered towards the fuel tank. 'Split up, keep them off me!' He said, pushing down on the handlebars.

A jet of blue flame burst from the bike's back, sending Aster directly towards the fuel cell.

The Seraphim followed the Black-ops just as Aster intended. Violet pushed to the head of her team, guiding them on her route, ducking and weaving past the onslaught of platinum arrows that soared through the air.

'Gentlemen, initiate crash sequence Alpha!' She said, turning sharply back towards the ground.

'Aww crap!'

'Not again, last time I came this close to dying!'

'Major, are you sure? What about Aster?'

'My orders are clear, Gentlemen.' She said, pressing down on the handles of her speeder.

The bike emitted a blast of blue flames as she hurtled towards the ground, her team following suit. Then, pulling up on the handles, the speeder stopped before it hit the ground. Flipping back on itself in a wide circular motion, Violet simultaneously produced a handful of maroon marbles, scattering them around the room. Oren followed suit, mimicking Violet's movements, scattering the same maroon marbles.

'Incoming!' Caspian said as he leapt from his speeder, landing on the back of Violet's.

'Tak now!' Violet shouted as the Seraphim darted under her, unable to slow down as they landed upon the ground.

'Roger!'

With a single shot to the engine of the falling speeder, it exploded in a ball of blue flames. Crashing into the ground, it stuck one of the marbles shattering it into a cloud of maroon dust. Each marble exploded in a chain reaction engulfing the floor in a plume of maroon dust that encased the Seraphim as they landed upon the ground.

Then beating their wings, the dust rose into the air, becoming thicker as it seeped into their feathers, until finally what was glorious white wings were now a muddy wine colour, dripping in maroon spores.

'Aster now!' Violet said, pushing the speeder as fast as possible towards the roof.

Aster appeared from being the rusty container. A trail of amber liquid poured from the primary holding cell as it wound its way across the room.

'She gonna blow!' Aster said, pushing his speeder as fast as he could.

The amber liquid poured across the floor, making its way to the flaming wreckage that was the econian speeder; as the slightest drop touched the flame, the liquid set ablaze in a stream of vivid green fire. The flames danced across the floor as they rushed towards the primary fuel cell.

'Major, aim for the lowest smoke vent. It's a direct passage out!' Aster shouted as he raced to catch up.

Violet flicked her wrist, producing a single M-ten, its barrel began to glow green. Then firing round after round of explosive charges at the vent, the metal frames began to collapse as the daylight sky pierced the darkened room. Finally, the sound of a shrill scream filled the air as the fuel canister began to dent gradually towards the ground.

'Major, it will destruct in seconds!' Caspian said, his knuckles turning a stark shade of white as he clung for dear life to the back of the speeder.

Violet remained quiet, biting her bottom lip as the speeder rushed towards the gap. Suddenly the canister erupted, filling the room with a burst of green flame, with the force of the explosion so intense it ricocheted across the room, thrusting the speeders out of the one person gap. The fire engulfed the room, melting the metal and causing the ground to rumble and crack.

'Major, the speeders are offline!' Oren said as he began to free fall, the inactive bike now silent as the blue lights cut out.

'And there will be no ground to stop us!' Takeshi said as the earth collapsed, leaving deep dark holes where the grassland once was.

'Come on, you piece of junk!' Aster said, punching the bike.
The speeder jutted, freezing in the air, the blue lights flickering on and off until suddenly it righted itself, hovering gently.

'Try them again!' He shouted, watching as the bikes slowly levelled off, just hovering above the hotels in the ground.

'That was close!' Oren said, wiping the sweat from his brow.

'Where are we?' Takeshi said, looking around the smouldering landscape.

'About ten miles from the citadel.'

'You said the weapon was close to the Capital?' Violet said, trying to gather her bearings.

'Yes, and it is, speaking of which.' Aster flicked his wrist, displaying his holo-screen. 'Gents, can you hear us?'

'Loud and clear, Commander!'

'Any luck on the God slayer?'

'Well, that's a question of two halves, you see….'

'In short, Leo!' Violet said, interjecting.

'No, not at all!' He replied

'Keep working on it! We need it to be operational ASAP!' Aster said, disconnecting his holo-screen.

'Fine!' Violet said, raising the bike into the air. 'There land towards that central tower, just a few miles from the citadel!' she pointed towards the ground.

The speeders flew through the air towards the tallest tower nearest the citadel. As they left the destruction of the tunnels behind, they focused on their next task; bringing down the God of War.

'Violet?'

'Serena!'

'Thank god, we've been comm-linking for so long. Where did you go?'

'We were… distracted. Where are you?'

'About one mile out from the golden citadel, we need back up. The Hellbourne has taken a lot of damage!'

Violet looked over at Takeshi, nodding her head.

'I'm sending Tak!' She replied, staying on route.

'Major, do you need us to go too?'

'No, there is still an army outside the castle walls. I can't afford to send you all!'

Approaching the tower, Takeshi veered off, speeding towards the castle fields to assist the Hellbourne.

'There!' Violet said, lowering her speeder towards the ground. As she approached, the sound of wings beating against the air gradually grew louder the closer they got.

'Looks like there's more of them than we thought!' Aster said as the golden army stood perfectly still upon the tower grounds.

Violet blinked, activating her in eye H.U.D, pressing firmly on the speeder handle, a shot of blue flames erupted, pushing her at high speed towards her enemy.

'Prepare for combat!'

— CHAPTER TWENTY-THREE —

FLEE!

Hordes of golden clad soldiers stood between Violet and the gates to the citadel.

'Increase speed. We head straight down the centre, do not stop till you reach the gate!' Violet said, pushing down the handles of the speeder.

Then, she activated her nano-bands, flicking her wrist, producing a single M-ten. The barrel began to glow a bright yellow, buzzing and hissing as she aimed into the crowd. Finally, she pressed firmly on the trigger and sent a barrage of yellow bullets through the air. The shot soared across the field, landing a strike onto the golden chest plate of the closest cadet. The shell erupted into a burst of lightning, jolting from soldier to soldier. Violet continued her fire as she pulled the speeder closer to the ground. Then, letting go of the handles, she produced her second gun, firing relentlessly into the crowd as the bike smashed its way through person by person.

Approaching the gate, she put one foot on the bike seat, then lunging back, she flipped into the air. Switching rounds, the barrels of her guns shifted to neon green. Opening fire, she sent a barrage of bullets at her enemies, killing all in a circular area where she proceeded to land. The in eye H.U.D began to glow red. The crosshairs darted back and forth as it registered each advancing enemy. Violet flicked her guns. The barrels shifted to a blazing amber, shooting bullet after bullet, each meeting its mark as she landed multiple perfect headshots.

'Incoming!' Aster said, jumping from his speeder, landing into the crowd of soldiers gathering behind Violet.

'Hold them back! I will access the gates!' Violet said as Oren and Caspian dismounted their bikes, opening fire with the newly materialised N-ten handheld railguns.

Walking briskly towards the gates, Violet produced a single block of nano-bots, attaching it to the black screen next to the entrance. A reel of numbers started to count down in her H.U.D.

'Three minutes!' Violet scoffed, shaking her head in disgust, 'Continue your fire!' she shouted, raising her weapons to the oncoming army.

As the timer counted down in Violet's eye, she and the rest of her Black-ops team held back the encroaching army of the Gods. A sea of bullets showed through the air as each soldier fell to the ground, their bullets striking with precise aim. Slowly they backed towards the gate, anxiously waiting for them to open.

'Do you think he knows we're here?' Caspian shouted over the sound of his railgun screeching as it continued to fire upon his targets relentlessly.

'Undoubtedly!' Violet said, scrunching her face in anger.

The gates clicked as the nano lens switched from red to green.

'The gates are opening. Fall back!' Violet said, lowering her weapons as she took off running into the darkened halls.

'Go, I'll hold them back!' Oren said, flicking his wrist to activate his nano-chip.

He produced two chrome poles and stabbed them into the ground, securing them in place. Then, he materialised a small drone, flinging it into the air. It began firing down a rain of bullets to any soldier who got too close. Suddenly a burst of red lasers emitted from the poles slicing down the golden hoard as Oren continued to fire his handheld railgun.

'Push forward!' Aster yelled as he ran down the corridor, entering a grand oval room.

'I've been here before!' Violet said as she tried to make out tapestries' scattered around the walls.

'Yea, you have.' Aster said, clapping his hands together once. The room sparked to life as the lights anchored to the walls came to life in a soft, warm glow. The tapestries dotted around the walls displayed the history of Eco, how they rose to affluence and their treaty with the Gods.

'It's the same room, the one you showed me.' Violet said, looking over to Aster as he finished taking in the familiar scent of rose and lavender that drifted about the air in the grand golden room.

A burst of air rushed down from the ceiling of the grand hall. A flash of white shot past them as seven winged men landed upon the ground.

'Congratulations on making it this far. You will go no. Further, one man said as he lifted off his platinum helmet.

'The Seraphim!' Aster said, clapping his hands together, producing his sword of black flames.

'Violet, go. We will hold them off!' Caspian said as he loaded his standard-issue assault rifle aiming at the Seraphim.

'That is something we cannot allow you to do!' The Seraphim said in unison, each one producing a white bow, they loaded their platinum arrows.

Violet flicked her wrist, producing a violet marble, throwing at the feet of the Seraphim. It exploded upon impact into a cloud of purple dust enshrouding the entire room.

Violet ran down the connecting corridor, leaving the sound of gunfire and metal on metal behind her.

A golden light extruded from the sole room at the end of the dimly lit hallway. Violet shrugged as she paused mid corridor. Then, turning back in the direction of the noise, she began to step forward.

'No!' she said to herself, looking back down the opposite end of the corridor towards the ominous glowing light. 'Let's finish this!'

Her steps started small as she activated her nano-lens, the crosshairs scanning the corridor for any potential threats. Then, widening her pace, she rotated her shoulders, loosening her back and cracking her neck. Her footsteps moved to a speed walk that broke out into a jog, then to a run. Now sprinting towards the light, Violet flicked her wrist, activating her nano bands, producing her M-tens. The barrels glowed their deadly red glow as the H.U.D changed from green to red, locking on its target.

'That's quite the drop!' She said to herself as she ran towards the ramp at the end of the corridor.

Then lunging towards the floor, she skids across the ground, sliding down the ramp at full speed. The slide ended with an upward flick launching Violet into the air. Flipping backwards, her eyes locked onto the white-haired man who stood nearly ten feet tall in the centre of the room, his golden hammer in hand, ready to attack.

Violet launched a barrage of red bullets from her guns directly at her target, piercing the gold armour and burrowing their way into his flesh.

Now plummeting towards the floor, her boots glowed a soft blue as she slammed into the ground, absorbing the shock of impact. Righting herself, she continued her barrage, snake winding across the room. Each bullet knocked the God back, his blood splattering across the ground as he moved his arms up to protect his face. Then, as quickly as her shots began, the bullets ran out. Her guns stopped firing as the red glow faded.

'Shit!' she said, flicking her guns, the barrels of her M-tens now glowing with vivid green light.

Not missing a beat, she opened fire again. Each shell exploded upon contact producing clouds of green smoke. Bellium dropped to his knees, the explosions disorientating him as he bled out on the floor.

Violet snapped her guns back, dematerialising them to reform the S.I.N auto rifle. She held onto the trigger. The barrel began to glow brighter with each passing second until it reached its full charge. Taking the shot, she sent a fully charged round at Belliums exposed head. The shockwave knocked him back onto the floor, his body twitching as a river of crimson red blood pooled around him. Violet paused, refusing to lower her weapons. Instead, she took slow and calculated steps towards her enemy.

'Don't get too close!' Aster shouted, running into the room.

Bellium rose into the air, springing from the ground; he swung his hammer. The edge of the hammerhead caught Violet off guard, shattering the S.I.N rifle and knocking her back across the room, then flipping in mid-air; she landed on her knees, unable to stand as the air escaped her body.

'Major!' Aster shouted.

Violet motioned her arm to indicate she was ok as she gasped for air clutching at her chest.

Aster sprang forwards, thrusting his blade of flames towards the God of War. Bellium's eyes flashed their blazing red fire as he swung his hammer at Aster, catching him off guard. The hammer connected with Aster's body. A thunderclap shattered from the sky, striking at the roof of the golden castle. Breaking the stone roof as gaps began to form, the thunder ignited the hammer into a fireball of red flames.

First, there was a crunch, then came a scream as Aster flew across the room, slamming into the wall above the second level. The ringing sound of a rail gun warming up began to whistle, the clang of a heavy weapon rooting to the ground ricocheted off the walls as Caspian loaded the anti-matter bullets into the barrel.

'Eat this!' Caspian said as he slammed the auto-lock on the side of his weapon.

A barrage of red bullets shot from the barrel like a sea of fire spraying across the room. Stumbling back, Bellium dropped his hammer, covering his face as he tripped under the onslaught of bullets.

'Major!' Caspian shouted.

'I'm fine. Get Aster!' She said, finally able to stand.

'Pathetic, if this is all you have, you never stood a chance!' Bellium said, lifting himself off the floor.

Floating into the air, he began to glow a magnificent golden aura as his wounds healed, his body ejecting the bullets as they rattled against the floor. Finally, the golden tear of Solus evaporated in a cloud of sparkling dust. Bellium opened his hand, the hammer swiftly left the ground, finding its way into his grasp. Then pulling his arm back, he thrust the hammer down towards Caspian, crushing the railgun as it struck the ledge.

'Go!' Violet shouted to a stunned Caspian, 'Get Aster and go!' She continued, rousing him from his panic-stricken state, 'Leo, hurry up, we don't have much time!' Violet said, preparing for Bellium's next attack.

'Yep, no worries. We are in full swing, yeah, baby. Just you wait and see, boy have we got a surprise for you! I'm preparing the finishing touches, and then we are away. So then, on my mark, get out of there!' Leo said as he circled the handgun scratching his chin.

'We're not ready, are we?' Zyair said, his arms folded as he leant up against the wall

'No... not at all.' Leo said, flashing a crooked smile at his comrade.

Leo bent down to inspect the gun. His prying eyes wandered over each nook and cranny as he made his final assessment.

'I have it. This thing is charged. It just needs a host to direct the charge. This button here is the activation button!'

As Leo clicked the button on the side of the display stand, the gun began to vibrate as it slowly grew in size.

'Ok, what's happening?' Zayair said, standing up straight, uncrossing his arms.

'It is activating!' Leo replied, staring at the gun, his mouth wide open as he started jumping up and down on the spot.

Small panels began to form from the base of the weapon stand. Then, they developed a metal shell that encapsulated the gun. Next, small steel balls flew up into the air spinning around the gun rapidly as they melted into a solid framework suspending the weapon from its base.

The roof began to jitter as the walls creaked. Years of slow decay fell from the ceiling as the hidden doors slowly opened, allowing the warmth of the orange sun to beam down upon the secret hole. As the platform lifted from the ground, the creaking steel pipes chimed as the God slayer continued to grow in size. The metal panels extended out, forming a barrel. Two small droids emerged from the holo pad of the display stand. Then latching themselves onto the back of the weapon, they began producing a glowing blue cage, big enough for one person to stand in.

'There we are, Easier than I thought!' Leo walked around the small ledge to get to the other side.

'Are you sure you know what you're doing, Leo? Even Aster didn't know how....'

'Look, the Commander is great and all but, let's face it, Zyair, he's not me!' Leo said, thrusting his thumbs back, signalling himself as he stepped inside the holo tube.

The gun had finished its growth sequence, now resembling an old fashioned sea cannon, and there it remained suspended many miles in the air, slowly pulsating with flashes of red lights. Suddenly a crack in the ground began to form. Running across the land, it reached the God slayer cannon.

'The planet has become unstable, Leo, now!'

A small black pad opened from the centre of the holo tube. Leo removed his glove, flexing his hand, ready to fire the weapon.

'Major! You may begin your evacu—' Leo placed his hand on the pad. A jolt of black thunder swarmed the cannon, running through the mechanics like black dye in a vein. It travelled towards the hand pad, swarming over his skin, snapping at his hand, burning his pale skin, turning it jet black. Steam vented from every pore as the black energy travelled up his body towards his face as they encapsulated his eyes.

Suddenly two bolts of electricity shot from each eye, the power of the God slayer was too much to control.

Leo loosened his grip just as the lightning struck him in the chest, jettisoning him from the platform down towards the ground below.

'LEO!' Zyair shouted, watching helplessly, as Leo struck the rocks at the tower's base.
The sound of a hard crack filled the air as the crimson warrior lay motionless upon the ground.

'Leo, update now!' the voice of Violet went unanswered as she shouted through the comm-link, the sounds of metal on stone crashed in the background.

Zyair pulled himself together; gathering as much courage as he could muster, he stepped into the control bay. There he looked at the control panel. He scanned the controls with a crack of his neck, hoping to make sense of the Econian words that flashed about the screen.

'There are too many, Major. We have pulled back; the Hellbourne has taken too much damage. We need to leave now!' Takeshi said from aboard the ship.

'This is it!' Zyair said, continuously flexing his hand.

Slowly he reached down, placing his hand gently against the black screen. The panel gripped him like an animal tugging at its prey.

A stream of black liquid seeped through his skin into his veins, flowing through his body. The black liquid made its way towards Zyair's face, dying his eyes and hair jet black. Slowly it enveloped him until he was nothing but a pitch-black figure.

The cannon emitted streams of purple light as lightning bolts struck the tower, sending rocks tumbling towards the ground. The purple energy began to centrifuge around the gun, drawing in the daylight; the clouds grew dark as the sun faded. The cannon was finally reaching its full power. The ground began to shake as patches of grass collapsed into the vast tunnels below.

The mountains let out an ear-piercing screech as the buildings tumbled. Then, they slowly collapsed, releasing plumes of dust into the darkening air.

The black energy slowly faded from Zyair as the canon suddenly fell silent. All energy stopped emitting from its core as it seemed to power down.

Then, a bolt of jet black energy shot from the cannon in a sudden burst. Its deafening boom echoed across the planet. The dark projectile sped towards the golden citadel, destroying anything in its path. Finally, the tower began to crumble. As the base turned to dust, Zyair snapped out of his trance.

'Major, missile on its way, proceed with evacuation!' Zyair said, pressing multiple buttons on the control pad, 'Come on, how do you deactivate this thing?'

The God slayer began to flake as bits of metal fell from the cannon, the barrel slowly turned to dust, dissipating in the wind.

'NO! NO! NO! Come on!' Zyair said as he slammed his fists onto the cannon shattering the screen. The gun fell apart. Each piece turned to dust in Zyairs hands as he frantically grabbed at the disassembled weapon, 'Leo!' He said to himself in a moment of clarity. 'Hold on, Leo!' He said, scaling the tower as he lowered himself as fast as possible towards the rocks below the building.

Grabbing Leo, he set off towards the citadel, pressing his emergency call button, hoping someone would answer his call.

*

Violet flipped back, avoiding the deadly swings of Belliums hammer. Suddenly it landed a strike next to her, causing the wall to crumble and collapse. With another swing of his hammer, Violet pushed herself away from the wall flipping over the jewel-encrusted weapon.

With a flick of her wrists, she activated her M-tens. The barrels began to glow pink, then a sea of pink bullets flew towards the God of War, each shell exploding upon impact into clouds of smoke. Bellium raised his hammer into the air, a sudden gust of wind blew the smoke from the room. Then raising his hand in a circular motion, balls of pure fire formed in the air floating by his side.

'Your tricks fail to impress me, be at peace, purple warrior, for you have fought gallantly, though, it shall be known in vain!' he said, motioning his hand forward, releasing the balls of fire in Violet's direction.

'Major, missile on its way, proceed with evacuation!' Came through the comm-link

'Time to go!' Violet said, turning on heels and breaking for the stone stairwell. 'Caspian, have you secured Aster?' she said, running up the stairs, the balls of fire striking at the ground, the flames whipping at her feet.

'Yes, I'm at the rendezvous point with Oren. We are on our way to pick up Zyair and Leo.

Bellium swung his hammer in the air, thrusting it with tremendous force against the walls. The bricks crumbled as he turned the hammer at Violet, destroying the support column. Unphased by the commotion, Violet continued to run, making her way towards the entrance corridor.

A blue pulse emitted from her nano-band as she ran towards the end of the hall. Seconds later, the econian speeder appeared by her side. The castle's roof began to fall as the floor rumbled and shook, the stones fell upon the ground exploding into dust and rubble. The walls started to fall as the citadel cracked and shifted, the one proud hall of the king now a desolate wasteland.

Violet mounted the speeder. Then with a firm kick, she shot into the air. Bellium, seeing their escape, spun his hammer aiming directly for the Major. But, it was too late! The black missile stuck Bellium in the chest, passing into his body. It encased him in a sheen of black energy. Bellium stumbled, falling back; his screams of pain filled the air as he dropped to his knees. The dark energy ripped at his skin, melting it away like ice cream on a hot summer's day. Taking his last breath, Bellium let out an earth-shattering scream. It ripped apart the land as eruptions of lava sprayed from between the cracks in the decaying landscape. Bellium fell silent as the dark energy dissipated, leaving behind nothing but Belliums golden hammer.

'We have Zyair and Leo!'

'Good, assemble at the Hellbourne!' Violet said, pushing the speeder to its limits.

'Incoming, we have company!'

The golden army began to beat their wings, now led by the seven Seraphim. Violet pulled her speeder to the side, preparing to intercept the hostiles. But, just as she pressed the handle on her speeder, Aster flew in front, blocking her attack.

'What are you doing?'

'Forgive me, Major, but now is not the time! Jax, initiate the orbital strike!', he said via the comm-link

'Are you sure? Diverting that much power to the orbital cannon again will drain the Hellbourne of its power. We won't have enough fuel to get back home!' Jax said, anxiously awaiting Aster's next order.

'Better stuck in space than dead on Eco, now punch it!' He said

'Roger, that Commander!' he said as he initiated the sequence.

The turrets on the ship aimed towards the ground, focusing on what remained of the army of the Gods. Finally, the base of the Hellbourne began to open. A cannon almost as long as the ship itself steadily locked itself in place. Then turrets began to glow, emitting a yellow light stronger than the sun. The artillery began to charge as Violet and her Black-ops team made their way towards the ship.

'Charging complete. Fire in Three - Two - One!' Jax said as the Hellbourne began to fire a barrage of yellow lasers from each turret, decimating the land below and tearing the planet to shreds.

— CHAPTER TWENTY-FOUR —

THE WRATH OF GOD'S

Violet sped towards the Hellbourne, her Black-ops team in quick pursuit. Then weaving through the blasts of yellow plasma, their speeders pushed to the max, daring not to look back at the mass destruction below.

'Jax, we're coming in hot!' Violet said as they moved closer to the Hellbourne.

'Landing bay is open, Major, ready when you are!' Jax replied.

The Black-ops team flew closer to the ship, the Seraphim still close on their heels, the orbital strike picking them off one by one.

'Brace yourselves!' Violet said, approaching the entrance doors.

With a crash, they hit the ground hard. The speeders lights cut out as each person flew from their vehicle, hitting the steel walls in the process.

'Close the doors.' Violet groaned as she pulled herself up from the floor, flicking her wrists to produce her M-tens.

Aiming, she opened fire upon the Seraphim. A sea of green bullets shot from her M-tens, the explosive rounds stunting the army from getting closer to the doors as they slowly retracted, sealing the Black-ops inside the Hellbourne.

'Major! A little help!' Zyair said as he pulled Leo from under the speeder.

'What happened?'

'He went to activate the God slayer, but something went wrong! I don't know what happened!' Zyair said as he laid Leo on the floor.

Violet bent down to look over her fallen comrade, pressing her fingers to his neck. She looked at Zyair as she counted.

'There is a pulse, but it's slow! Quickly now, we need to get him to the med bays, Caspian bring Aster!' she said as she grabbed Leo by the legs pulling him up with the assistance of Zyair.

*

Solus sat upon his crystal throne, the starlight reflecting in its many facets as it shimmered across the ground.

'My lord, it is as predicted! I feel a great disturbance on Eco. The lands are calling me out. I have not the answers.'

'My dear Paerminx, your mind is deceiving you, once again you speak of foul lands whispering in your ears, and yet the stars continue to shine, have faith, my dear, for as long as the fire of creation burns within you, you are safe, as are all my children!'

The moon suddenly appeared in the night's sky; its dim light shone blissfully upon the ground.

'The moon, she shines a dull light. Does this not bring with it signs of a dark future!'

'My dear, your power is far beyond that of a soothsayer, do not act like one. Your vision is of truth, but the whole story is yet to be told. Lunerios, my most precious start, will inform us of what she knows. Let that bring you comfort.' Solus said, rising from his throne.

A flash of white light shimmered across the sky. Suddenly, Lunerios plunged towards the ground, her body connecting with the crystal throne.

The throne shattered into a thousand pieces, exploding into a cloud of sparkling dust as Lunerios landed upon the soft grassy plain. Blood splattered across the field as she tumbled towards the cliff.

'Lunerios, speak of your ills, for we are waiting!' Parminx said with much disdain as she loomed over the Goddess of the moon and stars.

'I have been sent back by her witchery once more, the traitor's sidekick!' Lunerios spoke as she grasped at her side, coughing blood as she slowly pulled herself up from the lush green grass.

'Yet again, Lunerios, you have failed to stop a simple mortal from uprising against the Gods. So must I stand in your place once more and deliver true justice?' Parminx said with a bitter kick.

'Enough, my children. Tell me, Lunerios, who is this "Witch" you speak off?'

'The purple-eyed warrior, she holds a magic I have yet to understand, but I swear to you, my lord, I will make her pay for her insolence!' Lunerios said, her words burning the air as she spoke.

'I have no doubt, my most vengeful daughter. But for now, we must turn our attention to Bellium and his conquest.' Solus said, waving his hands in a circular motion in front of him.

A small glass orb floated in the air. Slowly it grew in size until it resembled that of a beach ball. It was of pure white, the centre reflecting the image of Solus.

'Show me the God of War and his conquests!' Solus said, waving his hand above the floating ball. The image of Bellium slowly came into focus.

'As you can see, my dear Parminx. His conquest shall come swiftly.'

Just as Solus finished his words, the orb turned black. Bolts of black lightning shot from the ball, striking at each of the Gods, landing a hit directly on Solus's chest. The power of the bolt sent him across the plain as he smashed through the stone bricks of the council chamber.

'My lord!' Croaked Parminx as she tried to stand, finding herself on the grassy fields at the bottom of the mountain.

Solus threw the rubble of his once glorious council hall onto the floor as he hovered into the sky. Then, producing two magnificent golden wings in a single beat, he blew away the shattered pillars. Landing next to Lunerios, who lay motionless upon the earth, two crystal shards protruded from her back, pinning her to the ground.

Solus remained quiet. His face began to crease in solemn rage as he clenched his fists. He loosened his hands to grip the crystal shards, pulling them free from the back of Lunerios. In his final fit of rage, he crushed the solid crystal shards in his hands until they were nothing but fragments of glass. Then, bending over Lunerios's body, he held out a single hand. A faint golden glow emitted from his palm, enveloping the God of the moon and stars.

The light penetrated the gaps in her back; the blood began to fade as a mystical force pulled her into the air. The glow started to fade as she dropped to the floor.

'My light in the dark, Lunerios, you have been healed!'

The moon began to glow brighter than ever before as the stars flooded the eternal night sky. Lunerios opened her eyes. She felt new, like she had just been reborn.

'Thank you. You're most benevolent!' Lunerios said as she bent at the knee.

'My lord, it as predicted! I have sensed that the God of War is fading fast. The power of the golden tear is all but spent! I'm afraid he doesn't have much time left!' Parminx said as she hovered above the shattered throne, her silver wings whistling softly in the wind.

'Await my return. I shall see to the end of this Violet warrior and the traitor, once and for all!'

With a flash of gold, Solus was gone, leaving Lunerios and Parminx alone in the pearly glow of the Petarian moon.

*

Violet walked into the cockpit of the Hellbourne. The doors opened with a swish to reveal Jax at the side panel, with Serena at the helm.

'Serena!' Violet said, rushing over to her, gripping her as tightly as she could.

'V, I can't breathe!' Serena said, patting Violet on the back.

'Sorry. It's just. Well, I—'

'I understand V. Believe me, all those feelings you have now. I felt every time you were on a mission. The sad part is, it doesn't go away!' Said brushing Violet's hair away from her face.

'Major, I hate to break the reunion, but the planet is breaking up!' Jax said, frantically pressing buttons on his control pad.

'Time to go!' Serena turned towards the helm, punching some brightly coloured buttons the Hellbourne blasted into space.

'Surprisingly quick for such a big bird!' Jax said as the G-force pinned him to his chair.

Violet sat on one of the chairs, looking out to the planet Eco as it splintered and broke apart. Plumes of volcanic magma rushed the surface as the planet began to cave in, shrinking from view as the Hellbourne soared into the deep dark of space.

'Do we have the location of the earth?' Violet asked, stretching her arms and putting her feet up on the dashboard.

'Yep, just inputting them now!'

'How long will this journey be?' Violet asked, resting her eyes.

'The question is not how long, but if?' Jax said as the computer finished its projection. 'At the ship's current rate, we will reach earth in approximately one year.' 'Although the ship has an interstellar drive, we can decrease the travel time by almost half if we use it!' Serena said, scanning the ship schematics.

'Then we do that!' Violet interjected.

'Just one thing, Major, we used a lot of energy during Eco. The system shows we don't have enough to even get to the Milkyway, let alone earth.

'Then what's the plan?'

Just as she finished her question, the Hellbourn began to ring its warning alarm. The screens started to flash red as the siren filled the ship. Bursting through the door came Caspian, Oren, and Zyair, their guns at the ready.

'What's the problem?' Caspian asked, flicking his wrist activating his holo-pad.

'There is a single target approaching from the west. It is gathering tremendous speed!' Jax said, moving his hands over the control pad.

Violet ran towards the window. Staring out at the vast darkness of space, she spotted a small shimmering object that moved towards them, gathering speed as it flew.

'Take cover!' she shouted as she leapt from the window towards the ground. The rest of her Black-ops crew, including Serena, lunged at the floor.

A golden spear pierced the hull of the Hellbourne, flying straight through the air began to escape as the vacuum of space pulled them towards the gaps it had made.

'Activating defence sequence Alpha.'
Slides of steel slid from the back of the cockpit across the windows then began to seal the gap in the hull.

'Whatever the hell that thing is, bring it down before it kills us all!' Violet said, climbing back up onto her chair.

The cannons began to mobilise, aiming at the golden spear.

'Fire sequence active, on your command Major!' Jax said, his breath short as the Hellbourne rattled in preparation.

'Fire at will!' Violet replied.
The cannons locked onto the golden speer, then firing a volley of dark blue lasers, they exploded on contact, each finding its mark.

'Ion shots are ineffective. So what do we do next?' Jax said as the speer passed through each shot unscathed.

'Activate the ship's shields!'

Jax placed his hand on a globe-shaped object floating at the edge of the control panel. A luminescent yellow shield began to form, covering the Hellbourne preventing a further attack.

'It worked!' Jax replied, throwing his hands into the air in celebration.

Just as violet let out a sigh of relief, a single ball of golden light slid into the cockpit. There it started to spin violently until a whirlwind of golden energy spiralled in the centre of the room, then in a flash of golden thunder, the ball dispersed, forming into the divine lord Solus. There he stood, his golden eyes burnt like balls of molten steel. Violet flicked her wrist, materialising her M-tens. Then, she fired a UV round at the golden intruder with a single shot.

Seeing the incoming projectile, Solus waved his hand; the bullet dropped to the floor. Then, with a twist of his hand, he gripped his fingers to form a fist. An invisible weight pulled the occupants to the ground, forcing them to their knees.

'You! Violet warrior, I, Solus, find you guilty of treason! Therefore, by the divine light, you are sentenced to death!' A golden spear appeared in his hand with a click of his fingers. Then, motioning with a single finger, he sent the spear towards Violet.

Unable to move, Violet closed her eyes, awaiting her final fate, but nothing, the sound of the whistling spear had stopped. The room fell quiet.

Violet dared to open her eyes, unaware of what she might see. Solus stood before her, encased in pure white light, his spear disappeared into thin air. Violet felt the pressure release, standing; she looked around in disbelief.

'How?' she said out loud.

Her eyes moved about the room, catching sight of a single white orb floating in the air next to Solus. The sphere began to spin, emitting a fog of white mist about the cockpit.

'The crystal!' Violet said, realising her pockets were empty, 'So this is why you gave it to me.'

'Pathic mortal!' Solus said, causing Violet to jump in surprise. 'You may carry the blessings of my brother, but that pathetic fool's creation will not save you forever. Mark my words, warrior, I will end you!'

Violet walked towards Solus, moving her face directly in front of his.

'I do not fear you! Have you not seen what I do to your kind!'

'The ignorant never fear what they do not understand. But listen now, mortal! You will grow to fear me.' Solus said, his body glowing a dark bronze as the white fog struggled to hold him back, 'Till next time!' he said with a final snap, then in a flash of golden thunderbolts that shot across the room, he was gone.

The orb continued to fill the ship with its white mist, seeping into each nook and cranny, coating each part with a thin white barrier. Violet looked around the room. Her crew lay about the floor as flashes of golden thunder jolted through their bodies.

'Major?' Aster said as he stepped into the room.

'Your awake, Aster quick, help me get everyone to the med bay!'

'What happened?' Aster Asked

'Solus!, come on quickly!' moving the bodies towards the corridor.

'Wait, Solus! He was here! Aster said, darting towards the main control panel.

'Aster, we don't have time for that. Come on!' She shouted.

'Listen to me!' Aster said, snapping at Violet, causing her to stop what she was doing.

In the five years, she had known Aster. He had never shouted at her, not once!

'If he was here, he knows who you are, where we are, and what we have done! You think what we have just accomplished can be easily replicated against him. You are wrong! Solus is a whole different ball game!'

'You weren't so concerned before he arrived. Surely you knew what all this meant, Aster. Bringing down a God will piss off the most powerful!'

'Yes, but here we are, in the darkest recess of space, no crew, no weapon, no hope. Violet, you must trust in what I'm about to do!'

Violet looked at Aster, his face as white as a ghost as he breathed heavily, his hands upon the control pad.

'When have I ever not!'

'Man, the far-right control pad. Press the black button on my orders.

Violet sat down at the control pad. A black screen materialised in front of her, mimicking the one in front of Aster.

'We need to do this in sync!' Aster said, holding his hand towards the pad.

Violet copied Aster. As they placed their hands simultaneously on the black screen, their eyes expanded in a pool of black liquid.

'Now, do you understand?' Aster asked.

'Yes!' Violet said, as her eyes began to glow like two fireballs in the void.

The Hellbourne turned in space, facing towards the direction of the closest black hole.

'Activate interstellar engine in three, two, one!'

In a sudden burst, the Hellbourne jolted forward, disappearing into the void.

ABOUT THE AUTHOR

Born in the United Kingdom, Douglas Shore is a British food writer. He is now stepping into the world of fiction with his debut novel, Violet Villin: The God Of War, the first of many books in the Violet Villin saga.

Follow his writing journey on Instagram
@doug_shore_
And his food writing at www.dougskitchenofficial.com

Printed in Great Britain
by Amazon